How to Design a Threshold

A novel by

Ted Bernal Guevara

1

The author wishes to acknowledge and express his gratitude to Humanity & Inclusion *(formerly* Handicap International*), an international non-governmental organization. It was founded in 1982 to provide help in refugee camps in Cambodia and Thailand. Headquartered in France and Belgium, since its creation, it has opened branches in six other countries: Switzerland, Luxembourg, United Kingdom, Germany, Canada and the United States.*

How to Design a Threshold
a novel published by Whispering Candle, F.E.

Amazon and the Amazon logo are trademarks of Amazon.com, Inc., or its affiliates.

ISBN-13 978-1-64199-091-2

Direct Quotations
Emily Dickinson, Gwendolyn Brooks

threshold *n.* 1: the <u>plank</u>, stone, or piece of timber that lies under a door : SILL 2: any place or point of entering or beginning: *the threshold of a new career.* 3: a level or point at which something would happen, would cease to happen, or would take effect, become true, etc. 4: *prevention*

To my sisters,

Maribel

Eileen

Jiji

Prologue

Uncle Dam

THE FUTURE. AS A MENTOR, HIS UNCLE gave advice on just about anything in the future. Whether it would be about school or girls or architecture, it had something to do with an item not yet taking place. "It's a gamble, that future," his uncle would say. "You can talk about it till you croak. But it's only a win when people listen."

In a matter of speaking, his Uncle Dam had the bigger ear. It was up to nine-year-old Howard Schoeff to recognize that those bigger ears had a bigger mind between them. Dam was short for Damien. Howard, as a kid, could not possibly figure all this out— till his fifty-two-year-old relative got out the Buddy, the new outdoors equipment of the day.

The pre-Weedwhacker was supposed to make people's lawns look like carpet once they were groomed, the radio boasted. In 1928, an ad on the radio would repeat twenty times a day, and Uncle Dam's Philco was at the window turned up high while the retired engineer worked at the barn. Uncle Dam had forty-two acres of land that he rented to a corn and soybean farmer. Shared profits from the farmer alone sustained a decent living for Dam and his wife. They were childless but had an abundance of nephews and nieces.

The wife would leave him twice a year on the average to stay with her sister in Indianapolis because of the blaring radio. News in the morning pepped up the bearings in Uncle Dam's innovative mind.

But it had been on an Easter Sunday when Dam, who was six-foot-three and had auburn hair amassing the back of his head and nowhere else, took young Howard and his cousins out behind the barn for a show. The fiddleheads grew desperately there all the way to the huge rusty tiller that had been abandoned by Mennonites long before the barn was ever built.

Uncle Dam was fond of current events and new things. It had been part of his wife Phyllis' lent resolution to remind him not to use any big contraption, like the tractor, just to cut the backyard grass. This was the first day he was conscientiously free to demonstrate. The kids looked around them on where to run to in case of danger.

"Now, friends, this is how to use the Buddy," Uncle Dam would begin. "This glorious machinery is no back-of-the-comics item but...quality tool." Phyllis, who was home, stood at the screened porch with her hand at her cheek, like Jack Benny expecting calamity.

Uncle Dam ripped at the cord. The trimmer screamed. The kids jumped back. He switched it off again. "First, we must wear protective goggles," Uncle Dam pointed out, taking a pair out from his bib, and placing them on. Howard had never seen him put on anything protective before. "With the Buddy," Uncle Dam continued, "we never know what can get into the eye. Grass, rocks, bug doo doo."

The kids laughed. This was Uncle Dam's forte, to make children laugh—but not so much as to scare the youth out of them.

When the Buddy came on again, the younger cousins jolted back once more. Howard himself tripped over a tire when his uncle incised through the morosely thick fiddleheads. Leading-edge as it was, the trimmer still shook a better part of Cass County.

Then, a premonition happened. Howard saw these blue pebbles shooting out from the Buddy. One nipped his arm and landed between his feet. His uncle cut the trimmer. Concerned, he walked over to Howard and inspected the oval object.

"It's a bunny egg," Jansy, a girl of seven, said.

"No, it's one of Howie's balls," said Milo, an older kid but friend enough to Howard to be invited to Easter.

Uncle Dam cupped what appeared to be a robin's egg.

"There's a couple here," said another cousin. When Dam asked if they were broken, they replied no.

Howard Schoeff, the eldest, except for Milo, saw worry in his uncle's face, as if the adult were receiving wavelengths.

"Someone must've watched over them," Howard blurted out and felt embarrassed about it afterwards. "It didn't want them to get whacked by the whacker." He expected his uncle to roll his dusty eyes. But Uncle Dam did not; maybe cursed needlessly, but still did not.

"They have the thinnest shell," Uncle Dam said. "Must have known the nest wouldn't stay."

Once inside, Howard thought what must have known? How could his uncle proclaim responsibility for the nest falling? It could have been just a slip of pronoun, Howard hypothesized. But why was there a pronoun in the first place?

The demonstration had ended with the children holding all the unbroken eggs. They had taken them in.

Aside this weird aura about him, Uncle Dam was a good advisor to Howard. On women he had yet to meet, maybe on all the women he had yet to encounter in twenty years. "You will meet your better half at the college," his uncle would say. "And you will lose your Mary before you will gain your Virgin Mary."

"What?" Howard wondered. As time went by, he would piece this together as losing his virginity before finding success in life. Maybe not earning enough to support the outcome of losing his virginity?

It would only be Howard feeling displaced in these talks.

He stood a foot shorter than his uncle and had to look up when the adult said, "Remember, Howard, you're flesh and bone before anything else. Don't let your rearing get the better of you. Your mother bakes great peach cobbler and teaches with dedication, but the lessons she passes on to you, they're still for the picking."

"Are you...sure?" Howard asked, perturbed.

Howard's father was always away on trips. His father contracted the disease of yellow fever while taking photos in Burma. The boy was only six when his mother thought it wise not to interrupt the beginning of her son's education by taking him abroad. So, parents and son were apart for eight months.

They could always catch up with the rearing, Howard's mother thought. Beside Dam and Phyllis's home provided all for Howard, who often slept over. Uncle Dam's explanation of his parents' absence eased the boy whenever he came home from school.

"Take caution when you'll meet a drugstore clerk from Maryland," his Uncle Dam warned him one day. These subjects were more important somehow.

"What? Who?" Howard said.

"Bright, red hair. She would have a veil that you would think she's pretty or him," Uncle Dam went. "And don't be political, poli...what's that term they're going to use?"

"When?"

Howard was eleven then, but to understand his uncle obviously required a higher aptitude. From the egg-saving event, he was convinced that his uncle was not a hundred percent there—

till probably the day Howard would graduate from Notre Dame University.

Hustling riffs and telling jokes were a way to pass the afternoon. Uncle Dam's talks were usually inspired by how big cities were, as compared to Logansport. He poked a lot of fun at New York City. Why that city? Howard wondered. Maybe it was the aspect of it ever growing, out of their sight but still grumbling daily on the radio at the window. There was actual fear in his uncle that Logansport would become a suburb of New York one day. Not Chicago. Chicago was moving west, away from Cass County. Uncle Dam would say, the bigger the town, the more sewage it would churn into fertilizer. Uncle Dam figured by the year 1990, their small town of Logansport would be a plutonium reservoir for the city of New York.

Howard asked where he got such notion, and Uncle Dam would say, straight-faced, that they were revealed to him in his sleep.

Uncle Dam had never set foot in the city of New York. He was from Young America, a town fifteen miles east of Logansport and where every philosophy had to be linked to fertilizer or the making of fertilizer.

Dam saw the Big Apple in his nephew, felt the city in him like it was one of his organs.

"Why do chickens cross the road in New York?" Dam would ask.

"I don't know," Howard said, twelve at the time.

"Because promiscuous pigeons think they're pigeons, too," Uncle Dam would answer. "How many New Yorkers does it take to screw in a light bulb?" he inquired.

"Forty-two," returned the boy at fourteen.

"One," Dam answered. "He just holds it over his head and expects the whole country to go around him."

And this one: "Why is there a Flushing in New York?" Uncle Dam asked.

"Because there's a Third, Manor and Scheidt in the streets," Howard answered.

11

"You've heard that one?" Uncle Dam was amazed.

Howard, at sixteen, dared not say but the progression of his uncle's joke-telling was leaning towards corny, especially at one time when Uncle Dam went too far with this clairvoyant thing. He told the boy that he must pick one event over another, and Howard's choice would affect New York City's future. In his deep assumption, there was an item Howard could not place a finger on, maybe for most of his bachelor's life: there seemed to be no spiritual faith in the adult. In all else there was. Uncle Dam, through all his premonitions, the boy thought, was free of God.

Howard, wide-eyed and wondering, still answered, "No. I dreamt it."

1

Zeyad

Premonition was hardly a cup of tea east of Logansport or New York City for that matter. There laid the open sea and dreaming of travel was more of a possibility.

In 1951, to be on the first Iraqi oil tanker to go to England was a privilege only a prince could have. Thirty-three-year-old Zeyad Nadeem Mughrabi was not exactly royalty but he had talent in ducking behind huge spools of rope. He was tall for your average shipyard ducker. It was plain to see that if he had any regal distinction, he would not be ducking in moors in the first place. Yet Zeyad wore dark clothes to hide himself. Before his leap from the pier to the mountainous boat, he had tied a roll bag full of his belongings around his waist. He spotted a line sagging from the rear of the ship. Zeyad thinking physics adjusted the bag around to his stomach, hoping he would hit the side of the ship with ample cushion. His *saffjjii* or carpet for kneeling was tucked between him and the bag. This alone should save any spinal injury. He checked the tautness of the rope and looked at the hull, which seemed a half football field in length.

When everything was clear, he jumped.

In the dark, physics escaped him. How could weight spin in midair when the line of tow was not the least perpendicular to the water? Zeyad thought. He had twirled and switched places with the roll bag before hitting the wall. The loud thud assured him that one of his shoulder blades was pushed in. He stifled his scream. The price of tasting taffy candy at an English amusement park was worth all the effort.

He had dropped out from Commerce in al Basra, and after working at the shipyard for four years, he decided it was time to see what was beyond the Persian Gulf. He had kissed his mother goodbye and kissed each of his brothers and sisters on the forehead without them knowing it. He prayed toward Mecca asking forgiveness for going northwest instead of east. His family's faith was not all that dominant in the city of al Basra. They were outsiders, but Zeyad as a Sunni remained devoted, and careful.

He scurried across the hull in the dark. He slipped into an empty iron cubicle where he had planned to stay for the length of the trip. After he felt the ship moving, he let out a sigh. The pain throbbed mercilessly. With a towel he soaked from a spouting hole, Zeyad wrapped the shoulder. He opened his bag and ripped at the loaves of Mogol bread that occupied a fourth of the bag. Zeyad figured the trip would last twenty days. Also, he took along Darjeeling tea with rum to help him relax and fall asleep in cold nights. With three hefty camel skins of water and two of medicinal tea, at three cups a day, he felt set. Tea with rum could only be medicinal when a Sunni took scary trips like this.

After the eighth day, he was wringing the last of the water pouches into his mouth, and half of the tea managed to lull his shoulder, thus far. He looked toward Mecca, begging for rain. He felt cooped up in the cubicle. At one point, had yelled out his frustration at the raging sea. No one took notice. He was at the opposite end of the crew cabin. Zeyad could have played his bassoon he left at home and still no one would hear.

On the eleventh night, he crawled out and climbed to the deck. As long as he was fasting, he decided he might as well get down on his knees and bow down to the rear of the ship.

His shoulder was better, allowing him to maintain his crouching position for hours. He was at a higher plateau spiritually when a horn from a tugboat blurted from below. He looked up and saw harbor lights. It could not be an English port, not this early, Zeyad estimated. He thought according to time this was certainly an undershoot, maybe Lisbon, Portugal, who knew. He scurried to the edge, leaned over and touched the lofty fu Manchu on his chin. He had a beard!

2

Mr. Antonisz and Wife

Premonition also did not have much purpose inland. Working for the existing day was all that mattered. A ticket to this laborious inland required special talent.

"Roll down the line, ace," the deckhand from the tugboat yelled. He thought Zeyad was also a deckhand.

Zeyad's eyes brightened in the dark. They dimmed again when he looked down. "You're not Portuguese? Or Irish?" Zeyad asked.

"No, no," the tugboat man said. "But welcome, we'll take all your accommodations. Now, throw down a line!"

"I cannot," Zeyad said. "I am just a passenger." He looked over his shoulder. "The ones who will help you are coming, and I better leave," Zeyad snapped. He hustled back down to his metal cave to retrieve his belongings.

"Passenger?" the tugboat man yelled after him. "What the…you mean stowaway!"

Zeyad came back, peered down again. "Yes!" he said, honestly. But the skyline to the south caught him weak in the stomach. He was about to climb down the ropy ladder. "What are those lights?" He pointed.

"Fucking Manhattan," said the deckhand.

At that instance, Zeyad tossed his bag down into the tugboat.

"Whoa, whoa! What are you doing?"

"Tell your captain, just to the lights, please," Zeyad said and threw a gold pendant to the man. Zeyad climbed down. "Just to the lights," he repeated. "Just to Manhattan, please."

"Do you have papers?" asked the man.

Zeyad only pointed at the pendant in the deckhand's hand. "Worth several hundred dollars," he said. "Take it home to your wife or…girlfriend." He darted into the tugboat's cabin. He crept up into a corner and curled up in a fetal position, startling the tugboat driver in a suit.

"Who in tarnation are you?" asked the driver with the bright-colored tie.

Zeyad recited his full name and mentioned that he was a shipyard man, too.

"Mr. Antonisz, I think you should take a look at this," the deckhand said, handing over the pendant. In turn, the baffled suited driver, who was in his late forties, took out a monocle from his breast pocket. He examined the pendant.

"You're the captain of this boat?" Zeyad said.

"When the first oil tanker from Iraq parks in my alley, I am. But by day, I am a jeweler. Where did you get this?"

Zeyad, with tears brimming in his eyes, looked toward the black wall of the ship he had come from, presumably eastward, and held out his hands in front of the suited man. Zeyad said, "From these."

"You made it?"

"Yes."

The deckhand brought a flashlight from below and shone it on the pendant for his boss.

"The detail, how did you manage?" Mr. Antonisz said. "And the amethyst, so polished...."

"No, ruby," Zeyad said. "Here is amethyst." He handed over another piece, a ring.

The suited man looked at him with discretion and looked at the second jewelry. "Tell me, how long does it take you to make one of these?"

"If the gold is warm, the stone solid, perhaps an hour."

"A phase?" guessed the captain.

"Apiece," Zeyad said.

Amazed, the captain-by-night asked for Zeyad's name again. Zeyad recited.

"All that?" said Mr. Antonisz. "Since you're in America, land of convenience, how about just Zed?"

"All set, boss," the deckhand who was now at the stern called.

"America?" Zeyad said. "Manhattan, New York ...is not England." He slouched back to the corner, conscientiously beaten.

The captain glanced at him, worried. "No, this is the U. S. of A., Eastchester Bay to be more precise. Persian Trade Pac signed a deal with Britain and us. Name's Raphael K. Antonisz."

"Darjeeling," Zeyad mumbled.

"What's that?"

"Knockout tea."

The moment the captain let out a sigh of welcome, Zeyad, exhausted, was free to maintain his sleeping huddle. He did so throughout the aligning and easing of the tanker at the harbor.

Mr. Antonisz, for all it mattered to his wife, to his employees and to his Jewish neighborhood, invited an adult Muslim stowaway to share his limo and ultimately his house in the Bronx.

Rapha told his wife that Zeyad was a skilled jewelry-maker from the Middle East and should not be bothered till the visitor had his rest. At the dining table, Mrs. Antonisz was stiff in holding back her comments, her hands clasped together in front of her as if praying for her husband's common sense. Zeyad, unshaven and

18

reeking of sea and sludge, was at the other end of the table eating prime rib. She had been quiet for the first five minutes. Her husband sat midway between them, ready to answer any questions.

"Does he speak English?" the wife asked.

"Zed?" Rapha said.

"Zeyad," Zeyad corrected. "Yes, yes I do."

"Rapha, does he honor the Sabbath?"

Zeyad nodded. "On Thursday at dusk, and again on Saturday at dawn, and again on Monday at noon. And on the third Friday of spring or autumn, and on every dawn of a new-moon night. And in fact, tomorrow morning, I will go to your nearest Mosque."

Gracie Antonisz gasped.

"Excuse," Zeyad said. "I mean tomorrow afternoon."

Rapha Antonisz grew concerned. "When do you make jewelry?"

"Tomorrow morning." Zeyad smiled, adding, "I brought along my basic tools and casts."

"How many casts?"

"Oh, four or six, and not very heavy, too. They are made of plastic."

"Plastic?"

Gracie, who had more silver hair but was more refined in the face than her husband, clenched her fists tighter, bothered by her husband's disregard for the completion of her interview. "Is he married?" she interrupted.

"No, I'm not," Zeyad said.

"Then, he cannot stay in this house," Mrs. Antonisz said. She got up and pushed her chair in, to accent her final decision.

"Gracie," Rapha said. "Don't you have any lending hand?"

"We have Chereb," his wife said. "Mr. Mughrabi, you will stay here for the night since it's late. Lizzy will make room for you in her quarters. She will sleep at the library sofa."

"What is a Chereb?" Zeyad asked Rapha, while Mrs. Antonisz went into the kitchen to talk to her help.

"Our daughter," Rapha answered.

19

"How old?" Zeyad inquired. Rapha stared at him.

Zeyad began to laugh, a high, childish laugh that seemed incongruent to a man of his height. "Excuse," he said again. "You need not concern yourself, my friend. I am Sunni and with Allah always. I am as good as a eunuch. You know what that is?"

"I do," Rapha said.

But Zeyad insisted on pantomiming a snipping act, which Mrs. Antonisz saw as she re-entered the nook. She glared with disapproval. Zeyad looked up at her. "Tonight, I will take the library sofa," he said. "Tomorrow, I will sleep at the Mosque." With this statement, Zeyad, taken in by a Jewish couple, retired from his first night at this new place beyond the England he had read so much about. Beside his interest in diversity and culture, he had a peculiar thought when he first set foot on the harbor of this city, Rapha mentioned as the Bronx, that would indelibly penetrate his curiosity.

3

Chereb

And premonition hardly existed in the limelight. It was the one culture Zeyad could never place his morale in, one that did not root from any heritage. That was the limelight culture—the Tavern-on-the-Green culture if you will. On Central Park West, a social tribe had gathered to toast a native queen. Juliane DeVoe, assistant manager and heiress to the DeVoe-Hilton Hotel, raised her champagne and beckoned Rose Mary Getty, a writer, and Rachel Browning, an actress, to do the same. "To Chereb," Juliane announced. "On her twentieth birthday. May she grasp the evening and shed sparkle on us all."

"Oh, Julie, don't be a cake," said a stark blonde girl in front of them, flanked by men, a film editor and a young cubist. "You probably hexed my ability to do so now," Chereb added. "Debbie Reynolds."

"Agreed," Rachel said. "But Debbie is a compliment, Jules."

"Well, excuse me, debutantes...of many sorts," Juliane said. "I just wanted to empty my glass. Who ordered four bottles of this stuff, anyway?"

"Don't you like it?" said the film editor with the sparse mustache.

"Yes, but not one and half gallons of it. Our table looks like a Portuguese basement."

"He wanted us to be hammered out of our minds," Rose Mary said, "so we can whirl around the park without our panties."

"Why, did he order another case?" Chereb said.

The girls laughed.

"Tell me, is your hair really that blond?" asked the cubist. "I mean no disrespect. It's almost tinsel on a Christmas tree."

Both Chereb and Rachel laughed profusely at this man's first line of the evening. Chereb winked at Rose Mary.

"Yes, Jared, it's real," Rose Mary said. "She's the first of her kind. Her parents had her head siphoned when she was little."

"I'm just curious," Jared said. "No joke intended." His eyes locked on Chereb.

Juliane tapped Chereb's foot at the base of the table. "Aren't we lucky on our birthday?"

"Control, if you please," Chereb whispered to Juliane.

"No, no," said the film editor. "You could kick Miss de Havilland out of *Heiress*. Couldn't she, Miss Browning?"

Rachel shook her head. "Or Gloria Grahame in *Bad and the Beautiful*."

"You wanted that part, didn't you, peach?" Rose Mary said.

"I would have done it better justice," Rachel whined.

"I'm just a dainty Jewish girl from the Bronx who

wants to get blitzed tonight, okay?" Chereb said. "If they want me, they can discover me at two o'clock tomorrow at Mabel's."

"Isn't that the time you have your pedicure?" Rachel said.

"Dainty, my ass," Rose Mary said. "Dainty, analogous to residue between your toes."

"Rose, gross!" Juliane said. "And you use such big words. Analogous?'"

Rose Mary looked irritated at first then reconsidered Juliane's capacity. "Virgin to nun," Rose said, "Rockefeller to Electrolux. Bing to…Bing?"

A round of laughter.

"You don't seem like the raucous type," Jared said to Chereb.

"Oh, I am," Chereb replied.

"She is," Rachel confirmed. "The night is young."

"Well, unattached is more like it," Chereb said. "I'm truly unattached tonight, and I wish everybody to be unattached along with me before this city rots to its core."

"She means free tonight," Rachel said to Jared, "not necessarily free, let's say, from uneven human relationships."

"This champagne tastes like the dialogue we're having," Rose Mary said.

"I vote for a little Red," Rachel suggested.

The men were quiet.

"Deal, Red Label for everyone," Chereb said. She waved down the waiter. When he came, Chereb ordered two bottles and Dr. Pepper. "You can bag those," she said to the film editor. Take them to your studio, for the cameramen."

"She's thrifty, too," Rachel said.

When the whiskey came and poured, Chereb lifted

23

her glass first. "Now, may every minute of this night be as happily lived as every sluice of this fine drink," she toasted. "And may we live happily unattached after twenty." To Rose Mary, Chereb said, "or after twenty-seven," to Juliane, "twenty-three," and to a scowling Rachel Browning, Chereb only raised her glass.

When the bar closed, the group moved on to Central Park. Rose Mary chatted with a carriage driver but decided against the ride since the six of them wouldn't fit comfortably. Juliane petted the horse at its hind leg. Rachel had her arm around the film editor, singing, "If I Knew You Were Comin' I'd've Baked a Cake." The cubist, Jared, had his hand on Chereb's shoulder and stole a kiss from her. "You can unattached yourself to anything you want to," he maundered. "Like painting, be as free as the colors. I'd like to paint you."

"I'm shapely," Chereb said. "You do squares and triangles."

"Tonight," he said. "I'd like to paint you tonight, while the stars are set in deepest violet. I live just around the block."

Chereb was guiding his walk, keeping him from going over the curb. "That wouldn't be a great idea," she said. "Our breaths would warp your canvas. Besides, I have synagogue duties tomorrow."

"That's funny," said the cubist.

"Which one?" Rose Mary asked. "Gesso warping or synagogue duties?"

"That's *hilarious*...," Jared uttered only.

Rachel Browning and her film editor passed them by in a clattering carriage, waving and toasting. The remaining three were obligated then to take Jared home. Chereb managed to get a street number out of him and hailed a cab.

24

After dropping him off for the doorman to take care, Juliane, who lived the nearest, invited the other two for the night. At Juliane's Park Avenue apartment, she insisted on a fire and popping corn. She entertained the group till dawn.

Before falling asleep, Chereb said, as if with a dying breath, "So much for nineteen."

4

How to Learn Voodoo

But those nineteen years were wiser than what any city street could ever bestow on a teenager. For one thing it involved a young Wall Street lawyer, between the seventeenth and eighteenth years. "Unattached" was the right salutation. It was from this that Rapha and Grace had taken a closer look at their only child's aspirations. Imagine, a young but still older man attorney calling the house. Him being married was never shared till it was heard from an *overgrown* grapevine. It had never entered the minds of Rapha and Gracie while it was happening.

It was ten till noon when she regained consciousness. "Hosting!" Chereb screamed, waking the other two. "I have to go."

"Stop with the obligation already," Rose Mary

grumbled.

"No, I have to host for Pop today, and he asked me to stop by Lindy's."

"Call him up," Juliane suggested.

"You don't even have your matador outfit," Rose Mary pointed out. "It'll be dinner by the time you get there. Tell him to host himself."

"Most people who go to the restaurant think of him as an admiral."

"And they see you as first mate?" Rose Mary quipped.

"Later," Chereb said, scooting out the door. At the lobby of Juliane's building, she phoned her father that she couldn't make lunch. "Calm, Papa, calm," she said.

It was four in the afternoon when she reached the restaurant and handed over the Nesselrode pies to the cook. By the time she got there, Andre Jacob, the host for brunch, had been called to duty. Chereb flashed a penitent smile and was free to go home.

At the north end of the Bronx, on City Island Avenue, her parents' three-story Spanish villa looked out to Eastchester Bay, as if it was a lighthouse. The driveway was a block off the street and was nearly a street itself. Chereb usually asked the cab driver to drop her off at the ingress, but not this time. She wanted to show that she was capable of earning her keep, by walking the distance of the driveway. *Please*, her mind went.

Her mother greeted her at the door instead of Sam, their butler.

"Good eve, Mama," Chereb said.

"Not exactly," her mother replied. "Where were you last night?"

"Juliane's apartment, but I had a chance to stay with a

cubist. Your good daughter turned it down."

"What's a cubist?"

"Someone who paints cubes."

"Chereb, seriously, there are hoodlums and bums and...Democrats out there, in every corner. My only daughter shouldn't be out half the night."

"You mean all night, Ma." Chereb walked by her and into the kitchen.

Halfway across the polished terra cotta tiles, she shrieked like a pig. Zeyad jumped out of the chair. Chereb turned around and ran out through the saloon doors back to her mother in the dining room. "I think there's an Arab with a Bunsen burner in our nook," Chereb said.

"Ah ay, that's your father's new discovery."

"What's he doing?"

"Melting our finest forks."

"Ssh," Rapha said at the threshold to the library.

Chereb greeted her father with a kiss on the forehead. "Sorry about this noon time."

Rapha ignored her apology and explained, "He is melting silver. He's a talented jeweler from the east."

"More east than Rhode Island, I take it."

Rapha pushed on the doors and found Zeyad standing. "How are you getting along?" Rapha asked.

Zeyad, who was now clean-shaven and had a maroon sheet over his head, nodded.

"That was our daughter, Chereb...or is," Rapha said, finding Chereb had followed.

"Our only," Mrs. Antonisz added. Chereb extended a hand.

"Zed," Zeyad said, grasping it.

"Nice to meet you," Chereb said.

"Mr. Antonisz, the silver is good," Zeyad said. "But I

have to do my tributes, soon."

"Tributes?" Chereb said.

"I have to find your nearest mosque."

This surprised even Mrs. Antonisz. Here it was, her daughter, obviously poised and attractive in every sense of both words, and all this ragged man, who still reeked of the sea, could think of was honoring his God. Maybe Chereb's voodoo blonde hair suddenly made him superstitious. "I think there's one on Grand Concourse," Mrs. Antonisz offered.

"Yes." Zeyad's face glistened.

"Chereb, would you like to drive?" Mrs. Antonisz said bravely, to her husband's utter shock.

No! Chereb thought.

"No," Zeyad said, and then stopped himself. "I mean I would not like to discomfort anyone."

"Would you like a cab?" Rapha said, easing the tension. "One could be here momentarily."

"Yes," Zeyad said.

"My daughter will be honored to take you in the big car," Mrs. Antonisz interrupted.

Chereb grinned weakly and said, "*Yeah*...just give me a moment...freshen up." She bowed, clenched her teeth, and left the room.

Rapha's wife turned around as if to check the shelf window and whispered to Rapha, "She could learn a lot from his ways."

Zeyad twitched many times while waiting at the foyer.

5

Ambassadors of Faith

In her father's big car, a blue Bel Air, Chereb drove well considering the awkward state she was put in, especially when her passenger clung to the door with his eyes closed as if he was about to leap out of a plane. Chereb was not herself also. She usually attempted to speak to calm a guest. The truth was she was not big on synagogues and churches, let alone, mosques. Her parents attended the earliest service on Saturday, and a synagogue duty to Chereb was bringing bon-bon pillows to her parents so they can sit for long during Congregation Moryas. Chereb would rather go to a UFO sighting in Blackdown, South Dakota.

She looked over to Zeyad, who was whispering a

prayer. "Do you ever wonder about beings out there?" she asked.

"Out there?" Zeyad flinched.

Chereb looked up.

"Certainly," Zeyad said, totally getting her meaning. His eyes were wide open now. "There." He pointed at a building with a gold dome.

Since they had been on Grand for some time, the building was as good as any to Chereb. The moment it was clear, she swung the car to a U-turn to park on the curb on the other side.

"You drive like a Pakistani," Zeyad thought to say before hopping out.

"I give you lift, and you say that?"

"No, no. Pakistanis are excellent drivers. That was a compliment."

"Will you be okay?" Chereb asked.

"*Yes*, now that I am at a mosque. Thank you very much for your kindness. Good-bye." He walked on ahead and slipped quickly into the building.

Chereb was left to scan the gothic doorway, with statues and etchings. A bulletin glass case hung in the middle of the huge doors. "Sunday Masses at 6:30, 8:00, 10:30..." she read, "Saturday at 5:45 P.M...St. Jude's Cath...."

She got out of the Bel Air and bolted inside. This church had a gold dome just like those in Persia or like the Taj Mahal!

Zeyad had already seated himself some twenty rows up, before the altar, bounded by turquoise pillars and candles. Chereb hustled up the aisle and excused herself going through the pew. When she got to Zeyad, he welcomed her to sit.

"No," she whispered. "This is the wrong place."

"I know," Zeyad said. "It is most certainly right to many people here, but a wrong place for me. But the atmosphere is good, all but singing. Will they sing?"

"What do you mean?"

"Sing?"

"Yes, they will," Chereb said. "Maybe later when they eat that stuff. Anyway, you are in the wrong religion. Wrong building."

"Yes. But I will stay."

"Don't you have a rule for not being in the right place?"

"Are you in a hurry?" Zeyad asked.

"Yes. No. Yes, I can...sit."

"Good. I am more at ease, thank you."

The priest at the podium with a stairwell took notice of this exchange. Embarrassment engulfed Chereb. She knew that the silence was due to Zeyad and her chattering.

The priest, a man with pudgy cheeks and a stocky frame, gave her a small wave. Chereb turned around, and when she looked up, the priest had kept his grin meaning that the start of his sermon depended on her settling in. "Hello," this priest said to the crowd. "I'm Father Schoeff, fresh from Indiana, South Bend to be more precise. You will be seeing my face in this parish Sunday in, Sunday out, for the next three years or so. And of course, on Saturday, a time for leisure, golf and having that hotdog cookout, a time for taking a date to Coney Island, hoping she wore pants instead of a dress so you could ride the Whirlee-Whirlee with no worries at all. And lastly, it's a time for priests on trial, to see what they've got. Lord or lard. Kingdom or boredom. Lamb or ham. The contract has been signed, sealed, delivered to your local and honorable bishop. The name is Schoeff, as in a baby's bottom."

31

Except for Chereb and three other humor-ready people, the crowd, bitten by this introduction, remained silent—including the Monsignor, who sat under the crucifix and was flanked by two open-mouthed altar boys.

"I am glad to be in this remarkable, ever-breathing city to share my good tidings," Schoeff continued. "Although the future is bleak, as it has always been, there stands a bright promise at the end of any time span. Stay with me. It gets better." He paused to focus on the smiles and grimaces he had caused. He checked on the Monsignor's. "My role is to let you take a glimpse of what is to come between now and that bright promise. Some of you may think I'm out of context an average priest clings to, if you will. But in truth, I am deep within that context. For instance, if I say the Yankees will win the World Series six more times this decade and then again in 1961, '62, '69, '78, '86 and the last of the nineties, you would say I'm off my mahogany rocker. His Highness above would never grant power on a disproportionate priest like me to predict sports events."

"Father Schoeff, may I interrupt you for a moment?" the Monsignor said.

"Sure, Monsignor Randolph, with my invitation," Schoeff replied.

"What does the future of the Yankees have to do with today's gospel?"

A priest had never interrupted another priest in the recent history of the church. All were captivated.

"I was getting to that, father," Schoeff said. "I'm still in my introduction. I figure I have time. Three and a half years seem like a millennium on the first day."

To this, the people murmured. Chereb in her bliss almost clapped.

"Is this unusual?" Zeyad asked her.

"I'm new to this as you," Chereb said.

"May I continue, Monsignor?" Schoeff asked.

"You may."

"Well, as I was saying, if a stubby Gaelic priest could map out the win column of the Yankees for the next fifty seasons, would he mention this gift just to help his credibility and make Catholics in the Bronx better bettors?"

The monsignor rose and walked up to the spiraling rostrum. At the landing, he bent forward, and Schoeff drew back as if to avoid a squirrel bite. The monsignor appeared disinterested and proceeded to whisper his message. Then he stepped down and exited to the backroom.

At this same time, a young man in a mesh overcoat gazed at Chereb from across the aisle two rows up. It wasn't so much his stringy hair that was conspicuous but the stagnant, sort of wet gray eyes the hair covered. Chereb, mesmerized, only noticed him when she clasped an earring, a habit she had formed from the constant changing of that accessory. The young man raised his missalette the instant Chereb looked his way, suggesting that she should read the one in front of her. Chereb gave him a blasé chin and focused to the front.

"In today's reading," Father Schoeff continued, "the prophet Isaiah couldn't wait to tell the people in the dark about little Jesus before He was ever conceived on earth. Isaiah came down from his sister's donkey he happened to take to the village that day and shouted, 'Guess what?' And the people in the dark responded, 'What?' Isaiah took a deep breath and said, 'Wonder-Counselor is going to be here!' 'Who?' they cried. 'You know, The Man,' answered Isaiah. The people were still stumped. 'Father-For Ever, Prince of Peace, He'll be the great, great, great, great grandson of

David, the One who will give you Light.' 'Oh? Oh!' the people chanted. 'When's He coming?' they asked. As you can see, Isaiah didn't really have the clout, nor any man of the cloth in describing the random future of this city unless he starts out with the Yankees."

After Schoeff finished and the assembly stood up, sat, kneeled, stood up and kneeled again, Zeyad attempted to get up when the people around him began to sing. Chereb convinced him to stay. "Where is the sun?" he asked, during the second verse of the awful song.

"Outside," said Chereb, looking at the stained glass on both sides, trying to see where it was brightest. The weather had been overcast. "Last time I saw it," she added.

"Never mind," Zeyad said. "I will stay, but I will not sing!"

They stayed through all the chanting of these Roman Catholics and through the communion, which Zeyad also didn't want any part of. In fact, they stayed after most had left the church.

Along the aisle, the young man with the hair tapped Chereb's shoulder. She caught his eyes, and he handed her his missalette.

"Who was he?" asked Zeyad.

"Don't have a clue," Chereb said and passed the booklet to Zeyad.

She walked to the back with Zeyad tagging behind. At the front vestibule, she saw a little girl talking to Father Schoeff under a statue.

"Go home to your mother," they heard Schoeff say to the child. "Tell your guardian that you have to be at your mother's reach at all times."

"You mean Oscaro," said the girl.

"Where is Oscaro?" At this instance, Schoeff got a

glimpse of Chereb and Zeyad at the back.

"Outside, he's *patinguilan*," said the girl. "He doesn't go in here."

"I'll walk with you in a minute," Schoeff said, and to Chereb and Zeyad, he asked, "May I help you?"

"Yes, my name is Chereb Antonisz and this is Zed Makarabi."

"Mughrabi," Zeyad said.

"I just want to congratulate you on your first speech," Chereb went on. "It was *with it*, almost in the line of striking."

"Thank you," Schoeff said, grinned. "But tell me, Miss...?"

"Chereb," Chereb said.

"Did you get 'random' in all I said?" Schoeff said. "I may have talked of specific things. But random is always there."

Chereb thinned her eyes and said, "Random is sensational." Zeyad bowed to Schoeff. Schoeff bowed back. "But...the humor was just fabulous!" Chereb exclaimed. "It was the *with it* in your message."

"Can't do it *without*," Schoeff said.

"It was *carpe diem*. Living it up to the fullest."

"Whoa," Schoeff said. "*Carpe humor...et rideo*. It's great to be in New York. Learn life ticks after every sermon in New York, Latin heaven."

"That's what I mean," Chereb pointed out. "There's life in everything you say. We came here by accident, and at this point, I'm glad we did."

The little girl, whose eyes were deep green, looked up to Chereb and said, "You, too?"

"Excuse me," Schoeff said. "This is Asha, and she needs to get home."

"I am here!" Asha said. "Oscaro, he wanted to go to the bay and talk to his *barcadas* at the port. He took me here instead."

"Is that so?" Zeyad said. "Are you Filipino?" he asked with a smile.

The girl just gawked at him.

"Well, maybe Oscaro could attend Mass next time," Schoeff said. "There's no point in lingering outside of church. Come, Asha, Oscaro shouldn't be waiting. Excuse us."

"This won't take a minute," Chereb insisted. "Here is my number." She handed Schoeff a piece of paper. "I'd like to invite you to Bitter End next Thursday at 10 p.m. We're having our monthly parfait there, and we could use a touch of philosophy."

"Bitter End," Schoeff said. "Sounds like a destiny."

"It's a folk music place, on Bleeker Street."

Schoeff folded Chereb's number and tucked it in his breast pocket. "I'll keep it in mind," he said. "But a priest-on-trial makes no promises." He made a twirling notion with his finger then pointing to the front where the Monsignor was. Schoeff bid his blessings and led the child to a side door.

Outside, Zeyad, curious, asked his guide if she had done the right thing. Chereb nodded and came to realize that as a guide she had not done her duty for the evening. She still had to find the mosque on Grand Concourse, whether Zeyad had said his "tributes" at St. Jude's Cathedral or not.

6

The Attendant

But there was no mosque on Grand Concourse in spite of
Mrs. Antonisz' thinking that there was. Everything was
bound to be on the busy four-lane, Mrs. Antonisz must have
thought. The nearest mosque was in Passaic County, New
Jersey, according to the patrol lady at the sidewalk. Muslims
were sparse in the Bronx, which Zeyad would hardly notice
for the fact that he was well received at the Antonisz house.
Chereb, still spirited, would drive him back to City Avenue.

Outside St. Jude's Cathedral, Asha's brother's face

was as hard as she had described it to Father Schoeff. Oscaro Gutierrez stood about the same height as Schoeff, but Oscaro was slimmer and his muscles were more evident due to his tight clothes. He squeezed his cigarette into a crevice on the wall when Schoeff and the girl came.

"How do you do?" Schoeff said.

Oscaro, in his Filipino dialect, snapped a sentence that made Asha step back, something about her having to bring the priest out.

"Does he speak English?" Schoeff whispered to Asha.

"Yes, I speak English," Oscaro said.

"I'm Father Schoeff. I don't mean to pry or intrude into personal matters. But I'm concerned about Asha's health. Does she have the flu?"

"No flu, father," Oscaro said. "Just the chilly weather we're having."

Schoeff bowed to the girl. "Would you like to light a candle inside, under the Blessed Mary?"

"So you can talk some *baingat* to Oscaro?" said the little girl.

"What is *baingat*?" asked Schoeff.

"Sense," Asha answered, making Oscaro look up in the dark sky.

The priest grinned.

"Don't you need money for lighting candles?" Asha said.

Schoeff winked at her. "It's on me," he said. Asha turned and scurried back inside. Just then, the wind rustled around the corner of the building and blew on Schoeff's frock. "You may be right about the chilly weather," he said.

"The *padre* should wear some coat," Oscaro said, "or he may get sick himself."

"That may be, yes. But, Oscaro, I also noticed needle

marks on Asha's arms. There are ones that missed her vein completely. I know they're not from flu shots."

"Padre, you are having visions."

"Who's been giving her the shots?"

Oscaro shook his head. "It wasn't me," he said, drawing closer to Schoeff. "Aren't you supposed to be crisscrossing bread inside?"

"I am not accusing you. But the person who is giving Asha the shots is doing a lousy job. Your sister is young, full of promise. We don't want to cut her off...."

"She's not my sister."

"I see," Schoeff said. "Asha looks up to you as a brother. Taking her to Mass on a Saturday before servicing cars is certainly a brotherly thing to do."

"How did you know I worked on cars?"

"Lucky."

" Padre, Asha is adopted. We got her when she was two."

"I see, and from the age of two, you don't know whatsoever of her beginnings."

Oscaro nodded. "Except for my mother and me, no one else knows in the Bronx," he said.

"I'll tell you this, and you have to have trust me when I tell you this. Asha is now your prized possession. Keep her from any harm no matter what the situation offers."

"What do you mean 'situation?'"

"You'll see."

Oscaro was speechless. His hard face eased a little. He wanted to speak, but the priest's genuine concern stopped every thought Oscaro had.

"Won't you get your sister inside?" Schoeff said. "She needs to be in bed."

7

The Monsignor

Monsignor Randolph had been with the diocese for seventeen years. He had kept the church in respectable order, considering the enormous influx of new parishioners, mostly Polish and Italians, in the last decade. A wing had to be added to the main building in order to meet the demand. Despite his asthma, a malady he had carried since youth, the Monsignor was always on his feet when it came to the well-being of St. Jude's Cathedral. That night was the first time he had hung up his sash before Mass ended. When Schoeff knocked at his chamber to re-evaluate the incident, the elderly priest felt thickness down his throat.

"Come in," the Monsignor said behind the armoire.

"Good evening" Schoeff said. "The light was on under your door, so I thought."

"Have you come to apologize for your comedy skit?"

"Not exactly. For I sort of planned it that way. It drew the attention I needed."

Randolph shut the doors of his armoire to face Schoeff. "It was preposterous," Randolph snapped. "These walls were designed to uphold the ceiling, store heat in the winter and avoid little squirrels from keeping their acorns under the pews, but they weren't made to muffle laughter."

"Your asthma," Schoeff said. "I don't want to trigger...discomfort." Schoeff drew closer to the bed.

"I can manage."

"But I feel..."

"Your homily belonged on Fiftieth Street and Sixth Avenue."

"Ah, Radio City," Schoeff said. "If it makes you feel any better, I pulled the same stunt in South Bend when I first gave Holy Eucharist there, a rougher version but the same idea. The one you heard was sort of a final draft."

"You write these things? 'Lord or lard' had to be written?"

"Oh, yes."

"Father, tell me," the Monsignor said, breathing harder, "You weren't able to finish your tenure in South Bend, did you not?"

"Well, my preliminaries were completed."

"The bishop there had to give you furlough, isn't that correct?"

"Yes, but I had a choice whether to stay or... "

"Because of your liberal approaches, your intolerable deliverances." Randolph had to sit on his bed. Schoeff went to the headboard and placed his hand on the Monsignor's

41

back. "Schoeff, why did you come to New York?" was asked between wheezes.

"Well, sir, it's hard to pinpoint. Perhaps, to protect these mountainous towers someday. In the early seventies, they will be erected in lower Manhattan. But if I happen not to be around when the time comes, well, the 40 Wall Street Building will do."

"What?" gasped Randolph.

"Ssh, rest." Schoeff looked around the room. "Where is your cortisone?"

Randolph closed his eyes and concentrated on the little passage in his throat.

"Your cortisone tank, father! Help me."

"At the annex," Randolph barely uttered.

"Okay, there are five," Schoeff said. "Five annexes make up the building." Schoeff started to pray, calling on two saints who were good in health care. He tilted the Monsignor's head back to widen the gap in the throat. "Oh, dear lord, don't let this man slip away. Please show me the annex. And if it is all possible—which it is in your eyes—pull that annex closer to this room."

The moment plunged into silence. Nothing moved. Nothing breathed. Schoeff kept his eyes shut, congregating a team of interceding figures in his head with Christ in the middle handing out manuals.

"Do you want him to repair the excavation damage, too," the Monsignor said, clearly.

Schoeff jumped back, nearly toppling the tiffany lamp there.

"What do you mean 'pull that annex closer to this room?'" Randolph said, sitting up in bed.

"Your eminence, you're breathing."

"Like you are. I just had a relapse. Happens every

time when humidity is up. It's in the north annex, my tank. Would you please retrieve it before I have another one?"

"Yes, your holiness."

Before Schoeff went, Monsignor Randolph asked, "Did you counsel children in Indiana?"

"A few, but not in a formal matter."

"That little girl lighting my candles, you seemed to have a lengthy conversation with her. Was anything wrong?"

"Well, she's sort of a lamb, father. She's safe for now, but there are wolves around her, I'm afraid."

"Ah, I've seen her in church before but not weekly. Get her to sign up with the CCD class."

"CCD class? Is there one?"

"No, but you'll be starting one in June. You seem like a good recruiter. Perhaps a CCD class will get you off the comedy binge."

"Perhaps," Schoeff said.

Never in his wildest dreams did he expect this. Not only did he sense a secure position in the highly attended New York parish, but he had an offer to teach children—plus an invitation to a folk-song bar from the Jewish girl and her Arab companion. This might go against Monsignor Randolph's new hope in him, but Schoeff found it utterly pleasing that his first sermon reached a spectrum of people. His Uncle Dam, fifteen years ago, had taught him to be frank about things. Just let it all out, by examples. Explanations would develop later by themselves.

8

Dr. Xya

Howard Schoeff, preoccupied with initial matters, set aside both the CCD class and the Bitter End bar, to look to the future.

He didn't use his first name. In fact, it only appeared on his certificate of ordination and his driver's license. He wasn't a big fan on being called Father Howard or Father Howie. Once, when a South Bend divorcee mother seeking pardon asked for his first name, Schoeff felt uncomfortable and had to say that Father Schoeff would do. To his amusement at first, the woman insisted on his first name, until it became physical. The woman shoved him against the divider at the rectory. He finally gave it, realizing that the woman didn't want to continue associating with a man likely to have the same name as her abusive ex-husband. Asked why he had scratch marks on his neck, Schoeff said to his superiors then that he was overwhelmed in a *mother-may-I* game. The woman had kissed him on the cheek as an apology.

Born to a photojournalist father and a schoolteacher mother, Schoeff was curious and motivated to learn about women early on. He entered the life of serenity at twenty-one and was ordained four years later. But prior to this, he had a college sweetheart who was both a pleasing memory and an instrument of wonder. He knew then that there were two paths at the end of youth, and he was certain he was on the right path with Jessica. When the relationship ended, he had no choice but to land on the other path, which he, in his deep belief, had never rejected. Jessica was just a deeper groove in which his humanness flowed. It could only be justified in his Uncle Dam's way of thinking. Schoeff wasn't a virgin when he took the vow of purity, and that had made Jessica an instrument.

If he had a chronic illness, this was it. He would lie awake in bed wondering why Jessica had given up her own virginity to him only to choose another walkway. She took on a reporter's position in Miami while Schoeff stayed in South Bend.

He never understood flexibility in women. As a counseling priest, he had the responses, but they would always be on the surface and never from his ribcage. If by chance Jessica would come to him now with a personal problem, Schoeff would likely sweat a quart in a half-hour's worth of consultation.

On Wednesday afternoon, four days after his first mass at St. Jude's, he sought his own counseling at a different level. He was in Hoboken, New Jersey, at an ice-cream social for an orphanage. He noticed the sun gleaming particularly bright on a window across the street. This orphanage was linked to St. Jude's since it was near and rather full in capacity. Half of the Bronx depended on the orphanage to take in its strayed children.

Schoeff shaded his eyes and read the heading above the door: Continental Pediatrics and Psychiatry. How appropriate, he thought. He gave his balloon to a youngster and walked up to the building. At the entrance, he looked up and the sun was gone. A few people were in the foyer, but they seemed to be preparing to go home, so Schoeff hurried in and caught an elevator about to close.

Impulse told him to go to the fourth floor since the sun seemed to have gone into that floor's window. The elevator opened, and Schoeff looked to his right and found a small hallway leading to a window atop a radiator. To his left, halfway down the rigorously polished floor, he saw a lit office. He walked toward that way.

R. G. Xya, M.D. was engraved on a v-shaped plaque sticking out from the top of the door. Before knocking, Schoeff felt his stomach bloat like the balloon he had. He wondered if he should knock, since the door led to a waiting room.

"Come in," said a fragile voice. Schoeff's dark clothing must have loomed on the frosted glass from the inside.

Upon entering, he automatically took off his shoes and set them aside. "Pardon me, I'm not trying to be customary," Schoeff said. "It's just the brightness of your carpet. Dr. Xya, is it?"

The man behind the receptionist desk bowed. Half balding and quite thin, he showed a characteristic trait common among Asian professionals, undefined energy,

Schoeff thought at first glance. "My secretary left for the day," Dr. Xya said. "But I'm at your service to take compliments on my rug."

Schoeff grinned. "Light turquoise?"

"Divine aqua." The doctor laughed and stood up. Schoeff came forward to shake both of his hands. "Brother Schoeff, I'm glad you came in." Xya stepped forward, placed his hand on Schoeff's shoulder and led him to the back. "If you don't mind, preferably, I like calling you brother over father. It's more literal, with this body, I mean."

"As you wish, sir," Schoeff said.

"I like sir, too."

"Pardon me, your..."

"Relax, Brother Schoeff, this is a medical office, not a mosque. And I'm a psychiatrist, not a rabbi." Dr. Xya showed him to a recliner. "A child psychiatrist to be more precise. I enjoy it to the fullest. I never had a clue that free will was so delicate in a child's structure. You know, that's the one thing I found dimensionless I left it alone."

"Deistic," Schoeff commented with a smile.

"Right on the money on that one. But remember, I'm always there. To seep in their little eyes at the beat of their little hearts and nestle in their tiny hypothalami. Well, I'm getting termy here. Tell me, how is the child?"

"I had hoped you'd ask...firstly," Schoeff said.

"It was in your mind," noted Dr. Xya.

"To be frank, my question is why a child?"

"Can you think of a better stage where the mind and soul, and the body for that matter, are purest?"

"She's a little girl."

"I cry with you, Brother Schoeff. If you foresee a tragic story, I cry with you in that. But I set the clock and left it ticking. You may think it's deistic, but I have to correct you on technicality. I do not leave things totally on their own. If you want things the way they ought to be, the Yankees would never win a World Series. Coach Casey Stengel would have a hard time breaking a tie in the fifteenth inning of the first game or in the fifty-first inning for that matter. But on the other hand, he would never acquire a stroke from a never-ending headache he would have. And same goes for the other coach, an equal to Stengel."

"I see, said the imperfect man," Schoeff said.

"Precisely," said Dr. Xya. "But that little girl would be your accomplice. She will lead to explanation."

Schoeff smiled. "By the way, how did you like my first speech?"

"I wasn't there."

Schoeff laughed.

"You didn't get to the point right away. You were a big hit on attention, but all that the people had put to understanding was that their Yankees would win a dozen titles in the next fifty years because their parish priest had said so. You left out the future of their surroundings, the things that needed to be foreseen."

"I figure I had time," Schoeff said.

"A minor difference it would make," Dr. Xya said. "Times didn't pick you because you were a parish priest, you know."

Schoeff, down deep, took pleasure in this. "So, I'm told."

"It was your sense of humor, your mannerism. It could easily have gone to Zeyad Mughrabi."

"Who's he?"

"The fellow you met with the Jewish girl. A submissive gentleman who has gone far, but not quite accepted in the place he had docked." Dr. Xya paused. "Or it could have been the Jewish girl herself. She's wonderful in appreciating what I've given her, life! But she lacks your discipline."

"So, they are part of the plan, like Asha?"

"Asha is your conscience. She is part of you. And these other parallels are as important as the next person you would meet at the curb."

"So, everything still coexists at random."

"Never at random. I am in everybody's hypothalamus, little cozy spot near the pituitary gland. Scientists will discover everything can burst in space from the size of a jumping bean. Your hypothalamus is my condominium, in which we share the maintenance fee."

"Ah," Schoeff said. "I don't quite get that."

"Brother Schoeff, I think our time is up for now. I have to attend to a boy with leukemia at City University."

"Leukemia?"

"A growing disease. It will come to knowledge in the early sixties, which reminds me, part of your message will greatly depend on another kind of disease, one that is deadlier than leukemia. Warn with careful choice of words. People will be confused. Your base is simple: I am, therefore, I care. And I don't cause."

"I'll do my best."

"But remember, the future can only be altered if free will is disturbed, which is impossible."

"Ah, ditto," Schoeff said.

"I'm with you," Dr. Xya bid with a smile. Schoeff shook his hand once more, and when he was about to walk out, the psychiatrist added, "Do enjoy the bar full of women."

49

9

Mr. Applestein

At the first hour of business, Rapha bravely turned up a marquee at his window that read, "*Genuine Arabian Finery.*" A day before, he pointed out to Zeyad that in order to obtain that word, "finery," the trinkets had to be crafted exquisitely, and that he should take his time on a piece, maybe produce only two a day. Zeyad, due to his quick strokes and the ample amount of jewels Rapha had acquired from a wholesaler, was churning out one every ninety minutes on the average, and they were all different from one another.

Mr. Applestein, owner of a fabric establishment and

an avid collector of jewelry, was in the lookout for brooches that particular Thursday. He had asked Rapha himself to show him the new line. Mr. Applestein got out his monocle and trembled upon picking up Zeyad's products. "How nice," he said, and this sold Rapha on the skill of his oil-barge discovery. "Who is your importer?"

"They are locally made," Rapha said.

"What do you mean?"

"Right here in the store."

"But the make, the detail is from somewhere Persian."

"They are," Rapha said. "Would you like to meet the maker?"

Mr. Applestein was confused but nodded. Rapha called for Zeyad.

With a green headpiece and a gray frock under a lab coat, Zeyad came out of the curtains to greet the miser. Mr. Applestein stepped back from the glass when Zeyad gave him one of his how-do-you-do nods. "I don't understand," Applestein said, and when Zeyad offered his hand, Mr. Applestein recoiled. "Raphael, what is he doing in your store?"

"He's my artist," Rapha said. "He made these gorgeous pieces."

"Just, looking today," claimed Mr. Applestein.

"Mr. Applestein, what does it matter?" Rapha begged. "Be reasonable."

"You be reasonable. There are codes to live by, walls to stay inside."

Just then, Chereb walked in. "What's up, Mr. Applestein?" she said, passing the man, who didn't say a word as he scampered out the door. "What's going on?" Chereb asked her father.

"I better finish the earrings," Zeyad said. "Once you

do one, you have to continue with the other right away." He turned to go back.

"Zeyad," Rapha called after him. "I know a lawyer who can work out your papers in order for you to stay."

"Thank you, my good friend. I am most happy still." Zeyad excused himself.

"What's going on?" Chereb asked again. "He looks drained." She had stopped by to borrow the Cartier necklace, which was displayed on the navy-velvet showcase at the center of the store. It had been there for a week, and it needed to be flaunted, she thought.

"Certainly, not. And it's an Antonisz once it comes in here," Rapha said.

"I need it tonight for a meeting. When everybody's wearing a Charivari or a Tourneau, you wear a Cartier. It's the law, Papa."

"I tell you what," Rapha said.

"No, I won't say to anyone that the necklace is for sale, not while it's on my neck."

Salesclerks in the store paused to observe Chereb.

"My daughter," Rapha sighed. But on his initial thought, he said, "Won't you take Zed with you tonight to this gathering."

Chereb laughed, but when she saw no one else did, she frowned. "No! What's with you and Mother about *this* person? He's like the Prince of Baghdad with two Jews holding up his tunic."

"Ssh…did you just see what happened?"

"Yes. Papa, usually you consider firing people who are bad for business."

"Mr. Applestein is just from the old neighborhood. He attends congregations and nothing sticks but traditions. And you should be more open handed," Rapha paused. "I can't believe I just said that. But the bottom line is Zed stays because he's a skilled craftsman."

"Open up the Cartier," Chereb resolved.

"No," her father insisted. "Have you seen our Arabian line? Maybe you can wear one of the pearl and citrine bangles. Very impressive."

"Great, I come in here for a Cartier and end up with a Mughrabi. What the hell."

Rapha scowled at his daughter. He had heard her profane before half a dozen times. This city could jade anyone. He let it go.

10

A Tour Guide

Never in Chereb's twenty years did she encounter such trite domestic pressure. Whether her parents truly wrung her hair of color at a young age, she had developed moods from it. She thought her looks were either alluring or remote, like the very thought of alien landing, depending on her state of mind the previous night. To have a Middle Easterner for a date would upset that balance.

From her father's jewelry store, she went to the salon and called Sam, the evening maître d', from there. She asked him to do lunch at the restaurant. When he insisted that he had a hair appointment himself, Chereb said she was on strict order from her father and must do her schedule that day. Sam said okay.

After she had her hair, nails, and a massage done, she went into Sak's for a hat. A derby in a bar, how wild is that? she thought. Lastly, she stopped at Bitter End and told the manager there to arrange the place like an amphitheater. Her presence, instead of just her voice over the phone, always made the manager give in. At four-thirty, she returned to her father's jewelry store. "Where is he?" she asked as she passed Rapha behind his desk. In the lab, she found Zeyad under a magnifying glass with tools in his hands.

"Well, are you in zest?" she said.

"What?"

"Ready?"

"Yes." Zeyad smiled. "Let me get in order, just one moment." He put away his things and retrieved the Qur'an from a small drawer at a desk.

"You won't be needing that," Chereb said.

"No?"

"Unless there's a mosque at the Empire State Building, which I doubt."

"Miss Chereb, I wish you wouldn't apply humor in accordance to the Qur'an. It's very displeasing."

Chereb bit her tongue. "I'm going to show you New York while it's bright."

"Pardon me, but I thought you were going to accompany me to my tribute."

Chereb saw in her mind the gross difference between her and this being. "Zed, you should cut down on the pardons," she said, guiding him out of the room and out of Antonisz's, before her father could make a remark.

In her sense of tour, she thought the subway would be more interesting than a taxi. She led him down to the nearest passage, bought tokens from a gawking lady and explained to him the power of the coins. While she was showing him how to operate the turnstile, two leather-clad boys jumped over the gates. Zeyad ignored them and dropped his token as he was shown to do. Chereb then told him that the tunnels were high-risk for unstable people and had ended many unwanted lives. Shock was a good ingredient to tour guiding, she thought.

"Upper East Side," Zeyad read the billboard on the subway car.

Chereb thought for a second. "You won't be kneeling in there, would you?" she asked upon seeing the word East.

Zeyad ignored her. "I like Mr. Applestein," he said instead. "His nature is assurance that I, too, would not change because of this freedom in America."

"He's a putz," Chereb said. "And that's a putz thing to say about…a putz."

Zeyad looked at Chereb in a hypnotic stare. "Miss Chereb," he said. "As a person of little western knowledge, I am pleased that you are taking me around. But as a person period, I am better to be on my own than with someone who tests my intelligence."

Chereb had no choice but to stop. They got on the next car that opened its door. They found a spot on the bench, where other passengers had scooted to the window to make space. "My mother always talked about Britain as if it were part of our country," Zeyad said once they settled. "She was there once during a very cold season, she told us, and all she could describe were the movements of Ferris wheels in lights and cotton candy on her tongue."

"We have Coney Island," Chereb said. The subway noise drowned her voice at times.

"Where is Bartholdi's lady of copper?" Zeyad shouted.

Chereb covered an ear. "Who?"

"In 1865, an Alsatian sculptor built a lady with forty-two feet of arm holding a lamp, as I remember from my French history."

"The Statue of Liberty."

"Yes, where is that?"

Chereb laughed. "I thought you saw it coming in from the Atlantic."

"I was asleep."

"Well, we're in the wrong subway for that."

"Don't bother. I have all the time here in New York City."

"Tell me, do you feel out of place?" Chereb asked. "I mean that man this morning was just an old Jewish dick. He's nothing to Pop except for business."

"And you are not."

"Not what?"

"An old Jewish dick," Zeyad said seriously. People laughed beside them.

"No," Chereb said. "I consider myself not even Jewish at times."

"An old Jewish dick, what is?"

Chereb looked up, whispered, "Forgive me. That's a bad impression I just gave you."

"No," Zeyad said. "The second thing you mentioned was a bad impression. Never say you are not Jewish at times. It is unforgivable to reject one's own religion."

"That's the difference between you and I," Chereb noted. "You feel guilt whenever you go out of line of your religion. I just feel guilty when I hurt another human being."

"In my personal belief, free will is God's worst gift to man," Zeyad proclaimed. "It gives us a way to reject him."

The subway car rumbled on. The lights went out twice before Zeyad observed the anger he had placed on his tour guide.

Chereb ignored his comment. "I mean here I am, twenty," she said, "trying to grasp everything life has to offer. I care about people. I respect my parents tremendously, have faith in what they do, and I am very grateful for what they provide. I am a cautious person. I watch my step. What else is there? Being Jewish is not only religion, by the way. It's everything. Don't you find it that when you say you're a Muslim, your world tends to be smaller? The places you go to become limited, the people you see or would like to meet are numbered, the food you eat becomes everyday stuff, and you become alone in society. I don't know about your country but here in New York, you're either an independent people-person...or a gloom tomb."

"What is the time?" Zeyad asked.

"Quarter to six."

"It's dusk." Zeyad looked at the individuals in the car. There were at least twenty. He reached for a handle overhead and pulled himself up. He looked down at Chereb and said, "Excuse me, just a few minutes." Then he kneeled at her toes, facing the front of the shuttle, and bowed with his hands out front. "I hear no *Muezzin*, but I think it is time," Zeyad said. "Forgive me."

"What's he doing?" asked a hefty lady with a checkered scarf. Annoyed, she pulled her feet in to avoid touching Zeyad. Chereb looked away stunned, subverted, but covering her smile.

11

Speaker on the Packard

She who had given up on the faith-absolving conversation offered to buy dinner. Lights were everywhere when they bobbed up to the streets. To her, a Bit of Bali seemed to be the logical choice after a public kneeling. She asked Zeyad if he cared for Indonesian food. When Zeyad said he had never tasted cuisine outside his ethnicity, Chereb said it was time to expand. American food was sure to dull, and she couldn't imagine that much difference among countries that ended in *i*'s when describing their food. She was certain none could match rijsttafel, a 25-course Bit of Bali specialty.

Zeyad ate from each of these twenty-five little dishes, and since his stomach wasn't lined with asbestos, he passed on the *sake*.

Chereb checked her watch. Her tour guiding didn't comprise too many places as planned, but she had to have a good hour's rest before the event at Bitter End. From the Indonesian place, Zeyad strutted ahead toward Seventh Avenue, feeling satisfied. "I see the point of your axiom," he said. "That might have been in me also when I decided to ride the oil tanker. Tell me, was I *limited* when I hid in the boat to come over to this huge city?"

"I guess not," Chereb said.

At the instant, a man with hooking sideburns nudged Zeyad from the back. Zeyad fell forward and scraped his arm underneath his cloak. "Excuse me, sheik," the man said. "Didn't mean to ruin your dress there."

Chereb stooped to Zeyad. "You did that in purpose!" she yelled at the man.

Zeyad grasped her shoulders, got up, and said it was okay.

"Mannerless ass."

"You got a mouth on you, bleach," the man said.

"You're from Jersey, aren't you?" Chereb pursued. "People in Jersey don't read. This man you just shoved is the new ambassador to the United Nations. His photo is on the front page of every major paper across the state, and you shoved him because his outfit offended you." To Zeyad, she said, "Don't worry, Shah Mughrabi, security is on its way."

"A good act, toots, but a little short of Broadway," the man said.

Just then, from Seventh Avenue, a siren whined and drew closer. Red lights flashed on the building wall. The man flicked his cigarette on the curb and ran off. Chereb took off her coat and wrapped it around the "ambassador," her pretense undeniable. "Don't mind stiffs like that," she said. It could have happened to anyone with a dress situation was her thought.

Zeyad replaced Chereb's blazer on her, and they both walked toward the sirens. On Seventh and Forty-second, a crowd gathered around what appeared to be an old ambulance. A man stood on top of that vehicle, speaking to the many. Chereb could not focus, but the voice from the megaphone seemed unmistakably familiar. Zeyad urged to go closer. "It's the priest," he said. "He's wearing a black turban."

Chereb squinted. "That's not a turban," she said. "That's a flap cap."

Father Schoeff also did not wear his usual black attire but a worker's jumpsuit, complete with the leather holster and tools. "If you're wondering how on earth this fine 'medi-sheen,' a term Harlem gentlemen would be using, oh, maybe in the late seventies, found its way here in the heart of Times Square, let's just say I have a friend at the top of a Hoboken clinic. He drove it here around five. I see that the police had finally noticed the meter had run out of it."

The crowd bellowed to its knees, applauding the three patrol cars at the scene. Chereb and Zeyad worked their way to the front.

"People," Schoeff said. "I come to you tonight not to sell chlorophyll artifacts or homestead lots or U.S. Bonds. Nor I am here to make a statement to run for sewer investigator for this great city of yours. I am here because it's a lovely night, so clear, so crisp that a whisper can be heard for miles if people would only listen. Many thanks, officers, for turning off your sirens. I speak to you also. In fifty years, your grandkids will be combing this area, and they won't be checking parking meters. They'll be cuffing sellers and buyers and hauling women of the evening by the dozen in trucks. They won't be checking locks on doors but will be on the lookout for lost children. In fifty years, someone will complain to the city why his daughter is found lying in a dumpster with a syringe on her arm. An artistic, bright young man will peer out of a hospital window counting stars and his days on earth because he has a viral infection bestowed from these streets. A kindergarten will receive a fatal wound to the chest by just riding in the station wagon. Individuals will stalk one another and kill and mutilate just because they are not in their neighborhood. A business woman will be raped in Central Park because she is diligent to her exercise program."

"What are you saying, Sam?" a man shouted from the side. "What's your credentials to be a fortune teller?"

"Sam, a certifiable name," Schoeff said. "As in Sam Walton, a billionaire who will come your way. But at this point in time, he's still driving his old pick-up in Bentonville, Arkansas, with his two hound dogs in the back salivating in the breeze. As for your answer, my credentials to tell of your future is the being who drove this ambulance, although he prefers to be called 'supreme.' He's not really picky on titles, like Miss Diana Ross in about four years, trying to find a name for her back-up singers. My credentials, my source, is the one who has asked me to slip on this carpenter's garb and carry these tools so I can mend the city of future ills. You just missed him. But then again, 'miss' is a mortal concept. Only *we* miss, but in truth, solution is all around us, let it come in our ear canals."

"What are you saying?" a desperately puzzled voice shouted from the crowd.

Schoeff visored his face and tried to spot her. "I'm saying that we should listen," he said. "Listen for the coming of tornadoes, as opposed to the storm. Tornadoes fling houses and little girls out of Kansas, but in this case, little girls fly out of the bright lights and into the blinding clear. That we may be blinded before danger hits. That is my message for the evening, people. Cringe, and danger will only have a fraction of happening in front of you."

"Blinding tornadoes in New York," said a feisty man up front. "Are you deranged?" People laughed around him. "Get down from that truck before you hurt yourself."

Schoeff ignored him and looked for the young lady. "Did I answer your question, miss?"

"Quite," someone said from the crowd--which little by little began to disperse. "Don't you have a bar to go to?" Chereb asked.

Schoeff grinned through his aching embarrassment.

"What she say? What she asked?" an elderly woman wondered out loud.

"Folk music, right?" Schoeff said. "Just let me finish up here."

"See you in a tad," said Chereb, suddenly the focus of the crowd. She took Zeyad by the hand and hailed a cab.

After a while, most had gone and turned to their evening affairs. A few waited for Schoeff still. He grinned and smiled and twiddled with the megaphone, which he no longer needed. "In conclusion," he said. "To what we can do in the present time, which is most...valuable, is we must open our minds, our hearts...take down fences. 'Love one another' is still as fresh...as salmon."

12

Jack

Schoeff climbed down from the white Packard, put his hands in his coverall pockets and sat on the curb. "Not even a reporter," he said to himself.

Someone patted him on the arm and kept on patting till Schoeff gave a gesture that it was okay for him to have company. Schoeff had been in the city long enough to know that these street citizens were just insisting on some change. The fellow with his shirt untucked and trousers ripped at the cuffs used Schoeff's shoulder as a cane. "You did good," the unshaven man said.

"I lost them."

"Lost them, find them. The odds are they'll come

crawling back and listen for more."

Schoeff looked up to the fellow and asked, "Did you get anything from what I said?"

The man sat down beside Schoeff then and batted his eyes as if a green-bottled fly was about to land on Schoeff's nose. "Live openly today, so the closed doors of tomorrow'll be easier to open," the man said.

Schoeff was amazed. He looked at the person and smiled.

"Yes, that's what I got from your talk."

"It's you, isn't it?"

"You who?"

"My credential.'"

"Look, Sam," said the man. "I just lowered myself here hoping you would spare me half a buck. I'm no credential nor do I work for a bank."

Schoeff laughed. "I'm sorry I've mistaken you for someone. It isn't you?"

The man stared at him, still awkwardly peculiar. "I'm Jack," he said.

Schoeff grinned. "Tell me, Jack...what's your story? You weren't once a priest who took a big-city assignment, were you?"

The fellow shook his head no, keeping his face a distance now. "Gambling," he said. "I once had a daughter who I lost in a bet. I had it in my throat. Anything of mine that can be uttered, my throat liable to place it on the table. She was only eight, my Heny. They promised they'd take good care of her."

"Who were they?" Schoeff asked frightfully.

"Just some people from upstate. They knew of a couple who were childless. So, my Heny was a gift, I took it."

Schoeff's heart sank a record depth. "Jack," he said. "I'll give you...this set of tools, brand-new Craftsmans, never been used, if you promised to have a self-consultation every time you have the urge to lay them on the table. If you keep this promise, you will have your Heny back five days after the tools are put to good use."

This time the man laughed. "Self-consultation?"

"With yourself," Schoeff said. "It's in you, likely."

"That was seven years ago. Heny could be anywhere north of here, maybe Quebec, Canada, for all I know."

"Did you try to look for her?"

"Two days after I came to my senses, I put her in the Times classifieds because circulation reach all the way up there."

"These tools have a wider circulation. Use them wisely and you'll have your daughter back, five days on delivery." Schoeff unbuckled the holster from his waist and placed the tools in Jack's hands.

"What are you?" asked Jack. "Some kind of a...patient?"

"No," Schoeff said. "I'm a messenger, like your paper boy. I have a day job as a priest in the Bronx. Come see me sometimes. We'll play musical pews."

Jack stood up from the curb, straight-faced, a little confused about the whole encounter. He walked away. Before Schoeff could look over his shoulder, Jack had disappeared behind the Cyclone Ace Cigarette ad, propped up between two buildings.

"Lord, what did I just commit?" Schoeff said to an empty street.

13

Women

He walked on Broadway, some eight blocks from where he had made his speech. His heart was doing the rumba. He still couldn't believe that the invitation was "confirmed" by Dr. Xya, meaning that he was allowed to take in unblessed chardonnay. "Folk music," he whispered to his chest. "Not Brazilian."

At the doorstep of Bitter End, his hand wandered to his neck. He didn't have a collar. He checked his watch and turned around. Twenty-three till ten. What a timepiece, he thought. It even lured his eyes to the precise minute. No Rolex could do that. But what was he doing? Twenty-three minutes would only get him back to Times Square and the spot where he had fizzled. He went to the entrance with a canopy. Two women who were obviously members of Chereb's society met him at the crossway. "Hello," they said, amused.

Schoeff nodded and let them by. He followed, his composure renewed by the thought that he was an honored guest. He was begged into this shindig, and that should give leeway to his carpenter's garb.

The place was quiet and dim. The tables were all set around a stage that could hold a piano. Only five tables were occupied at this time. From the one nearest to the platform, Chereb stood up in a white dress, completely made over from two hours ago. A maroon derby, elegantly placed on her head, accentuated her whole appearance. "Hello, father," she said. "Glad you're here."

Schoeff shook her hand. "Miss Antonisz, ecstatic to be here. But with all the commotion that went on out there, I'm not exactly in tune with or well-attired for this place."

"You look great. For the painter's overall, Cesar will take care of that." She waved at Cesar by the door.

"Tell me, Miss Antonisz…"

"Chereb."

"*Yes*, Chereb, tell me, who's playing tonight?" Schoeff asked.

"You are."

"How wonderful," Schoeff said.

"Your philosophy fitting into mine. Remember?"

"Philosophy. How wonderful."

"Are you nervous?"

"I certainly…am."

"Would a Tom Collins help?" Chereb offered.

"Is that by chance a name of a personal cab driver? Miss Antonisz, I mean, what should I say once I'm up there? I know the Gospel is a powerful thing, but the people here have three more days till they'd want to hear about it. Not that I'm willing."

"You have a way with words," Chereb said. "You were fabulous out there. Tell this crowd something of what you said out there. These women are normal, father. They give in to the slightest talk of magic, for instance."

"How many are women?"

"Except for Cesar and three or four waiters, all are."

"Oh."

To have the future in mind, Schoeff had to ask whether place or time mattered. He had divine consultation in between sentences with Chereb, who led him to the center table and introduced him to a budding writer, the daughter of a hotel magnate and an accredited actress.

The topic that came to him was shopworn, but it proved to be of interest among women, if not in public, in conscience, so he had hoped.

"Chereb tells me you're some kind of a brilliant soothsayer," said the writer.

"I don't know about brilliant," Schoeff said. "Come to think of it, I don't know about soothsayer." He laughed. "I relay messages."

"What kind of messages?" asked the magnate's daughter.

"Prophetic, of course," the actress said.

"Somewhat," Schoeff said. "Let's just say I'm not a person who dwells in the past."

As the room filled slowly but surely with members too well-dressed even for a wedding, Schoeff planned his speech by closing his eyes. The tropical fruit drink he ordered made him feel less self-conscious. Chereb patted him on the back and went up on the stage. "Dear ladies," she began. "As your delegate, I have a little surprise for you this evening, and it's not concerning spring fashion. Ladies, please welcome my discovery, Father Schoeff."

"Holy kitchen, Reeby," Rose Mary Getty whispered once Chereb sat down. "Couldn't you be more elaborate? He came all the way down here and un-collared himself and all you can say is he's not 'concerning spring fashion?'"

"'Holy kitchen,' that's a new one," said Juliane DeVoe.

"That was elaborate enough for me," Rachel Browning said. "A little more appeal won't hurt."

"Appeal usually has ties to sex."

"Rose Mary, please."

"Oh, grow up, sex is as part of religion as death. Isn't that right, father?" Rose Mary called.

"In the right context, Rosie," Rachel said for Schoeff, upon checking his compact but structural body. "Anyway, appeal is not necessary. Chereb has no hots for anybody here. Right, Reeby?"

"Pardon them, father," Chereb said.

Schoeff listened to this little parley before stepping up. He crept to the mic, enthralled by the hearty applause these cultured women gave him. But he sensed, from Chereb's circle of friends, that culture talk would also be boring.

"Thank you," he said. "I'd like to sing you a song right now, but my ukulele is getting restrung at this point, and I can't possibly go *twing twang* with my mouth and sing at the same time." With this opening line, he dared not pause for response. "Anyway, Miss Antonisz, Chereb." He nodded to her. "Has asked me to share a little life with you and on how to deal with it. I'll *not* do that."

The place went silent, captured.

"I'm sure each of you has a unique way of facing the morning, or whenever you open your eyes and say, 'Oh, life, it's you again.' Who am I to tell you another way? I am flesh as you are, a little rigid, fatty at some areas, but…."

Someone whistled.

"But you can observe," Schoeff went on. "Chereb heard me speak not too long ago, and after that speech she told me that I've patterned her way of life into sacred words, and my mind went, 'Alleluia, someone understood me!' She brought forth this phrase that sounded like stale river fish. You ladies know it by heart. But Chereb has picked it up from me as a fresh idea, which was completely unintentional in my delivery. It worked for her. I'm not saying lecture does not work and all the gurus, rabbis, preachers and priests of the world are mere mumbling fools to be heard. No, I'm saying there is another way that they can be effective, and in the long run, their messages creep in and breed like cute little rabbits in April. Which brings me to the subject I've chosen for tonight.

"Cute little bunnies in spring. They happen. Miraculously, yes. Accidentally, yes. Even from uninvited forces. In the 1980's, not one thinking rabbit, male or female, will avoid this great vacuum hose that will knock on their front door and suck them out of their decisions. Ladies, I'm talking in animation here, but what I'm about to relay to you Disney won't give me a time of day for, until 2024 when production of that year will actually portray rabbits having to face the lingering scale of abortion."

Juliane gasped.

I don't know women, I don't know women, Schoeff thought.

"C'mon, father," Rose Mary said. "Where did you pull this one from? Your midnight prayers? I mean, Snow White can't even pretend she has cravings for Dopey instead of the Prince, let alone bleeding rabbits."

"Rose!?" Juliane said.

"Forgive me," Schoeff said. "Things will be different in thirty years. And I, by no means, am not hiding the cruelty of it. But in the same token, I've brought up this subject no different from a construction worker installing a yield sign before an onramp. I am just telling you of what is to be."

Rose Mary flung her glass of bourbon on stage, splashing the cuffs of Schoeff's trousers. "Who will yield to what, father? If the subject is brought up then, who are we to yield to?" she said, standing up. "They'll be the same people who would judge the female-rabbit trash thirty years before. Nothing will change. Righteous people will always be stiff necks, insensitive only to the fact that it happens, no matter. Tell me, father, what is to be?"

Schoeff felt shivers up his back and looked into the woman's teary eyes. "That there will be *choice*," he said, making sure his face didn't crack as well. The room was dead silent. "Miss Getty, may I continue?" Schoeff asked.

Rose Mary nodded, slowly sat down, Chereb frozen at her side. Her thoughts ran wild about the whole idea in bringing in a surprise guest. This was supposed to be a time for happiness, a time for resourceful entertainment, as she had planned. But one of her friends had thrown glassware and all she could do was stare at the man behind the mic, hoping he would step down.

"I will," Schoeff said, as if reading her thoughts. He looked at the crowd, observed what he had done. The faces were held, but they weren't in good humor. He watched his step going down to the floor and seated himself.

"That was interesting," Juliane said.

"Thanks, Miss Devoe," Schoeff said.

"Disney in the future...how fascinating."

Schoeff laughed.

"Father Schoeff, I was just at Times Square, oh, around five in the afternoon today," Rose Mary said. "And I swear I saw a man on top of a Fleetwood who looked just like you, but his voice was different."

"Oh, it must have been those chlorophyll tablets I took beforehand," Schoeff said, hoping the mood would turn to cheery. "Like the ad says, it 'refreshes clean on the scene,'" he added.

"Well, jet sets, sorry to leave early," Rose Mary said, "but I have a chapter to edit."

"I thought you do your writing in the morning," said Rachel.

Rose Mary shouldered her sequined bag. "I suddenly had the urge to do it evenings." She drank her renewed bourbon empty. "Father, I'll see you...in the future."

Chereb felt disowned. To Schoeff, she said, "She's usually not this way."

"Go with her," Schoeff said. "I'll be here when you get back. I'll keep this candle lit for you." She frowned, trying to get his meaning. He grinned. Then she realized her responsibility as a host to him suddenly was no more.

14

Rose Mary

Outside she caught up with the writer, who was about to enter the glimmering Rolls. "Hey, you, get in," Rose said. Once Chereb was inside, Rose said, "Early departure, but I couldn't hack the...let's leave it at that, I couldn't hack." She tapped a gold cigarette dispenser and lit the smoke.

"What was wrong?" Chereb asked.

"What was *wrong*? Night was wrong. Your priest turned out to be a *regular* priest. Behind that mumbo-jumbo future crap, there's a stalking, little priest ready to slap the back of your conscience. Didn't quite turn out the way you described him to be."

"Sorry."

Rose Mary coaxed Chereb to have a cigarette herself.

Chereb took a hit from the one in Rose Mary's hand.

"I have to get back in there," Chereb said.

"It's a special blend from Havana," Rose Mary said. "It's like silk with the bourbon." Chereb took another hit. "Hold it in," Rose advised.

"Yep," Chereb said.

"His righteous was showing. To my gut, where it needn't to be."

"I'm sorry." Chereb said. "Next time, I'll find a more wrongful priest. One that wouldn't offend my friends."

"Remember Harley, the guy I used to go to lunch with? Tall fellow from Cornell? Unbearably moody but had a mind cultured as pearls."

"When was this?"

"Oh, about three years ago."

"I've only known you for two."

"Oh. Anyway, Harley had a flat in Chelsea. College students have dorms, graduates have apartments, but Harley and his brilliant, temperamental breed had flats. Anyway, henceforth, in this flat, he had a corner just for me to delve into my imagination. I produced some of my best pages from that corner when Harley was out of his flat."

"Rose, could you get to the point. I have to…"

"Attend to your priest, I know. It gets better. When Harley was in, I had produced something else, and it wasn't fiction. Harley described it to me as a gigantic lima bean with ears, nose, fat cheeks."

Chereb gasped. "You had…"

"Here's the climax, kid. Harley was a last year medical student who had access to every lab, observatory, torture room in Cornell. And since the timing wasn't right, three more years of this fucking residence, marriage was clearly out of the question. I was Harley's…first outpatient…well, in and out." Rose Mary held back, which in turn dried out her eyes. "And that moody prick thought describing the thing to me was a consolation prize." Rose Mary then groggily told her chauffeur to buzz up the divider.

15

Seeking Inside

Yet in this revelation, a secret among her circle, Chereb still could not grasp reality. They were in the momentum of a worry-free world, out in the limelight, with no shortcomings to drag down their morning hours. When she went back inside and realized that her priest friend knew through his clairvoyance that Rose Mary needed to therapeutically tell her sad past, Chereb began to feel that her own mind had been invaded.

Back inside, Schoeff asked, "How is Miss Getty?"

"You should know," Chereb said.

"I have no idea."

"How did you know she had an abortion?" she said close to his ear.

"I did not," he said. "But there is intuition. We have it if time calls for it. Miss Getty was the only one who responded the way she did. I think she benefited from it."

"Benefited from it?" Chereb said but was stumped after that. "How did you come to choose such a blah topic anyway? I don't usually go for blah, let alone promote blah."

Schoeff felt her green eyes piercing. "It was sort of blah-ish," he agreed. "Miss Chereb, to tell you the truth, I don't know women, especially a nightclub full of women. Women in my life are either biblical figures or relatives who come and bring me fruitcake."

Chereb was tongue-tied again. Juliane, in the background, resorted to goo-goo eyes, which Chereb ignored.

"So," Schoeff said. "Where is Mr. Mughrabi tonight?"

Chereb ignored this as well. "Forgive me," she said. "But was there *no one* close at all?"

Schoeff made an awkward laugh. "Once," he said, "but that's another club speech." The ladies beside him laughed. Chereb, on the other hand, fell like a soft stone. Her otherwise street-brass heart at twenty couldn't be more curious.

16

A Radio Announcer

Schoeff did regret the topic. It stayed with him long moments after. But he felt his Uncle Dam would have been ecstatic about the examples he was utilizing. Just then, a person in a dark gray coat and a parrot-spotted tie approached their table. "Excuse me," the man said. "But I couldn't help overhear these ladies addressing you as father."

"Yes," Schoeff said, reaching for a handshake.

"Father?"

"Schoeff."

"Father Schoeff, my name is Edwin Fuller, and I'm from Metro Voice, WDDS, a talk station. Were you at Times Square around five, six today?"

"Yes," Schoeff said, overjoyed.

"Were you that man?"

Schoeff opened his dinner coat and revealed the

carpenter's overalls for Mr. Fuller.

"Glad to meet you. I've been searching the whole night just for a clue on how to get in touch. You see, NYPD had barricaded all reporters from that vicinity. They were afraid you'd draw more people if cameras were going off. Would you confirm the nature of your speech, now that I know you're a man of the cloth, as prophetic?"

"That question has come up quite a few times from these girls. I'm afraid I have to tell you the same," Schoeff said. "I'm just a messenger."

Mr. Fuller took out pad and pen. "A messenger from whom?"

"That's a question with an obvious answer, isn't it?"

"*Yes,* but for the record...never mind," Fuller said and put away his implements. "I'm a radio announcer, not a press man, for God's sake. Would you like to be interviewed, on air?"

Schoeff didn't answer, awestruck by the turn of events happening to him in the bar.

"Go for it," Juliane said.

"We are a prestigious station," Fuller offered. "We've interviewed personalities such as Burt Lancaster, James Agee and most recently General Wycoff on the fall of MacArthur."

"Gee," Schoeff said. "Anyone from Sweetser, Indiana?"

"Pardon?"

"A remote town. Few people live there and it's totally out of context here."

"He does this at times," Juliane said. "It's a trait of his magnetic charm."

Chereb looked at her.

"When?" Schoeff said.

"We'll have you live this Sunday evening."

"How appropriate," Schoeff said.

"Yes, it has to be Sunday, father, best time of the week," Chereb said.

"Tell me, father, what is the prime target of your say?" Fuller asked. "I mean what is the goal? It all seems to pertain to the next century, some fifty, sixty years from now."

"Do you know that Walt Disney will produce a film about abortion?" Juliane said.

"Say again?" Fuller asked.

"In what year was that, father?" Juliane said.

"Don't mind her," Chereb said. "She's rocking a wild horse tonight."

"I'm not." Juliane siphoned her drink with two hands on the straw.

"Mr. Fuller," Schoeff said. "Throughout time, the past has always affected the present. Well, thousands could have dealt with the great flood, which only Noah and family survived, if generations before were told of how infidelity could create monsoons."

"Sure," Fuller interrupted.

"The Civil War could have been avoided if people were aware of civil rights a decade before. We have boys in Korea now because some of us have not learned from the depths of the war that would end all wars, and the person who had coined that obviously didn't do his social studies homework."

"Whoa, father, save it for the interview," Fuller said. "But that's the right material."

"You mean you're preparing this city for catastrophe?" Juliane asked. "I just had it in mind that the big one will drop. Let's see, in fifty years, I'll be approaching sixty-four..."

"Seventy-four, you bee wax," Rachel Browning said. "Anyway, it wouldn't matter. Seventy-four will be like forty-two in fifty years due to the advancement of medicine, and Juliane, honey, you'll feel death like a forty-two-year-old."

"The big one will never drop again," Schoeff said. "A greater mind than ours has engineered our minds to learn from the worst and will grant the Japanese the token of great engineering for our mishap. No, the catastrophe I'm talking about is more like slow erosion—and a choice at that."

"Oh," Juliane said, somewhat disappointed.

"Father Schoeff, we could set the interview on one-to-one contact with the city," Fuller said.

"That's very enticing, Mr. Fuller, but I have to ask permission from the Monsignor."

"When can you be sure? Here, I'll give you my card, and you can ring me tomorrow, or better yet, I'll ring you at the parish."

"I'll give you a call," Schoeff said, taking the card. On noticing everybody at the table wordless for once, he smiled, sending off Mr. Fuller.

"Was that what you wanted?" Chereb asked.

Father Schoeff looked plagued for a moment. "I don't know," he said.

17

Doctors in a Boat

Oscaro, the foster brother of Asha, had managed to hide behind the huge incinerator just yards away from the fence of his sister's elementary school. It was the parochial school north of St. Jude's, and the nuns there were particularly strict about the welfare of their children in the more hustle-and-bustle part of the Bronx. Oscaro knew an escape route out of the playground for his sister to take whenever he needed her. When the preparatory graders were rung outside for their two o'clock recess, Oscaro knew exactly how to get Asha's attention, without him getting noticed. He would poke an apple on the wire fence. Asha would spot it yards away. It was her cue. When she saw the red crab apple that day, she was heartbroken.

"*Manong*, not now," she begged when she saw him. "We have election bid, and I don't want to miss it."

"Asha, these doctors have appointments. There's

election bids every week."

"It only happens once a year!" Asha said.

After Oscaro stretched out the corner of the wire fence to let his sister through, he then guided her toward behind the incinerator where he had parked his Indian two-cylinder. He lifted her up to sit on the gas tank. Only when it roared and spat did the nuns take notice of Asha's leaving.

Oscaro drove west on 155th Street to take the Hudson Parkway, clear out to Pier 80 by the newly dug Brooklyn-Battery Tunnel. Down the musty abandoned pier, he let the bike rumble till he saw the usual three men in dirty-white lab coats, one always carrying an oversized black bag. Oscaro could never figure out why these men had to ride a boat from Brooklyn when they could swing around West Side Highway in a car.

"We have a mild one for her today," one of the doctors said. "It's a new phase of a fairly reliable opiate."

"Skip the big words," Oscaro said.

"Is she more relaxed today?"

"She's okay," Oscaro claimed.

"How are you, sweet?" asked the man who would perform the task.

"I don't want it today," Asha said.

"Don't you guys have pills?" Oscaro said.

"These aren't gumdrops, kid. Everything has to be intravenous to take effect. Do you want to hold her or shall we?"

"No!" Asha screamed.

Oscaro hugged his sister and pulled her stiff arm from the cradle of his stomach, around his back, so that it was exposed without her seeing the needle.

"Don't worry, kid, your sister is a gift to all children. If she responds right, the society will forever be in her debt."

"Make it quick," Oscaro said. If these men were so professional, he thought, why did the padre' find mistake in the needle marks?

Asha yelped, and it was over. Her body hung softly on Oscaro. She was speechless, but he knew the only thing in her mind was sleeping in her bedroom and waking up for school again in the morning.

"Call us if there's any vomiting, cold sweat, fever," the doctor said. "She should be more adaptable to this one."

Oscaro was handed an envelope from the black bag. It contained an amount equal to a month's pay at his night job or two weeks of their mother's seamstress position at the local Dupont.

"Till the first Wednesday of June," one of the men bid.

Oscaro kept his silence. He strapped his slumbering sister against his chest and drove back to the Bronx. She was a bright girl being watched and schooled by nuns, who were meticulous about grades and uniforms. Asha's last marks were all excellent. She had run for Class Police Person, which Oscaro did not quite understand. But at her age what could be better than being a gift to all children? Oscaro kept in mind.

18

The Way Dark and Rainy

Asha missed Mass on Saturday, and Schoeff, from all his other appointments and affairs, grew concern. In his room, he wrote a memo to himself to have a talk with the Monsignor about the radio show. He went to the telephone in the South Annex. Before dialing zero, he said a prayer for guidance. The operator came on, and Schoeff asked for a listing for Francesca Gutierrez, Asha's mother. It didn't exist. Then he asked for the ESSO station on Lorillard and Third. There were at least three ESSO stations in the Bronx. The one on Lorillard was the closest.

"Good evening," he said. "Does a Mr. Gutierrez work there by chance?" He believed nothing was by chance, and he regretted using the idiom--especially when he was committed to trust.

"Yeah, but not here tonight," said the man with a husky voice.

"This is his night off?" Schoeff had a feeling that a

young man like Oscaro would rather be in front of a jukebox grill instead of a grill of a Buick fixing radiator leaks.

"Nah, he called in sick. Stomach pains or the likes. Could be heartburn. The kid went for a lot of tamale, even for snacks."

"Would it be possible to have his residence number?"

"Who is this?"

"Schoeff. Oscaro knows me as a priest from St. Jude's."

"Well, father, it's possible if he's connected the phone. I think the kid is the provider for the family and I don' t think he's the telephone-connecting type. Hardly misses work. Is he in some kind of trouble?"

"No. I'm sort of a guidance to his little sister, and I was concerned why she wasn't in church this evening."

"It's Saturday."

"Yes, time for Ferris wheel," Schoeff said.

"Well, I can give you the address he jotted here."

"Please."

"Right down here on Selwyn. 186 D, next to Rexall's, where the kid probably takes his calls."

"Thank you, Mister...."

"Pinelli. Georgie Pinelli. Greetings to Oscaro and his sister. Take care, father."

All these idioms! Most of them based on luck and wishing well guesswork. People said them all the time, not knowing the outcome of their take care's, break a leg's and bon voyage's, and the ones who accepted these faithless locutions were in for a big surprise if things happened the other way around.

Haunt wasn't a related word, but that seemed to be the verb which these idioms were doing to Schoeff. He kept postponing speaking to the Monsignor about the radio interview, which he was supposed to confirm with Mr. Fuller that evening. And now Schoeff had a gut feeling that something was terribly wrong with the girl.

He hurried into the main vestibule and ran into with Father Merrill Lamantiaragski, who was standing on the marble font, preparing the altar for Palm Sunday.

"Father Schoeff, why the strides?" the lanky, frizzle-haired priest said.

"I have to be going," Schoeff said. "If the Monsignor wants me, tell him I've left to see a potential CCD recruit." Schoeff hurried and turned around again, almost tripping. "Not that I've accepted the position. I haven't decided yet. Nor I have denied…anyway, that's a lovely donkey. I must go."

Father Lamantiaragski (Laman for short), alarmed by Schoeff's urgency, plunged his left foot into the font's water to keep his balance.

In his room, Schoeff rummaged for a coat, an umbrella, and a black hat he seldom wore because it made him appear old. He checked the money in his wallet. He scurried back into the main room, unaware of how much noise he was making.

"Father," called Father Laman, who had both feet in the font now. "The Monsignor wants to see you. He was just here with a face of displease you won't believe."

Schoeff halted but went on. The urge to comment on Laman wading in holy water occupied him for a second. He shook it off and said a convincing good evening.

Father Laman had the most refined profile in his Master of Divinity. Laman was valedictorian for all his prep school years. Plus, he received a loyal award upon ordination. He could wade in the purest water all he wanted, Schoeff thought. He was most priestly among them.

The rains of April had started. Schoeff sprung out his umbrella and flipped up his lapels to go into the streets. Lightning and thunder ravaged, and Schoeff's environmental physics class in college came in handy. It was a huge, dark cloud with lots of floating negative ions clashing with a fair maiden of a cloud, thus big noise. It had nothing to do with the buzz he had from Bitter End.

He caught a taxi two blocks from the church. "Where to?" the driver asked.

"Let's see," Schoeff said, reading a piece of paper. "Selwyn Avenue. 186 D."

"You sure?"

Schoeff handed him the address.

"I mean that's a harsh neighborhood."

"Let's just say I'm a tourist, out for a once-over," Schoeff said.

"You'll see a once-over all right. In this weather, I pray it ain't a last-over."

"Your prayer is being processed."

The cab driver laughed as Schoeff settled in. "Where you from, father?"

"The Midwest. Good and corny Indiana."

"Long ways, aren't you?"

"I'm a New Yorker now, with lots of New Yorker things to do. Hello, Father Schoeff at your backseat." Schoeff extended a hand. The driver shook it.

"Donald Bodine. But don't be shaking anybody's hands once you get to this address. There's lots of people there who looks somewhat like me but don't have the same friendly chin."

"Thanks for the tip, but aren't you going to drop me at the doorstep?"

"Nope, Jerome is blocked off at that section, some

88

kind of a road repair going on there for months. I have to drop you off about a block or two from where you want to be. That all right?" Mr. Bodine checked his rearview mirror.

"Yes."

Within minutes the scene drastically changed. Out in the wet alley, lit only by flickering pole lights--a few were bent at the base from cars hitting them--small houses loomed over in tight spaces, some abandoned and some with windows glowing, as if from candles. No one was out, and it was not due to the rain. In the back of the houses, there stood a huge building in the distance. It appeared to be a hospital. Mr. Bodine parked at the entrance of the alley without turning into it.

"What do you think, father?" he said. "This is it for me. Selwyn is over that barricade."

Schoeff paid him and prepared his umbrella. When he got out, the running water came an inch above his ankles, drenching his socks. He bid farewell to Mr. Bodine and skipped on upturned pieces of concrete to get to a dry spot. Steam came from the ground also. Schoeff hiked over rubble with metal prongs and all. The fog allowed only a short distance to see. Schoeff stuck close to what appeared to be a ledge in the alley, not quite a sidewalk. But he still collided with an old school desk.

"Hey, watch it," someone spoke, jolting Schoeff out of his walking balance.

"Sorry," he said. "Didn't see." He rushed to the middle of the alley, his umbrella collapsing in the process. His heart rattled, incongruent to his breathing, making him take stretching steps toward the nearest lamplight.

"What are you afraid of?" said a voice in the dark.

"Who's there?" Schoeff said.

"Don't worry. You're safe. It's only us soaking in this

rain. You should have been here last month. The bones numb at a certain degree, and the body feels like it's a Barcalounger."

Schoeff tried to spot where the voice was coming from.

"Come closer," said the voice. "I'll show you how to sit in nights like this. I'm at the dumpster."

Schoeff leapt back to the ledge. A tattered man in his sixties was pressing his back against the dumpster. His face had a scar that mowed a line down to his bearded chin. He wore a torn tweed coat and two sweaters underneath, his trousers leaking at the hems.

"Usually, there's three or four of us out here, especially after dinner time when that corner Chinese place swings their pails of variety this way. What's the matter? Cat got your tongue?"

"I'm just..." Schoeff started.

"Don't worry, mind works even in the rain. There are more important things than idioms. And cats will always go after tongues."

Schoeff kneeled down in a hurry and grabbed the man by the shoulders. "It's you!" he said, above the drumming pour.

"In your mind," the derelict said but blocked Schoeff from embracing him. He began to weep uncontrollably in front of Schoeff, and Schoeff clasped the man in a hug anyway. "Never in my unending, unbegun life have I felt so miscast."

"How do you mean?" Schoeff said. "Isn't what you're feeling now only experimental? That you chose to be in this position?"

"As you see me now, I was born this way and have faced the ills, the failures and the downgrade of an unheralded citizen. I live and breathe the musty air of this alley. Look around you. Do you see anything by choice?"

Schoeff asked, "Are you warm, sir?"

"I am on a Barcalounger," said the derelict.

With restored empathy, Schoeff laughed. "It still gets me, having no beginning. Having no end, I can grasp. But having no beginning means you were around when brontosauruses walked around here."

"Not here, maybe in the Memphis area. They were afraid of the sea."

"You were around when only protozoa lived on earth, or when the earth was just a spitting fireball thrown from the sun. How fascinating."

"I was around. Just like you, and Jesus and my other offspring's, Confucius and Muhammad and Maitreya and Moses and David and Inari, Honen, Caleb, Kabir, Ramakrishna, Buddha and his predecessors, and your Saint Christopher and Saint Paul. What differs me from these bodies of mine is memory while in the flesh. That and mind are expendable…"

"Thank you," Schoeff said, "for including me in that great company."

"I would have included that man you just tripped over by the wooden desk if you have the time."

"Ah," said Schoeff. "Modesty is still best."

"For a priest, your knowledge of prehistory goes beyond what is expected of you."

"Uncle Dam, he liked things open-ended."

"It is who you are."

At this point, Schoeff was like a sponge. His nose dripped constantly only to be washed off by the cold rain. He shouldn't worry. Curing congestion was a small item to ask, if not already included in fringe benefits.

"Sir, how am I doing?" he asked.

"Attainable," said the derelict. "But you need to be organized, make loose ends meet. So far, what you've described to this city is a lot of future mishaps. There's no binding tie, and your solution tends to be at a lost because of the lack of tie, especially since you've forgotten to call Mr. Fuller."

"You do want me to go on the radio!"

"Certainly. I prefer *Today* with Katie Couric, but she won't be attending broadcasting school for another nineteen years."

"A television show?" Schoeff asked.

"A television personality."

Silence came over Schoeff as he hesitated. "Sir, I hate to bring this up..."

"She is awake, just three houses to the left. The rain will stop in four minutes, but your clothes will be presentably dry in three. You could knock on the door then, grant her your concerns."

"As for yourself, you'll be alright?"

"What is due to this body would surely come. Decreasing sense of touch, sense of pain, of vision and hearing, decreasing blood flow to the brain, weakening of respiratory muscles, loss of teeth, cyanosis, prostate problems, arthritis, diabetes, denial, anger, rage, depression. Other than those, I'll be fine. Your worry is the predecessors of this body. Go on, brother, save your life."

Schoeff stood up. He lifted his shoe from the silt and walked away. He looked back at the derelict. For the first time that night, he had encountered a person whose name he didn't ask for.

19

Cavalry

The windows were lit. Burly curtains dimmed them. With water streaming from the roof, it was hard to make if there were people inside. In the porch, Schoeff felt his coat and hat lighten, and when he stepped up to the paint-peeling door, clumps of soaked spots diminished from his shirt and trousers. His collar, though he felt no heat, was pressed-dry by the time he knocked on the door.

Locks were disengaged. The knob creaked and the door opened. Asha's mother, a small woman with smooth complexion, looked up at Schoeff. She seemed too young to have Oscaro as her eldest.

"Good evening," Schoeff said. "I apologize for this late visit, but I was concern about your daughter, Asha."

Mrs. Gutierrez was still in her seamstress uniform. She uttered no words but relegated them to her son, who was behind her. Oscaro got in front of her, nodded at the priest. Oscaro wore a cutoff shirt, showing the brawn of his arms again. "Can I help you, father?" he said, puzzled.

"Hello, Oscaro," Schoeff said. Suddenly another face appeared from behind Oscaro's legs, a boy of three or four. Schoeff squatted. "And who might you be?"

Oscaro held the boy on the shoulders, turned him around and marched him back into the living room. "Father, I know it's too early for a Christmas visit, and I know we didn't call to have our apartment blessed. So, why are you here?"

Schoeff grinned. "I came to see how Asha is coming along. I didn't see her at mass, unless she was hiding in the confessional booth."

"It's Saturday. Most people go Sunday."

"I've heard. But with your job I thought you might only have Saturdays to take her to church."

"Busy today," Oscaro said.

"When you do have time, why take only Asha to church, Oscaro, when you have a mother and other siblings?"

"Asha needs it the most."

"May I come in, Oscaro? I came all the way here through the construction."

Oscaro let him by.   "But you're dry, and with a broken umbrella," Oscaro said, touching Schoeff's coat. "What is this?"

"Perma-press."

"There's something hocus pocus about you, padre`. I can't figure it out."

"Please, where is Asha?"

"In her bedroom. She is fine, just a little tired. That's why I couldn't take her. She might get sicker with all this rain."

Schoeff passed another girl in the carpeted hallway, patting her on the head. He was midway in the house before he realized the place was exceptionally adorned. The wallpaper was bright. Portraits of the children were hung in stained metal frames. The candleholders and the full-sized mirror matched in brass tone. He saw a phonograph out in the living room with yet another girl listening to an evening program, and in the kitchen, he had a glimpse of an all-white contraption that seemed to be one of those easy-rotate dishwashers Sears & Roebuck had on the front page of their catalogue. Schoeff greeted Mrs. Gutierrez again at the door to Asha's room.

"Excuse my mother," Oscaro said. "She only speaks English when she needs to at her work."

"That's okay," Schoeff said upon seeing Asha, awake in bed. Her eyes were deep in their sockets. She was hugging what appeared to be an elongated compress that stretched from her chest down to her knees. Schoeff knelt by her side and took away the compress from her hands. "How long has she had this fever?" he asked. He spotted new injection marks.

"She has no fever," Oscaro said. "You mean how long has she been this manic."

"Is that the right term, Oscaro?"

"You should know, padre`. You're the one reading all the minds around here."

Schoeff turned to the young man. He stared at the eyes, trying to find a clue. "Oscaro, how did you know about that word, manic? I mean since I am here now and have seen the state of your sister's condition."

"It came with the package," Oscaro replied. "You don't sign anything unless you have been educated about the experiment, right?"

95

"The experiment?"

"Yes, with papers. These doctors meet up with us once a month or so, and try new medicine on Asha. Everything is recorded, plain and legit. And what you said about the injection shots not being in the right place, well, there are other roots within the skin, and not all medications go into one vein. You had me worried." Oscaro met the stare of the priest. "Padre`, you didn't hear me. This is all *legit*! All you see is a little girl sleepy in bed." Oscaro talked with his hands swatting the air. His little brother and sisters had come into the room and were peering up at him. Mrs. Gutierrez stayed in the hallway. "In a couple of days, Asha will be up and jumping as she always does after the medicine wears off. Look at her, you're seeing a...a pioneer. My sister will be a landmark in science!"

"Oscaro, is that what you really feel?" Schoeff said. "All I see is a helpless being. It's in her eyes, her face, the color of her skin. Her body can't take much, and it's showing. Don't tell me you don't see suffering."

"What do you know?" Oscaro said. "What made me let you in when all of this is supposed to be a family secret? Are you Asha's guardian angel?"

"Is your mother in need of money?"

"Father, she was in need. Believe me, we were all in need, but the bucket was filled after two trips to these doctors, and what you see in this house, on the walls, floors and ceilings, are extras. Things most of our relatives back in Zamboanga never set eyes on." Oscaro's body broke down to shaking. His pained voice drew his mother back into the room. She knelt down beside him and touched Asha's arm at the same time. "See this?" Oscaro went on. "We still both work. We don't want to go soft on that money. We still bring in."

Asha stirred in bed. *"Manong,"* she spoke, calling for Oscaro. "There are too many people in the room. I can't breathe with all the other noses in here! Oscaro, please, make them go out. All of you, except for Father." She spoke to her mother what sounded like an apology.

"See, father?" Oscaro said. "She even knows hospitality. She is still bright."

Mrs. Gutierrez stood up and nodded to Schoeff. She then led the little ones out of the room. Oscaro got up too and followed his mother. "Father, I will leave you with my sister, and you can say your blessings." Oscaro then pulled on the door.

"Promise me, Oscaro," Schoeff said. "Next time you have a meeting with these doctors, call me."

The scowl on Oscaro's face re-emerged. "Why would I do that?"

"If everything is legit, this team of professionals wouldn't mind if a policeman accompanied you, let alone a priest."

Oscaro paused. "Sure, father, I'll call you." He shut the door without another word, leaving Schoeff a chance to console with Asha, his first recruit for St. Jude's CCD.

"You see, father, my mother doesn't need me by her side," Asha said. "She has a whole cavalry doing that already."

"Cavalry, what a grown-up word," Schoeff said.

"I know what you're thinking. But the 'l' comes after the second 'a' on this one, and I don't have to make the sign of the cross every time I say it."

"A vocabulary tip for me," Schoeff said. "Advanced minds of fifth-graders these days." Schoeff made the cross sign himself. Asha laughed through her aches and pains. "Tell me, do you like these doctors?" Schoeff asked.

"They're funny sometimes but not like you."

"How are they funny?"

"I don't think they're funny the way you're funny," Asha changed her mind. "It's not the same."

"You, my friend, are blessed. Do me a favor and get a good night's rest."

"That's easy for you to say. It's thundering."

"Ah, but it's a good thunder. It's one from a good cloud fading away. A bright, elderly fellow outside is making sure that it's fading away."

Asha rolled her eyes. "If you say so," she said. "Wish me a relaxing dream."

"The most relaxed," Schoeff said.

He left the Gutierrez' apartment at one in the morning, far more invincible than he had been all of that week. The moon was out, and it was unmistakably crescent.

20

The Citizen

The following Monday morning at the Empire State Building, Rapha Antonisz' lawyer requested that Zeyad shorten his name so it could fit in the certificate.

"Just think of it as your American name," Rapha said. "New title for a new beginning."

"Thank you very much," Zeyad said. "But I like my name at the present time. It is my birth name. Thank you." He nodded to the lawyer, then to Rapha, and then to the lawyer's secretary.

"Well, that won't be much of an obstacle," the lawyer said. "Rebecca will just put the typeset on a smaller scale."

Rebecca, the secretary, then asked Zeyad to sign the prepared document, handing him the oath to recite. Zeyad thanked her but gave the pledge back.

"What's the matter now?" Rapha asked.

Zeyad put his hands together at his chest as if Rapha was a sacred pillar. "I do not want to be an American." He bowed down, ignoring the air of embarrassment he had caused in the room.

"But this is the chance of a lifetime," Rapha said. "Most foreigners have to go through immigration, years of waiting. Mr. Seufert here is offering you a citizenship right off the bat."

"Yes, why not just immigration?"

Rapha excused Zeyad and himself from Mr. Seufert and Rebecca. They went out in the hall, Zeyad clipping his cloak to his chest. "There seems to be a misunderstanding in your thinking," Rapha said. "You arrived in this country by fault, I know. But you are illegal, because you came in a tanker, for Pete's sake. What this man is offering you is immediate freedom, and if you don't take it, it's immediate deportation."

"That is if they find me," Zeyad pointed out. "Rapha, when I first had England in mind, I wanted to just see England, not live and grow old in England."

"Yes, yes, but things didn't work out as you planned. You drank potent liquor, overshot England. There was a little miscalculation involved, and that miscalculation turned out to be a good thing. It led you to me and a job that you were doing in Basra as a hobby. Now you got your picture in today's *Post* under the Arts & Crafts. You're famous. Your identity is no longer your own business."

"How long do you think before they find me?" Zeyad asked.

Rapha placed his hand on the doorknob back to the lawyer's office. "Believe me, Zeyad, it's a wonderful country," he said. "A lot of things have happened since the Emancipation Proclamation. "

Zeyad, thinking nothing about England and much of his homeland, went in and recited the oath.

21

Ira

It was true. Zeyad was a celebrity. Albert E. Thomas, famed columnist from the *New York Post*, had visited Antonisz Jewelry on a Monday and noticed the bold yet refined details on the dragons and camels from the Arabian collection, and within the week, Zeyad's photo and life story were in the paper. The newspaper thought it exotic to have an artist with such a zestful cognomen.

The first eager shoppers at Antonisz Jewelry after the article came out were none other than two members of Chereb's society circle.

"Where is this dark craftsman?" said Juliane upon entering the store.

"Hush, Julie," said Gigi McCormick, a tag-along from the art world of Greenwich Village.

"What? I say that as a compliment," Juliane said. "I know at least a dozen handsome *muchachos* at the hotel who don't mind being called dark."

"This is not a waiter," Gigi said. "This is a reluctant artist."

"May I help you, ladies?" Chereb said.

"Your darkest phallic stone, please," Juliane said.

"Excuse me?"

"Don't mind her, Reeby," Gigi said. "I didn't know she could use such terminology in a sentence. So...where is the man and his craft?"

"The man is behind those people, and his craft, all eleven pieces of them, are sold out. He's taking orders now."

"A hot commodity, isn't he?" Juliane said, peering over other browsers.

"Which is he?" asked Gigi on her toes. A gentleman in a duffle coat behind Chereb blocked her view.

"Come, I'll introduce you." But as Chereb turned with Juliane's arm, a slightly familiar face met hers with an undeniable eye-to-eye contact. "Pardon us," Chereb said.

"Reading the missalette lately?" the man inquired. He appeared not older than twenty-two, and the duffle coat assured the girls that he was a college boy.

"I saw you once at a very appropriate place," he said to Chereb.

"Oh? What place was that?" Chereb answered.

"As if you don't recall."

"No, not really."

The man gave a swift, choppy laugh.

"Pardon us," Chereb said again.

"Pardon me," said the man. Chereb pulled Juliane on, and they didn't see if Gigi had stayed to chat.

"What appropriate place was that?" Juliane whispered to Chereb.

"Beats me. He looks like a certifiable townie. It could be a beatnik bar."

But Chereb knew exactly where it had been and had seen that off-season coat before. Gigi was behind them, and Chereb felt relief. She hurried to the counter where Zeyad entertained brooch enthusiasts. "Zed," she called.

Zeyad excused himself and came to her assistance.

"Ah, more friends," he said.

"Yes, I'd like you to meet Juliane and Gigi. Ladies, Zeyad."

"Our pleasure," said Juliane. "It must be glorious to be a newfound artist."

"Thank you. Newfound yet old."

"Zed, look over my shoulder," Chereb said. "You see a man in a long, tannish coat?"

"Yes, the man praying at church and wanting you to pray, too."

"Are you positive?"

"Quite," he said. "I remember his smile. It is not too keen, as you would say. That much I see."

"What's this?" asked Gigi.

"Would you do me a favor?" Chereb said to Zeyad. "Would you go over there, introduce yourself and find out what his business is here?"

"Relax," Juliane said. "So he stumbled in here to look at earrings for his cousin. Not every joe who happens to mingle with you has intention to ravish."

"What are you talking about?" Chereb said. "You've heard that conversation. The man thinks I was somewhere appropriate, and he doesn't even know my name."

"He has to know your name," Juliane said. "The call of the wild needs to know Chereb."

Chereb looked at Juliane's eyes to see if she was stoned, but Rose Mary Getty had gone to the Virgin Islands and couldn't have possibly shared water pipes with Juliane this morning. "We'll talk about this another time," Chereb concluded.

Zeyad took off his black velvet apron and proceeded at a task he saw as essential to Rapha's daughter, though he hadn't the slightest idea how to introduce himself. He got behind the long "tannish" coat and started clearing his throat. "Excuse me," he said. "May I be of help?" The person obviously didn't hear him. "Sir, may I be of help to you?"

This time the man turned around and scanned Zeyad's loose apparel, which included a hunter green headpiece held by a panther pin with sapphire eyes. "Impressive," the man said.

"Hello, I'm Zeyad."

"Yes, Fatima`. Have you heard?"

"Excuse me?"

"Did you know that was the town where the Blessed Mary appeared in front of three children?"

"Yes, yes." Zeyad, surprised by this man's spontaneity in choosing a topic. "Actually, that town in Portugal was named after a daughter to the prophet Mohammed."

"Right you be. But our Mary utilized the place, do you see that?"

Zeyad avoided going further into this obvious clash-of-faiths challenge. "May I have the privilege of knowing your name, sir?" he asked.

"Certainly. Kublai. Kublai Kahn."

Zeyad dropped his hand. The man then bowed down to hide his smile, which would be a disparaging insult if this person were in Iraq, Zeyad thought. Then in all seriousness, Zeyad said, "Sir, the woman with whom you just had a small conversation, I believe, is the daughter of the Antonisz' and she is concerned about your affair here. She would like to know what exactly do you want."

"Mm, could you point her out to me?"

Zeyad did, though he knew it was nonsense.

Chereb avoided the glimpse with a quick reflex. She

pretended to be displaying a tray of bracelets to Gigi, who cooperated. Juliane had her face to the wall, excited in the suspense. "What if Zed brings him here?" she asked. "Then you'd know if he's dangerous or just a plain-joe admirer."

"Or something in between," Gigi commented.

"What would that be?" Chereb said.

"Horny."

Juliane giggled. "That's typical of a plain joe. They're likely to be that."

"I don't think he's a plain joe," Gigi said. "I spotted a Philip Patek and a gold pen clipped to his lapel. With that prep look, you may be talking Fifth Avenue and Columbia University here."

Zeyad managed to get back to the subject of names, and though the man did apologize for his sarcasm, he still did not provide a name. "Then you have business here?" said Zeyad.

"I frequent jewelry stores," the man said, showing a gold bracelet to Zeyad.

"Would you like something I would make in the future, another bracelet perhaps?"

"Yes, but you'd be an arm and a leg."

Zeyad was puzzled.

"Costly," said the man.

"Oh no, if you give me enough time, I will give it to you as a token."

"Are you real? Never mind, just tell Miss Antonisz it was my pleasure." He patted Zeyad on the shoulder and hastily walked out the front door, the musty draft blowing in.

"Who was he?" asked Chereb.

"Nameless. He would not say."

"Well, that eliminates horny, I'm afraid," Juliane said.

"He's reserved. Reserved people can control themselves till they get to their pads, then they let out the heaves."

Zeyad looked at Juliane in confusion.

22

Juliane

Chereb never wondered to the point if Juliane had a
permanent loose screw in that head of hers. As long as
Chereb had known her, she was formal, informal and
occasionally ditsy. According to Juliane's father, the hotel
owner, Juliane was a splendid Assistant Manager. When
Juliane had stepped up to that position, her father knew that
she couldn't possibly wander off to other venues outside of
the hotel business. She was the model Assistant Manager, a
queen on the middle step. When she waved adieu to her
peers that afternoon, she was totally unaware of the
edification into which she was about to enroll in. And to
think her vocabulary had just expanded to "phallic."

She had parked her Jaguar three blocks from
Antonisz Jewelry, and she was not about to hike Bronx'
slanted boulevards in a pair of heels. She tried, but at the
first sight of a yellow taxi, her hand sprang up involuntarily.
The cab stopped, but not for her. The man in the duffel coat
got it first, and Juliane froze where she stood, clutching her
sequined bag in front of her. At the last instant, he looked
her way and called out, "Care to share this?"

"Thank you kindly," Juliane said. "But there're

others."

"Not as dent-less as this one. Anyway, we both hailed it at the same time. As rules go, ladies get the privilege. Since I'm a man of the liberal, functional society, it'll be my pleasure to share it."

"C'mon," the cab driver snapped. "Can't you see that bus up my ass?"

Juliane, who was never an independent adventurer, darted for the opened door of the taxi. Inside she left plenty of room for the gentleman, who had not taken his eyes off her yet.

"Where to, lady?" said the cab driver.

"Up Maldoogan."

"This *is* Maldoogan."

"Yes, I know. I parked my Jag a little ways from here. That crumbling concrete is unbearable to walk on."

The gentleman smiled his slanted grin. "I know what you mean."

"Why? Do you have heels, too?" Juliane said.

"Not exactly, but I'm going farther." Because of his lanky limbs, he had no choice but extend an arm on the ridge of the backseat. "May I ask what your destination is after you get into your Jag? This will be a quick acquaintance if nothing…transpires now."

"What is your name?" Juliane asked. "You know, that was a great… mystery back there."

"I know. The star craftsman was investigating. Ira. Ira G. Othem." He offered his hand in such a suave manner that Juliane automatically took it. "But before mentioning your name in return," Ira said, "say your destination first."

Within an hour, Juliane made it to the Devoe-Hilton but not to her usual employment corner. Mr. Othem beckoned her to show him the best room the place could offer, so that he might recommend it to visiting friends in the future.

"I can't believe myself." Juliane laughed in the elevator. "It was radical enough to bring you in with me. But now I'm showing you the penthouse."

"Well, it's likely to please me," Ira said. "Among other things."

"Will I need the bellhop to look after me?"

"What is Miss Antonisz like?" Ira asked.

"Chereb?"

He nodded.

"Well, she's nice. She's just turned twenty, and her parents own a sizable portion of the Bronx. Oh, I see. She was your first target, and since you've missed, you had to settle for me."

"Not at all. I never see women as targets. The ones who are beautiful are just destined my way."

"What's your major in college? Analytical English?" The elevator opened to the penthouse. "This is it," Juliane announced.

"Do you need my assistance, Miss DeVoe?" asked the elderly elevator attendant.

Juliane looked at Mr. Othem suspiciously. "I'll be fine, Rudolf. Just bob up in fifteen minutes or so."

"Certainly, Miss DeVoe." Rudolf closed the elevator doors.

The large room was of French and harem decor. At every corner there was an exquisite piece of furniture, and mauve candles accentuated the dark wood. Mr. Othem walked in ahead, checking trinkets and curtain material. Juliane was starting to think he wasn't a campus boy at all.

"I'm a poet," he said. "The working kind, not the kind who writes three lines in the morning, walks the park in the afternoon and feels he can woo women in the evening since he had an inspirational, productive day."

"Published?" Juliane asked.

"Do you know that's the most degrading first question you could ask one who writes?"

"My apology."

They drifted into the open-door bedroom without realizing it. There, the huge bed with the sheer canopy reaching the ceiling came between them.

"I've published a volume at eighteen," Ira said.

"How old *are* you?"

He walked over to Juliane's side and gently touched her neck. She wasn't shocked. Her first thought was that he was a seasoned toucher. "That's the second most degrading thing you could ask." He slightly brushed her temple with his lips then caught her mouth, a bit lengthy for a first. He kissed her a second time, and she pulled away to catch her breath.

"This is so sudden," Juliane said.

"Shall we call Rudolf?"

"No!" She underestimated the tone of this response and was deeply embarrassed by it. What would her friends say? Getting acquainted with a dignified mystery man from the street, yes. But this?

Her "no" permitted Mr. Othem's hand to go down the glossy folds of navy satin between her thighs. She withstood it by trapping his paw with her legs. The hand persisted to move. The sensation was unreal, and so new, that Juliane fell to the bed, helpless beyond her grasp. How can vulgar be so finesse, and the moment be so...rare?

23

Modesty of Night

Schoeff had enough confidence in Asha's health for the time being to turn to other affairs. At St. Jude's, as he was soaking an infant's head over the font, he drew the conclusion that Oscaro, although misguided, had a legitimate reason to choose Asha over his younger brother and sisters. But Schoeff realized he was giving leeway to a matter so dreadful it didn't deserve second thought. He wasn't completely himself when the monsignor asked to have a word with him in the south annex.

"A fellow named Fuller called and left a message twice asking my permission to interview you on the radio," said the monsignor. "May I ask what possible jamboree could he be interested in in doing so?"

"Yes, jamboree, here I come," Schoeff said.

"Just last Friday, I was at Daphne's Café, and I heard someone speak of an unwell man in farm clothes preaching on top of an ambulance and making random predictions on just about anything. Was that you, Howard Schoeff?"

It was the first time he had heard his full name spoken by a clergy without "father." To this, Schoeff said, "Monsignor, your holiness, you are speaking to an endorsed premonitionist."

"Is that so?"

"When you had that asthma episode and I was at your side, that wasn't all me that brought you back to breathing."

"No?"

"You were sinking, and you were somehow spared."

"Spared?"

"Maybe you have a role in this mission I'm in, or maybe for the benefit of the parish, I'm not quite sure."

"Hold, hold," the monsignor said. "What mission, precisely?"

"That, Monsignor, I can't fully pinpoint. All I know I have constant guidance, a sort of a day-to-day instruction, and in that, constant proof."

"What proof?" The intensity on the monsignor's face doubled, or was the Monsignor being sarcastic? Schoeff couldn't tell.

"Well, aside from your sparing," Schoeff said.

"Yes, aside that."

Yep, the monsignor was mocking. "A couple weeks ago," Schoeff continued. "I was in Hoboken at an ice-cream social when the sun shone particularly bright on a window of a medical building. I went in and searched for the room of that window, and sure enough, monsignor, I met a child psychiatrist who knew me inside and out. Even his carpet was stark bright. The man knew my thoughts. Thoughts I have kept for most of my life, going back to my childhood in Logansport. Parables and visions, made-easy. Not an overview of that book, but a concise, detailed portion. That child psychiatrist in Hoboken knew exactly why I came. Your grace, are you catching any of this?"

"Relax, father."

"My fear comes when people don't believe in what I have to say," Schoeff said.

The monsignor stared at him. "All I know is—and you may take this as assurance—that my doctor today told me I don't need albuterol anymore before each sermon. He said that the synapses in my brain have become potent, beefing up my respiratory system. I have been doing the routine since I don't care to remember."

"Hallelujah!" Schoeff burst out. "Are you pulling my leg, father?"

"If I could, I would not," the monsignor said. "Tell me, for what purpose do you prophesy? Is it in any way related to the Second Coming?"

"Not that...precise. But, thank you."

"Cut the plain priest modesty. If this is happening to you, this must be documented, and parallels from higher references must be found, and the Vatican comes next."

"I feel it's in early stages. And modesty is as comforting as things happening in random, and certainly nothing official has been granted."

"Certainty has not been granted?" Monsignor Randolph said and dwelled on it a little. "Well, then, you have my permission to go on radio," he said. "You realize after this interview, a hailstorm would be at our front step. Your modesty would disappear then, that knee-scraping on concrete you will feel." The gray-haired monsignor paused to use the easy function of his lungs. "As for me," he said. "It hasn't been a bed of roses, you know. I've also stepped on thorns to get to where I am. This modesty you're talking about, it doesn't blend with the fruit of your foresight."

Schoeff's throat bobbed up. "Thank you," he said.

"And I am sure this envy will eventually subside. Now I must say good evening."

Schoeff looked him in the face, and by its stillness, Schoeff thought it best to just leave.

24

Door by Design

In the afternoon when the sun was beginning to provide agreeable warmth, Oscaro walked through Wild Asia with his younger brother and sisters. The Bronx Zoo had opened their gates for the first time after a long winter, and the exotics were most curious and funny at this time. Oscaro reminded the kids to hold hands. "Pilu!" he shouted when he saw his brother getting too close to a huge tortoise.

"I think that thing is safe," Asha said. She was on Oscaro's shoulders as if she had a cast on a limb.

"I don't know," Oscaro said. "That thing looks like it had no breakfast yet, and Pilu may look like cabbage to it."

"Yeah, but that gate doesn't swing out," Asha said. "That tortoise can't even bull head its way out."

"I don't know," Oscaro joked, with Pilu contemplating to go closer still.

"Pilu!" Asha shouted. "Get back here...now!"

One of the sisters retrieved Pilu and rejoined him in the chain. With their mother at work, they had a couple of hours to enjoy the lovely zoo. Oscaro was feeling at ease also. He wasn't due at the ESSO gas station till six.

"Oscaro, was Papa *patinguilan* like you?" Asha

115

wondered with a laugh.

"Excuse me?" Oscaro said, squeezing her shins. "Hey, don't use that word in front of the padre'. He might not know what it means, but he's wondering. It's embarrassing."

Asha laughed. "He doesn't know."

"Oh, he might. All those priests are what you call bilingual."

"You mean multilingual. Our dialect, if he knows it, it's one of many."

"And don't be a smartass. We're not paying those nuns good money so you can be a smartass."

"But was Papa like you?" Asha wondered still.

"Yeah, he was like me. But we should not be thinking of him anymore, the shit."

"Is he coming back?"

"No, maybe, when he feels like it," Oscaro said. "He's got to take over my spot here, take you kids to this stinking zoo for once." Oscaro realized he was punishing Asha again for speaking her mind. Vania, the six-year-old, stopped walking in front of them.

"How come, *nong*, Asha gets to be on your shoulders?" Vania protested. That "nong" means honorable older brother.

"Because I'm sick," Asha said.

Oscaro, still deep within himself, ignored the two. The talk about Asha being adopted, which Asha was not aware of, was just in passing or it might have been just Oscaro's weak defense when he was questioned by Schoeff. But in truth, these doctors wanted a bright child, and Asha had been that, obviously.

Anyway, they were close-knit as siblings at the zoo. The exit gate was in sight, and they had to catch the bus.

Those kids would have plenty of rest on the way home. Oscaro allowed his father in his mind a little longer. He wondered if the old man--who was living in the U.S. territory of Hawaii on a war pension the last time Oscaro heard--ever carried a kid on his shoulders.

25

Air Men

WDDS was on the twentieth floor of the Flatiron Building, a range height that could reach Cleveland. Schoeff was treated like he owned the Holy Grail upon entering the studio. The weatherman shook Schoeff's hand and asked to be blessed. Mr. Fuller told the weatherman to save his haggling and let the priest get ready.

"I'll be introducing you as an associate clergy at St. Jude's," Mr. Fuller said. "Things like modern-day prophet and awesome outlook, well, that's all up to you, father. Would you like to rehearse your opening?"

"If I rehearse," Schoeff said. "I can't guarantee what I say would be the same as when we'd be on air."

"Ah, divine thoughts at the spur of the moment."

"Just plain thoughts," Schoeff said.

"He's modest, too," blipped in the weatherman.

"Mr. Javier, disconnect Mr. Pyle, please," Fuller said.

The sound room was a tiny place with a La-Z-Boy, a barstool and a huge mic hanging from the ceiling. The walls were matted with what seemed to be egg crates to Schoeff.

"Now, father, when that blue light flashes, that means calls are coming in."

"Ah, K-Mart dawning."

"Pardon?"

Schoeff shook his head nothing.

Fuller placed his headphones. He suggested for Schoeff to drink water if needed. Mr. Javier signaled sixty seconds.

The first thought in Schoeff's mind was the floor underneath them was on fire. He was nervous. Fuller felt it and mimed to him to make use of the La-Z-Boy, get comfy. Javier pointed, flagging that they were on air.

"A pleasant good evening, New York," Fuller began. "Welcome to Metro Voice, brought to you by Chloro-Eze. If your head's not at peace, try Chloro-Eze. Available in tablet or syrup. Our guest for tonight may well be a personality in the future, in a sense that he could foretell. Last week some two thousand of you witnessed his becoming from the top of a Packard ambulance just south of Times Square. Welcome, Father Schoeff."

"Thank you," Schoeff said.

Mr. Javier signaled for him to speak up.

Schoeff spoke louder with, "My appreciation, Mr. Fuller, glad to be here."

Fuller nodded. After mentioning Schoeff's day job and Indiana background, he asked, "Why appear on Times Square in a ho-down carpenter's garb?"

"Laundry day," Schoeff said. "But with meaning. The garb signifies gusto, and the ambulance meant urgency. Put two and two together, you make a strong statement. Moses did it with a staff and sandals, and he made people walk to their freedom."

"You said it, not me, father. So, there is that word...prophecy."

"Well, it's in the buildup of the mind, like an

119

architect drawing up a blueprint. He adds more detail as he sees fit, and function."

"Hmm, but wasn't there more significance in the driver of that ambulance, as I recall?"

"Yes," Schoeff said. "My credential, singular. He is the one behind all this. He is what I am nurtured and raised to be about. He picked my apparel and the spot where I was to speak. I am here now on my own will, but his persuasion is something, more liberating than Monsignor Randolph's permission."

Back at St. Jude's, the monsignor, four other priests and a flock of nuns gathered around the RCA with the volume turned up. Monsignor Randolph turned to a sister and asked, "What in the world is he saying?"

Fuller crackled, "Tell me, father. Who is this credential and what is his occupation? I want to hear it from you."

Schoeff didn't expect this question to come so early. He looked around the studio, looking for the weatherman behind the glass, maybe postponing his gut answer. "Let me put it this way," Schoeff began.

The wrinkles on Fuller's temples smoothen at that instant. His complexion lightened of the red he started with, perhaps, from a day of stress. "What are you afraid of?" Fuller said in a deeper, more content voice. "Speak of the Mind truthfully, and I will energize yours. This moment is only between you and I, but there are waves of ears out there once you become audible."

Then everything returned. Furrows deepened again on Fuller's face. He was back to himself. "Go on, father," he said.

"Mr. Divinity himself!" Schoeff shouted. "His occupation? Why, eternal Nanny, of course! What do you want from me? People think He's slow on the watchful eye, but they don't know he has eyes even in his ears. Physiology, we don't know!" Schoeff shivered, then calmed down, causing silence in the radio station.

"Whoa, father," Fuller said. "And I thought he was a chauffeur from Evenings Unlimited."

Schoeff managed to catch his breath. "He may well be," he said and leaned forward. "Mr. Fuller, he was you just now."

"Excuse   me?"

"Do you remember saying, 'speak of the mind truthfully?'" Schoeff asked. He examined Fuller's eyes up close. "It should still be in your short term."

Fuller gawked with an open mouth. He cued Mr. Javier to cut to an early station break. "We will continue in two minutes with Father Schoeff and my answer to his entrancing query. And now from our sponsor." The jingle for Chloro-Eze ran. Javier signaled clear. Fuller pursed his mouth. "Father, if it's not too much to ask, knock off the psychic bit. It's clearly out of context here."

"You remembered."

"Listen, I have been at this all day, preparing a credible line of questions in the hope that New York might buy it. Something like this comes up and throws everything off, totally uncouth. Get my drift, father?"

"He spoke through you telling me not to deny Him. Evidence that there has to be a minding...if you will."

"Look, my kid has just been admitted to a clinic with the clap, and all my ex could jabber about over the phone is how her corgi is in dire need of obedience school. I'm a divorced man, father. The last time I respectfully went to church, Roosevelt was still in office. Why would divinity wallow in the throat of a calloused, scheme-as-long-as-it-is-

121

safe radio man?"

"You'll voluntarily train the corgi yourself," Schoeff said. "Not a demand but a fact. And despite all, you visit your son with the acute syphilis and tell him everything would be A-Okay."

The blue light flashed meaning calls were coming in. Javier waved five seconds. Fuller, still baffled, said, "Welcome...Metro Voice. Here with the reluctant soothsayer, one Father Schoeff. And yes, I had promised you an answer to his asking. Yes, I do remember the line 'speak of the mind truthfully,' but I don't recall ever saying it."

Javier behind the glass showed a face of disapproval but contained himself not to get involved.

"He thanks you," Schoeff said. The blue light lit on.

"Compared to the old," Fuller said. "As one in the Bible, if you will, your outlook seems to be more widespread, no boundaries, sporadic. Like for instance, you talk about the intensity of crime in forty years one moment and the next you would be describing a deteriorating man in an infirmary suffering from a yet undiscovered disease. How is that?"

"Yes, all will be funneled into one." Schoeff thought of mentioning that all started with his Uncle Dam. But that would only confuse things.

"Your credential?"

Schoeff smiled.

"Divinity?" Fuller restated.

"Well, it all fits in. My message has something to do with everything in forty some years."

"Okay, hold that thought," Fuller said. "Let me clarify my question for the audience. To Moses, it was to free the Israelites from oppression. To your St. Paul, it was to turn men to Christ. Do you feel within that company?"

"In a sense that these men slept, ate and would have enjoyed the game of Scrabble. But beyond that, no way."

Fuller held on. "What is Father Schoeff's goal in his prophecy, or to put it in a more non-suggestive manner, what is the divine duty bestowed upon you?"

"To put a threshold on New York. Maybe clean it up a little."

"A threshold?" Fuller stammered. "You mean like a doorway?" His faith in the priest was in muddy waters again.

"More like a door jamb."

"What the hell do you mean, father?" Fuller said. "I know you mean it symbolically, but the Mayor wouldn't know what to do with symbolic."

"Yes. But I'm talking about picking up soda-pop bottles. We're in the same page. This city is growing apart from itself. Its citizens are forming groups and building walls. In Brooklyn, it's the Italians and the Jews. In the Bronx, it's the Polish and the non-whites. And there will be more ethnic groups moving in and forming their own villages because they're not allowed to settle in where they want. As it is showing now, languages will become fences, and there will be pressure if one person communicates with another person of a different color. Crime will grow twenty-fold in fifteen years. Drug abuse will be so widespread that one out of every nine children will die of drug-related misfortunes. This will be due primarily to grouping. People will help one another only when there'll be a great moment of bang, none before. People will be homeless by the thousands. 'Homeless' is not a household word yet, but it will be in forty years. The rest of the country may be a world power, but New York will be third world. Pago Pago could beat it in housing development."

123

Fuller, amused by this sudden outburst, smiled skeptically at Schoeff. Schoeff grinned like a freshly redeemed comic. "Are you saying that the root of all problems this city will face years on are due to racial tension?"

"Not all. I think the covid flu in 2019 will be due to closed-in nursing facilities not released to a more space-worthy battleship."

Both Fuller and Javier remained silent.

"But seriously," Schoeff continued. "All the major ones will be. People will have to realize that segregation is a drawback. It may be comfortable, but in the long run, it ignores the problems, plaguing the community as a whole."

"You make it sound unsettling," Fuller said. "But I guarantee you that ninety percent of the people out there disagree."

"In due time, that will change. My worry is there won't be effort. The days I see are not here yet. The buildings I see aren't built yet. I just have to stick to example buildings."

Fuller dropped the thought of asking Schoeff to expand on this allegory. "I've always thought that the future is unchangeable," Fuller said instead. "All depends on chance."

"It is, and it does. Free will has the authority on that, but free will can be enhanced, and that is my primary duty. To me, I've always thought the future couldn't be seen in a physical, structural kind of way till I read it, envisioned it and shook hands with it at a psychiatrist's office and in an alley and felt the gravity of it in my skin. The future is under my skin, and it feels clammy."

"In an alley?"

"On a Barcalounger."

Fuller dropped it, sighed, signaled for Javier to cut.

26

Twenty-Nine Callers

Fuller reminded the city that Father Schoeff would welcome insights after the break, adding, "if there is any room on our switchboard already." He turned to Schoeff and said, "Put on your thinking cap, father. You might have to sing and dance."

"Yes," Schoeff said.

"Do you have any aspirations of being an entertainer?" Fuller asked.

"It's not in me per se, but if Hope and Crosby need a third leg, I'm game."

The red light came on, and Fuller welcomed back his listeners. He waited for Agnes, the caller editor, to cue in the first inquirer, and she brought forth a young man from the Upper East Side.

"Hello, you're on Metro Voice," Fuller said. "Your insight, please."

"Yes, I would like to challenge the father. What worthy function does anyone have to tell of a dying gruel in some hospital forty years from now?"

"Father?" Fuller said.

"For short, there'll be a line of dying gruels leading up to this, and the number will multiply exponentially from December 8, 1973 on. I assure you that this dying individual won't be alone."

"What event would take place on December 8, 1973?" asked Fuller.

"Patient Zero will pass away due to lobar pneumonia. That's classified. Even Encyclopedia Britannica will not record this bit of fact." Schoeff winked and pointed up. "Only."

Fuller, perplexed, clicked on the next caller.

"Hello, this is Martha Amore Davis from Brooklyn, New York."

"Hello, Martha," Schoeff said. "How are you this splendid evening?"

"Not too bad. How do you do, father?"

"Oh, perspiring at the moment, but my shirt is perma-press."

Martha laughed. "Father, I'm a colored person in a colored family who happens to live in an all-white neighborhood, and they treat us just fine. I mean we being here in contrast with the rest. Mrs. Cacenski, the lady next door, even sent a house-warming bouquet the first day we got in. My son is an internist down at Mercy, and he himself hasn't even been bothered when he comes walking down the sidewalk. Now, as opposed to your prediction, aren't we a good sign for mixing in the future?"

"Yes, you are, Mrs. Davis. You live in a good neighborhood."

There was a silence of wonder in the studio. Schoeff smiled at his interviewer.

"Hello, you're on Metro Voice," Fuller welcomed the third caller.

"Mr. Fuller, this is an exec from the Chrysler Building. What kind of fools do you take us for, putting a hocus-pocus quack on your program?"

"I think this one will have to go unanswered," Fuller said, beckoning Agnes. Agnes mimed back that the man had switched his question.

Schoeff said that he would like to answer. "Sir," Schoeff said. "Mr. Fuller is a committed radio personality who is concerned about tomorrow. As for you, sir, you will be saved from bankruptcy by a fellow named Lee Iacocca. But I think you'll miss your chance to be on Metro Voice since you will defy Mr. Iacocca, questioning his trust in leading the company, him being an ex-Ford man."

Agnes cued in the fourth caller, a twenty-three-year-old mother of four who feared the bleak images of the city Schoeff had described. Schoeff told her to mind-see her children as grownups and live well in these kind days.

"That colored lady just proved you wrong," claimed the eighth caller. "People will have no trouble mixing in neighborhoods. No one's going to fight over which territory is his."

"For sure not Mrs. Davis," Schoeff replied. "But in 1995, the so dubbed 'trial of the century' will occur and it will split the nation in half. An O.J. will be accused of murdering a Nicole and a Ron. I will not tell you the verdict. I will only tell you what Ron's father will say after the verdict. Ron's father will remind us that 'the *country* has lost rather than the prosecution,' meaning that the big divide separating this nation with race will still be big that late in time."

"Father, what's an O.J.?" Fuller asked.

"It stands for Orenthal James."

"Therefore?"

"Therefore, Orenthal James will be accused of murder, of the two."

"What would make this trial earn the name, the trial of the century? Obviously, O.J. will be somebody famous."

"Correct," Schoeff said. "He will rush for the San Francisco Giants."

"Ah, city football?"

"Yes."

"Okay. O.J. is accused of murdering Nicole...and Ron?"

"His ex-wife," Schoeff said. "But you're not doing bad on the future scope."

"But still, father, it seems trivial. To split the country in half, I mean, it would take some kind of disturbing political...ingredient."

"Beats me," Schoeff said. "It's certainly not for the fact that O.J. is black and Nicole is white and Ron will just be returning a pair of sunglasses."

Mr. Fuller jumped off the stool to cover the mic in front of them, and Schoeff thought it would take more than two hands to edit what he just said to New York. Mr. Fuller mimed for him to cut the thought.

"Not good for Mrs. Davis to hear?" Schoeff whispered.

The radioman ignored him. After sighing deeply, Fuller let go of the mic and checked the clock. Fuller estimated he had time for two more calls, perhaps enough to sway his audience to forget the trial of the century. The switchboard was lit up like a Christmas tree, still. Mr. Javier, after regrouping himself, talked to Agnes.

"Father, this is Jack," said the present caller. "Jack, from the curb."

"Good to hear you, Jack," Schoeff said.

"I done lost the tools."

Schoeff signaled Agnes to keep Jack on. "How?" Schoeff asked Jack.

"Same old deal." Jack began to cry. "I've gambled off Heny again. I done lost her."

"Jack, Jack, those tools come with a warranty. Come by St. Jude's tomorrow after four and we'll see what we can do."

Over the break, Schoeff explained Jack's dilemma to Fuller. Mr. Javier said it would be wise to extend the program for another fifteen minutes because of the incoming calls. "I think a third of the city is listening. Sponsors will be ringing in tomorrow by the dozen." And when Fuller still didn't look too content, Mr. Javier added, "No one really heard it in full."

Metro Voice ran an extra hour and a half that Sunday evening. Father Schoeff answered most of the negativity the best he could--from the little capsule in his head.

Monsignor Randolph, back at St. Jude's Cathedral, was in the rhythm of his snoring when one of the nuns got up and switched off the radio.

27

The Desk

Even as a young published poet, Ira G. Othem was steadfast on everything. For one, his name, which he thought was undauntingly poetic, graced the cover of his first volume, in spite of his mother's wish to replace Othem with Clareaux, her maiden name. It sounded more literary and lasting. Ira had the habit of penning free verse at all hours of the day especially after waking from a nap. But this evening he didn't need energy from sleep. He tossed his mesh coat on the sofa, switched on the light over his school desk and began writing. It was more like scribbling, as if his bottled ideas would fly out the window if he didn't place them on paper quick enough.

"Where have you been?" his mother asked.

"Good evening, Mother. Your bad back, I assume?"

"It's nearly two in the morning."

"So, it's not your back. It's waiting for me that's keeping you from sleep."

"Where have you been?" his mother persisted.

"A woman at the DeVoe-Hilton," Ira said. "The

daughter of DeVoe himself."

In her embroidered robe, his mother stood appalled. "I beg your pardon?" she said.

"Yes, I was with a damsel of stature." He paused. "But I wouldn't call her fully-developed. No, I wouldn't."

"Four nights?"

"It took me that long to get *her* number."

"Look at you, all stooped up over that pupil's desk like a living gargoyle."

"It's my status symbol, my metaphor. Brooks toyed around with a rocking chair when she published her first book of potato-and-grits poems."

His mother walked off toward the nook of their West Side apartment. "Are you hungry, dear?" she asked. "Who is this DeVoe girl anyhow? What makes her appealing besides being well-off?"

Ira suddenly felt his mother's questions had no relevance and left them unanswered.

28

Assistant Manager

There were six telephones in the Antonisz' house with four different numbers. Two were basically Chereb's personal lines, and they were strategically located in her bedroom and in the spa. The latter was meant to be for anyone's convenience, but after years of teenage chatting, it simply became Chereb's phone by the Jacuzzi. She never gave the number in her bedroom to boys or to first-time callers. They had to work their way up to that level. Only her three closest friends knew of the number at the moment. The young Wall Street lawyer whom she had an affair with knew it, but he had faded off to Pennsylvania with his family. Zeyad, of course, memorized it the first week he was there, in case he had to wake Chereb to pick him up from the mosque in Passaic County. Zeyad wasn't considered a male prospect. He was more like an asset, one of great importance, like the mailman.

"Miss Chereb," Zeyad whispered at the door to the study. "My apologies, but Miss Juliane is at the phone by the water."

Chereb looked up from bending her back and to the front again, doing her every other day stretches. "Why would she call me there?"

"I don't know. She followed her instinct that you were in the study and not in your bedroom. It has been known to occur between devout Muslims."

Chereb went down to the spa and took the call. "Julie, are you a Muslim?" Chereb snapped.

"No," Juliane emitted.

"Then hang up and dial me upstairs. It's hot in here."

"No, this can't wait another moment."

"Go on."

"I don't know exactly how to put this. Oh, help me."

"Is something the matter?"

"Oh," Juliane moaned. "Oh, Reeb, you know last Friday at your Arab friend's jewelry exhibit, that man in the long tan coat? He picked me up."

"Picked you up?"

"Well, dazzled me off the street. Actually, he needed a ride." Juliane went on to tell her the whole interlude. "I offered him the penthouse, but he insisted on being closer to the office where I work. So, I put him in the Guilliam Suite, and Chereb, every break I had, he would know and come after me. It was tyrannical, on his part, anyway."

"Hmm."

"The third time we did it, it was in the lounge by the pianoforte."

"Miss Juliane!" Chereb said. "Not by your father's pianoforte."

"Yes, isn't that unlike me? It seemed like a long roller coaster ride."

"Well, I'm happy for you, Julie. I hope the relationship grows."

"Did it ever."

"Juliane, let's *not* forget ourselves!"

134

"Oh, I gave him your phone number."

"What?"

"He wants to invite us to an upcoming writers' ball at the Waldorf."

"Why couldn't he just mention it through you? Juliane, my numbers are strictly for us."

"Mm. Anyway, he has ties with a Harrison somebody, an upbeat novelist I'm sure Rose Mary knows, and Ira wants this person to interrelate with you."

It was this unyielding openness in Juliane that Chereb could take a vacation from now and then. In her own cautious corner, Chereb was glad to avoid any utter that might have hinted envy, which she believed she didn't have an ounce of. This Ira person might have just skimmed at random, and Juliane just happened to have crossed his path in convenience. "What am I thinking of?" Chereb said to herself after she hung up the phone. "I don't want to cross paths with that louse."

29

The Patriot

In Rapha's den, which was adjacent to the jacuzzi room, there was a life-sized Spanish Armada statue with sword and all. Zeyad ducked behind it and straightened himself once it was safe. He asked at the door, "To whom are you speaking?"

Chereb jumped. "Nobody. To myself, to the air! That has been known to occur with Americans alone in spas." On another thought, Chereb turned around and said, "Forgive me, Zed. Some people just can't keep their erotic adventures to themselves." She felt irate and at ease at the same time in Zeyad's presence. "Don't tell me you need to go somewhere," she moaned.

"I do."

"Zeyad, you're a star jeweler. You can afford a full-time chauffeur. Talk to Dad about a loaner."

"But I need your company only, not a ride. I need to walk to the school down the block where the flag is."

Chereb knew what he meant. She kept a straight face and turned to him. "Zed, listen, we don't worship the face of Eisenhower or the Statue of Liberty or the American flag at some school yard just because we got a note from the citizenship bin telling us to do so. These are the Fifties. Happy times even for Muslims in New York, get my definition?"

Zeyad bowed down. "It's not my wish to worship the flag. I worship only Allah."

"Forget it, Zed. You're standing on lush, well-built and well-decorated lush, that happens to be the Bronx. That's enough land kissing for all of us in this house. So, just say your Pledge of Allegiance where you stand. I'll slip into a bathing suit and have a spiked chocolate Coke out in the patio."

"As you wish."

"Right you are."

"I will leave this room now." Zeyad walked off.

"Zed, no hard feelings."

"No hard feelings. Enjoy your cola."

*

Under the cool sun before noon, Zeyad stood in the backcourt of a school. The band of children playing in the distance saw him in a white dress, looking up their flagpole as only an immigrant out for a walk. And when he squatted on the ground, Asha just took him for a brave soul, unlike her laughing classmates.

Zeyad, deep within himself, saw the sky darkening. He was there on a mishap, a five-thousand-mile miscalculation, and now he was part of it, the land of the free and blue jeans and big, bloated Chevrolets and women with uncovered faces. He couldn't place the tears he shed. Were they for his mother and siblings? Or were they for the decorative fences that suddenly slithered around him, like the Great Wall of China? His homeland with its dry heat and occasional dust storms couldn't be more enticing at the moment.

Upon returning to the Antonisz' house, the one uncovered face he had seen the most was lying on a narrow bed under the scorch of the sun. Her flesh, the shape of her limbs, her skin so white. Why did she expose herself to eyes that were accustomed to sacred things? Such contrast was hard to take. He pushed himself away from the balcony.

Chereb caught a glimpse of his frock through her cat-eye sunglasses. She thought nothing of it and applied more oil on her shoulders. She basted till four that afternoon, just enough to show a touch of Caribbean on her skin at the beginning of summer.

30

A Gentleman Caller

Chereb did not see Zeyad again for the rest of the evening. She dined alone with two candles over lamb chops and vino. She had yet to start on Rose Mary's manuscript, a freshly written novella she had promised to read and give an opinion. She placed it in front of her in the study. Upon seeing the word "trammel," she wondered what she had been drinking when she granted Rose Mary the favor. One of the phones rang, and she couldn't track which one. She listened more intently. Since her mother was in the master, likely to answer the phone in there, the rings were definitely coming from her bedroom. She hustled up the stairs. The caller was patient.

"Hello," Chereb sighed.

"Good evening."

"Likewise. Who's this?"

"I've never had the pleasure of meeting you, Gwendolyn. But my colleagues tell me it's my heart's content to know you."

"Wrong number, *monsieur*," Chereb said and hung up. Within the minute, the phone rang again. "Hello."

"Isn't your hair white as stationery? Pardon me, I

don't mean to interrupt. But your hair complimented your whole existence when I saw you."

"Who is this?"

"That's not important right now. It's just that mere communication should be established between us, and in due time other things would fall into place. I needed to hear from you."

"Look, first of all, I'm not Gwendolyn. Gwendolyn is at another phone anxiously waiting for you to call her, I'm sure. So, hang up and dial another number."

"Are your legs, may I ask, as bright as your hair?"

Chereb thought of saying *Hell yeah, and they'll kick in your member into your stomach, understand?* but she clicked the man off without another word. She left the handset unhooked. This city got on her nerves at times. When it was this detailed, it was usually due to her prank-making friends.

That call had the likes of one Rachel Browning, Chereb thought. It had the dramatics. Ah, it was Jared, the cubist, who knew the film editor, whom in turn adored Rachel. At the thought, Chereb placed back the handset, certain that it would ring again.

31

Sons and Daughters

At the ESSO station down Jerome and Burnside, Oscaro contemplated on using the pay phone. He was in the garage under a Pontiac with an oil leak, a drop light at his side. It was a clean pan, all things considered. The lugs still showed their pewter color. It was senseless loosening them just to find the gasket was unbroken. Oscaro lay motionless on the crawler.

"I don't hear any ratchet," said George Pinelli, his boss. "What's the matter, kid? Lost your nap today?"

"No, I'm awake. Just that..."

Georgie looked under. "Clean, huh, kid?"

"Yeah, it is, Mr. Pinelli. Hey, do you have any daughters?"

"What kind of a question is that?"

"No, I mean young kid daughters. Maybe granddaughters?"

"I do."

"Just thinking," Oscaro said, working on the first lug. "Do you give them whatever they want?"

"Hm...what?"

"Like if they wash your car or shine your shoes?"

"You got the wrong offspring, kid. My boys do that."

"That's what I figured."

Oscaro loosened three lugs and found the gasket ripped at one corner. The owner of this vehicle must have his boys spray the bottom every time the car went through a puddle. It was a quarter till eleven when he had finished, too late to ring up St. Jude's. He knew he wouldn't get the padre' first on the line anyway. Oscaro clocked out and rode home to his own offspring's.

32

An Arab at Prayer

"It'd better be spectacular," Chereb moaned from her hour-old sleep.

"I'm sorry to wake you...."

It's *him*! she thought viciously.

"...But I've been thinking of you. The moment I saw you a little over a month ago, I couldn't, well, satisfy the burden inside me till I have your number. "You don't know what this...."

She hung up and when it rang again, she pulled on the wire. On the third yank, it came off the wall. "Why can't people be crazy at eleven in the morning?" she said and tried desperately to fall back to sleep.

At the glimpse of day, she got to her feet and called for Zeyad, who was nowhere to be found. She flounced around in her silk robe and furry slippers asking maids and gardeners if they had seen the Sheik of Jewels. She realized it was Friday morning. Zeyad should be at the mosque in Passaic, she decided, but that was twenty miles away. She ran back upstairs and slipped into jeans. She left the house with her hair uncombed, which she noticed in the rearview mirror in her father's Bel Air. She drove fast, and when she arrived in New Jersey, at the mosque's parking lot, she looked around for any item in the car that would hold her hair up. One of Rapha's hats was in the backseat. She put it on, repositioned it till she thought it was conservative enough for the religious.

Inside the mosque, she found Zeyad on hands and knees, his scalp toward the altar. The rest were looking at her at the door. "Zed," she said not immensely loud but audible to the farthest person from her. He seemed sedated. She had no time for this. "Zed?" Each of the dozen people there had taken a second look at the Jean Harlow look-alike, with the gangster hat, all except for Zeyad who remained in his stooped position. Chereb got the message. With embarrassment, she walked out. Five minutes into her wait, she began pacing.

Zeyad was one of the last to leave the building.

"I'm sorry," Chereb said, as he walked by her. "But I had to see you first thing, to talk about the weirdo."

Zeyad kept on walking.

"Zed?" Chereb caught up to his side. "Why didn't you wake me to drive you here? How early did you get up? Listen, you have to help me on this."

The Arab refused to talk.

"Hey, I'm sorry. I know this place is strictly for praying, and I should have been more in control...vocally."

Zeyad was a walking mannequin.

"All right, all right, if you have to be stiff about it...."

Zeyad stomped his feet and turned, whiplash fashion, brazing his nail on Chereb's arm accidentally. "Ouch," she said.

"Sharia does not permit me to speak to you," Zed said.

"Who's she?"

144

"I am sorry, but we are of different backgrounds. We cannot communicate. It is law."

Chereb nodded, biting her lip. She knew of this nature, had understood the origin of anger. "Listen," she said, suddenly disturbed herself. "I've told you that I'm not attached to that different-in-background crapola, nor do I have a burden on my back about the afterlife while I live and breathe, you understand?"

"No, you understand me," Zeyad lashed back. "You are not here if not for Creation."

"Creation what?"

"Creation this," Zeyad retorted, pointing at the cleanly swept sidewalk. "You do things *not* of creation, like burning your skin and wearing little garments and going to Meadowland Park hoping to witness alien! There is no good *function* in these everyday things you do. You are fighting the very purpose of what you are."

"It's called tanning and bikini and Martian mania, and it's none of your beeswax," she retorted. "You call what you're wearing functional? Zed, you're wearing this, a dress, on Grand Concourse this morning where every sicko was still on the watch for something exotic?"

"We do not think alike."

"No?"

"It's better to leave Creation…beliefs out of our talks," Zed admitted.

"Well put."

"What couldn't wait?"

"I don't know if I should even bother."

"Forgive me."

"Are you calm now? Are you in control of yourself?" Chereb asked.

"Yes."

"Zed, I need for you to stay in my room tonight."

Zeyad frowned. Sweat accumulated at the inside brim of his cap.

"That person at your jewelry jamboree. Juliane, ditsy alien herself, has given my bedroom number to this person, and he made two calls last night!"

"Prank?"

"Yes! Zed, I think he's a sex fiend, and he wants something from me." Chereb looked at another puzzled expression. "Sex fiend, sex fiend...uh, do you know how you would want to clothe me if I'm half naked?" She did a charade with the little garments. "This person wants to take them off...." She mimed the rest. "And he is the same gentleman you spoke to."

Zeyad, at immeasurable loss, nodded. "Yes, I will stay at your room tonight," he said and walked off.

33

The Mechanic

Schoeff paid an extra five dollars in cab fare to get to the Sears & Roebuck. At the tools section, he examined sledgehammers and pulleys and electric chop saws before he found the set of common tools he wanted.

"Aren't these on special?" he asked the tools representative.

"Oh, yes," said the young man. "From seven-fifty to six even."

"In that case, I'll take nine sets."

"Nine? But, father, these are Craftsman. They're guaranteed for life. You'll only need one set."

"Generous young man, you're underselling yourself. The man at the office is not St. Nick listening in to your good deeds. He's the boss with your commission check."

The boy nodded.

"By the way, are these guaranteed against loss? If that's the case, hold on to the nine sets and replace the one a friend of mine had lost over the weekend."

The boy grinned nervously till Schoeff said he was kidding. From yonder, poundings on a stuck brake drum could be heard.

"Ah, automotive," Schoeff said.

"Yes, sir. A garage connected to the store for your convenience."

"How grand," Schoeff said. He paid for the sets and asked the young man to hold them while he browsed on. At the next aisle he crept up behind a person watching the brake work at the window to the garage. This person had a nice white shirt on, with sleeves for once, and no jeans that looked like a truck had ran over them. "Fascinating, isn't it?" Schoeff said. "It's amazing how air produces such wrenching power."

The person turned in a snap.

"Father, don't do that!" Oscaro said. He stepped back and caught his breath. "I'm lucky to be inside here!"

Schoeff smiled, said, "You're an equal to the other shoppers, my friend. Your confidence in knowing that make them lint off your suit."

"I have no suit," Oscaro said.

"Imagine," Schoeff said tapping on his temple. The fact that Schoeff just popped up no longer surprised Oscaro. It was angering his sister's guardian angel--which Schoeff could well be--that frightened Oscaro. "Father, don't tell me. You just happen to be looking for an air filter for the monsignor's Ford."

"Nope, tools," Schoeff said. "Oscaro, why haven't you called?"

"No need."

"If I knew you were going to be here exactly this minute, wouldn't you think I'd know if you were telling the truth?"

"That question is like if you were a savior to my sister, why wouldn't she be safe?"

"Ah, wise. Is she safe?"

"All comfortable in bed."

"It's a school day, Oscaro."

"Answer my question," Oscaro threw. "If you were Asha's guardian angel, why is she still in danger?"

"Because she will be mine, Oscaro. *My* guardian angel," Schoeff said. "I don't expect you to grasp that right away. But in the meantime, your weakness is being used."

"I have to go see my business." Oscaro started walking away.

"Mr. Pinelli doesn't need that distributor till tonight. Talk to me, Oscaro. When is your next meeting at the harbor?"

"What do you mean my weakness?"

"Simple. Just think of balance. If a lug nut feels too tight, you hate it but force yourself to loosen it with a vice grip. You have no choice but to go counterclockwise. If there's day, night has to come. If there's clean, corruption has to interfere. You remember the way you think is vulnerable." Schoeff grasped his chin. "It's not really the hunger for money. It's more like the indigestion of money that is *your apple*. Oscaro, you don't realize it, but you're addicted to what your sister provides. For you and your family, the abundance of money. But the sad thing is, Asha is getting addicted, period."

Oscaro's face broke a little. He held back his tears. Desperados in the Bronx like him never showed emotions. "Monday, around midnight, Pier 60, behind the old lumber yard," he said.

Schoeff clutched on Oscaro's shoulders for giving him this valuable information. Oscaro let him only for a second.

At the aisle, a clean-jumpsuited Sears mechanic approached them. "May I help you, gentlemen?" he said.

Schoeff raised a finger as if to give advice but decided to hold on the thought. "A little before your time," Schoeff said. "No, thank you. Keep up the honest work."

Schoeff believed that honesty could be anybody's tool. It had the flexibility of a stomach compress. Good people should cling to it for dear life, and shady people could use it at times in their schemes. He had known where the meeting would take place. He just had to know how flexible Oscaro was.

34

A Dying Man and His Son

When Jack from the Curb, another citizen on the teeter-totter, showed up at the front vestibule three days late, Schoeff was ready to give him a second set of tools.

"Remember, Jack, take better care of this one," he said. "You must keep it for yourself or you'll never see your daughter."

"Father, you got to understand the place I live in. There's no guarantee I'll be all to myself. People in every corner with dice jingling in their knuckles. They rattle the walls every time you pass'em."

"Stay at home, build a chair."

"Build a chair?"

"Or fix a neighbor's bicycle with your fine tools."

"I got no neighbor with a bicycle."

"Jack, the first time I saw you, I knew how sincere your longing for your daughter was from your eyes. And I still feel that longing in you. Now promise me you'll hold on to the tools."

"Five days after, ain't it?"

Schoeff nodded.

"Five days after what?"

"Five days after you feel that you're definitely the proud owner. That they're definitely a keeper."

"Five days, then I see my Heny?"

"Yes."

Jack grasped the new set with trembling hands. "Why if I booze up and forget?" he asked.

"Don't booze up," Schoeff said with a smile.

The worried look on Jack's face did not fade as he struggled with the doors on his way out.

Schoeff turned around thinking he was free to have his evening solitude of prayer when Father Laman stood there, blocking his way at the foyer.

"Father, did you just promise that man the return of his daughter in exchange for hammers and wrenches?" Laman asked.

"No, those were pliers, two screwdrivers and four wrenches. The homeowner's deluxe set included a hammer, but it doesn't go on sale till Memorial Day weekend."

"Wasn't that a little risky? Don't tell me this is part of your mission."

"Actually, Father Lamantiaragski, you yourself could have made that promise if you have enough faith on circumstance. It's what we are made for."

"Yes."

Schoeff tried to squeeze past him, but Lamantiaragski placed his hand on Schoeff's shoulder.

"Do you mean if a dying man with a son comes to this church and asks for sure salvation for his young boy, you would grant him the promise?"

"I don't see the connection."

"Under the same circumstance," Laman said. "That young boy would be completely unprepared for salvation."

Schoeff, at a loss, referred to a prognostic thought.

Laman was older than him by seven years and perhaps had been in the priesthood longer. In Schoeff's vision, statistics were involved, and chances were slim, even in fact, if the hidden allegations of present day were made public. In fifty years, liberalism in the church would open gates for anyone within the compound of circumstantial private matters, which was good, Schoeff thought. Individuals, like abused altar boys and oppressed nuns, would be free to speak out. Then again, Schoeff was jumping to conclusion about Laman. With all seriousness, he asked the fellow priest, "Is the boy unprepared spiritually and...or physically?"

Laman peered at him. "What could he be unprepared for physically?"

Schoeff felt a surge of embarrassment. Was it the fact that Laman doubted his promise to Jack from the Curb after all the radio interview, the speeches and prophesies he had made? It had been a long Thursday, with the shopping at Sears. "Forgive me, father," Schoeff said. "I am over-reaching for a simple answer to your speculative question. Yes, I would give hope to the dying."

Laman, not at all satisfied, simply said, "Hm...well, good night."

"Yes, I need it," Schoeff said.

35

A Giver of One Sock

In his sleep that night, a remarkable dream eased off his worries from the hectic day. It was about Jessica, his forever ex-girlfriend. There was a wedding reception going on, and it was at a lodge. It took a while for him to notice that Jessica was the bride, and even though he knew that he wasn't the groom--because he was seated looking up at the entourage--Schoeff felt happy for her. But it was when she approached him afterwards that he had become perplexed. She handed him a knitted sock with the word "Dildo" embroidered on it. He woke up shortly, trying to figure out the significance of the sock. In fact, he wrote it down. Why "Dildo?" Why a sock, and why just one sock? He never once received a comical gift from her. She was always stately. She had little capacity for humor, unlike him.

During Saturday's Mass, he started out by saying, "The future still holds Christ's love as always, and it is felt in the present. I'm sure some of you have that feeling of guarantee that the one closest to you, whether it be that uncle who always dresses up as Santa, or your mother or father, girlfriend or boyfriend, husband or wife, would always care for you, and *you* not worry about it, even in the strangest of circumstance, even if they are no longer there. If they have given you socks, always feel the warmth in them, none but."

36

Popeye

When Rapha asked Zeyad why he had requested for a cot
from the servants, Zeyad told him that Chereb's bed was a
little soft on his back. Chereb was in the dining room at the
time and had to scamper through the kitchen into the den to
answer for Zeyad. "He was testing Sealy ingenuity, Papa,
but he prefers that canvas feel in his room," she said. "It's
what he's used to in the climate of…his country."

Rapha, bemused, said, "No, let Zed speak. I know
that nothing of mishmash is going on here. Why the
running into this room?" Rapha told for Zeyad to go on.

Zeyad peered at Chereb, who looked anxious. "I was
testing the bed in her room this afternoon," Zeyad said. "I
find it very bad for my posture. I was going to test the one
in your bedroom, but your wife was taking her afternoon
nap at the time."

Rapha, who still had his admiral's cap and jacket on,
leaned forward and said. "Does the missus know about this
bed testing?" he asked.

"Pop!" Chereb snapped. "Obviously, you think
something is out of whack here."

Rapha thought for a moment. "I do when my
daughter causes a religious man to lie," he said.

Zeyad closed his eyes.

"Okay," Chereb surrendered. "Some weirdo has been calling me in the middle of the night, and I want Zed to identify him, so he stays in my room. I've slept in this room for two nights already. I don't know the person. He's not someone I've met at a party. And if you don't believe that, you're not my father but some bonehead from Jersey."

"Who, who is this weirdo?" Rapha asked.

"If we knew that," Chereb said, "Zed wouldn't be sleeping in my bed, would he?"

Zeyad stood still. The shackles at his shins were loose but locked. Chereb held the keys.

"What has he been saying this weirdo?" Rapha asked.

Chereb's eyes narrowed. "You still don't believe me," she said. "Zeyad's guidance on me is not working, Daddy! I'm ruined!"

"Hey, hey, I'm only asking," Rapha said.

"Rapha, the man called once last night," Zeyad contributed. "And clicked off immediately after I spoke."

Rapha tried to focus on what his employee was saying.

"I think he's an associate from the Tavern," Chereb said. "We were at the place the other night. I think I caught his eye when I danced on the table. You know men, they always think you're vulnerable when you're a Jew princess, so they bottle up their passion and drive..."

"Enough!" Rapha said. "We trust Zeyad, but when he's testing beds in my house, I have to ask."

"... And relieved themselves on the phone in the middle of the night," Chereb whispered. Her father didn't hear this. She knew for certain that her father had not forgotten the married lawyer.

"May we be excused?" Rapha asked and regretted

157

him asking in his own house. "Zed and I have business to discuss."

Chereb wanted to tear the long curtains off the windows. "What else?" she barked by the huge cabinet, thinking the two would leave the room. But Rapha, two days out from sea, in his admiral suit, blended well with the velvet French sofa. This was his estate this time for staying put. Chereb tap-tapped on the cabinet with her fingers before she left the room.

Her mother noticed her swift steps up the stairs. "What's the matter?" Mrs. Antonisz asked.

"Your Popeye, okay!" Chereb said.

"My Popeye?"

It was in these moments that Grace Antonisz herself were perplexed about the life her daughter led. For one, Chereb's lingo was a sure sign that she was beginning to create her own brand of higher education.

37

The Envious

It was in these situations that Chereb molded her mother into her father, like one of Zeyad's casts. They were just one parent with a brain overloaded with what used to be: Brooklyn during the Thirties. Struggling Jewish immigrants gallivanting from brownstone to brownstone, and when they finally settled in next door to each other, *viola`*, get out the jewelry box and the old recipe book. We're going into business. They never counted on a buoyant daughter. So thought Chereb.

Her independence couldn't resurface from horrendous self-pity. In her future, she would be an object of longing passion from one too many occasions, and it seemed hard not to get involved in a relationship or two. One thing for sure, this self-pity was so unlike her. When her phone rang at a quarter after two that night, she had no will to resist.

"Yes."

"Do you know careening with a man other than your own kind makes a lousy, overexposed picture?"

"What the hell are you talking about?" Chereb said, deeply bothered.

"I mean at your wedding day when the photog snaps away and delivers you a white leather-bound album full of pictures with dark blotches on them."

"You're talking caca."

"Isn't he a little Haile Selassie for you? I mean, darling, I would never have guessed you for a Persian rug, not for just anybody."

Chereb grasped the handpiece, listening as if it was news of war in Europe.

"Are you still there?" the voice wondered. "Okay...I'll just mingle with your hotel friend. She's entertaining. I'm sure she'll spring up the real story behind you and Haji. Bye for now, my..."

Chereb hung up, regretting that she had listened. The fact that she had offered her voice racked her mind in misery. Or was it flattery that she felt? In a sordid way? Juliane, poor, romanticized Juliane. How could there be so much cushion in that head of hers?

Chereb then realized the lack of Juliane's face and the rest of the faces that she was accustomed to on weekends. It was Saturday. A call from one loser usually didn't put her in a nerve-racking mope.

38

The Drugstore Clerk

At dawn before the eight-thirty Mass, hordes of people crowded the steps of St. Jude's Cathedral, as predicted by the monsignor. Some carried banners with messages in Latin, others with rosaries in their hands. Women in bright-colored veils, men in suits and children beyond their Sunday best lined up at the entrance.

"Whose idea was it to lock the doors?" asked Monsignor Randolph, who had been awakened by one of the altar boys.

"Mine, Father," Father Laman claimed. "I thought they came to protest."

"Protest what?"

"Our thing with Father Schoeff."

Randolph turned to his right and looked at his priests. They were all at the choir balcony, where there was an opening at the stained-glass window of Saint Peter holding a basket of fish. The crowd below stretched clear to the next block. *"Euliji santi crucifix,"* the monsignor read one of the banners. "'God ascended from the cross.' As you can see, Father Laman, they're an educated, peaceful lot. None of them are carrying bayonets or tommy guns. Also, notice that their faces are new. They're pilgrims. I imagine some of them have come from out of state. It's the first Mass after the radio interview."

"But it's not Father Schoeff's Mass," Laman said.

None of the priests were in celebration garments. "Whose Mass is it?" Randolph asked.

"Mine, father," said Laman.

"Are you ready?"

"Under this unusual awakening, it's hard to say I am. My homily is not for this group."

Still weary-eyed, Randolph looked at Laman. "Would someone wake up Father Schoeff?"

"He's over at the ordinance building climbing steps," said Father Gado, a transfer from Arizona. "He mentioned something about car-di-o-vascular activity, and stair-climbing as a way to the future in exercising the heart."

"Exercising the heart? Why would he worry about his physical health?" Randolph said. He turned to Alan and Wayne, the altar boys, and told them to unlock the doors. "This is a church, not a fort."

Wayne jumped to this, beating Alan down the loft.

But as the monsignor looked down, the murmuring crowd wasn't so eager to come in anymore. Instead they formed a doughnut-shaped assembly around a figure who seemed to be running in place in the parking lot across the street. This figure had a towel around his neck and a black shirt and a pair of boxer shorts.

Caught in this garb as he was jogging out of the alley, Schoeff had no choice but to face two reporters, who took him right away for a priest from St. Jude's. Only an ordained man would wear black in the humid ending of May. As for the boxer shorts, the reporters had their first inquiry. Schoeff stayed mum. The locked doors of St. Jude's at nine fifteen in the morning he hadn't envisioned. Now he was jogging in place, trying to whip up an explanation of why.

"As you can see, people," he began, "I am training my body. It will be called Aerobics, and I am not doing it for track or football, but for myself, to better my reflexes, my stamina and my thirty-four-year old heart. And I assure you, you didn't come all the way here from Lewisburg, Pennsylvania and Perry Point, Maryland and Boston, Massachusetts just to find the famed St. Jude's Cathedral closed for business and settle for a priest in shorts."

Randolph, Laman and the rest stepped out to see how the invincible Father Schoeff would take care of this one. As they made their way into the crowd and found a spot, Schoeff was already in the future with the importance of cholesterol reduction.

"Be Jewish if you will," Schoeff said. "When it comes to food selection, they have their reason not to eat pork. It's beneficial to the arteries. And as for my jogging, I'm timing myself to see how long I can keep it up. 'And God rested on the seventh day.' To tell you the truth, I had nothing to do, and nothing to do makes rest a boring thing. My next Mass will be on Thursday...."

The monsignor frowned at this.

A broad-shouldered lady with a copper-colored veil down to her shoulders asked, "Are you the one who spoke on the radio?"

"Yes," Schoeff puffed. "Father Schoeff at your service."

"Well, you can't be," said the lady, dark welts under her eyes, behind the veil which she shouldn't have been wearing outside. She looked meek but still huge with the voice. "You're sweating like you're on something," she said. "No right-minded saint does that in public."

"Well, like I said you caught me by surprise," Schoeff said. "And by no means am I a saint. That's why I'm jogging. I have to keep fit."

"Are you on drugs?"

Schoeff paused, stood still and looked around as if sensing a *different* being in his presence. "My dear Jesus," he said.

"Did you hear him?" the woman laughed. "He took God's name in vain."

"You did, too," Schoeff said. "Excuse me, are you by chance from Baltimore?"

"You betcha," said this woman. Her orange veil dimmed her smile. The people around her looked on. This was clearly unexpected. The confidence of this person was beyond reason. Reporters stuck microphones to her face and toward Schoeff, who still couldn't grasp the fact that he was enmeshed in a gathering at this time. "What's the matter, father? Ran out of explanations?" the woman said. "You haven't fully justified your jogging on the sabbath to these people."

"What is your name?" asked Schoeff.

"What is your problem? Can't tell when you're dying? That's one thing you can't do. That's why you jog."

"It's just that," Schoeff replied. "Verify, I'm a little rusty on definite. You look like Glessie from my junior high. Kind lunch lady."

"Or a beefed-up Winona Ryder in *Beetlejuice*," the woman said.

"Ah, a future flick."

"You're not ready for what is to take place, are you? For instance...." The woman pointed up at the Roster & Soard Building facing the gravel lot and the cathedral across the street. A person could be seen up there on the ledge, desperately hanging on for her life six floors up. No one noticed her till now. She appeared to be a brunette and had a green dress on. Schoeff sent her a prayer. The crowd went to pieces. Some dispersed, covering their heads as if it was going to rain debris. Others stayed to watch.

The veiled woman stayed put. "Say, father, can you tell that gal's future?" she said. "She's had a rough week I'd say. She's married to a hotshot attorney at the Mercury Firm. A CPA herself. Got two kids, one at Durham and the other just stays home being tutored. What could be wrong with this picture?"

"Spare her," Schoeff said.

"You're talking to the wrong person, Howie. By the way, I'm Agothe Mir. I'm the drugstore clerk. Can you believe it?"

"Why are you doing this?" Schoeff said. "You don't have to involve anybody."

"You mean this is *not* right?"

The woman on the ledge up above yelled something, released her hands from the protruding cornice and took a step forward. Her silent fall ended when she landed on a parking meter, puncturing her chest so that her ribcage bulged from her back. Women and children screamed. Schoeff bent down to his waist to release what could have been a plea for the woman's consideration, or a cry for mercy to this Agothe Mir. She was all too familiar but his uncle had never expounded to this bleak moment.

"Don't look at me," Agothe said. "I had nothing to do with it." She took off her orange veil. Schoeff saw her thick bangs soaked in sweat. He sensed that she was trying to keep a straight face, but her grin blurted at him. "Look, she may have been on the rebound," Agothe said. "There're a lot of beautiful secretaries at that Mercury place. I'm sure her husband looked up a few skirts, or this may well be a vision of your little darling, what's her name?"

"Bite your tongue!" Schoeff roared.

"It's bitten," Agothe replied, clamping her upper lip. "By the way, father, that was a great explanation you gave that flip boy of why he's screwing up his adopted darling sister. It pleases me to see a priest defend *moi*."

"Miss Mir, I gave Oscaro the truth to benefit himself. Other than that, I being a priest had nothing to do with it. I mean God could have picked you. You seem to be outspoken."

Agothe shook her head as if to discard Schoeff's idea. "You know, your little sweetie won't make the cut," Agothe said. When Schoeff ignored her, she added, "And you're in no shape to deliver this city, not with that attitude."

Schoeff walked toward the body. He released it from the meter, making everybody around him squeamish. Blood dripped down his arm, soaking his black shirt, staining his shorts. He laid the body down on the grass. She was nobody to whom he had spoken before. The comeliness on her face was familiar only that she might have been a member of St. Jude's. In his veneration, he asked that her suffering was over. There were two words to be uttered. "Forgive me," Schoeff said.

Randolph and the other priests came to his side, offered the soul their own prayers.

The church doors were open. The pilgrimage moved inside.

"You better let that homo priest carry it as planned," Agothe shouted at Schoeff. She walked backward as the clergymen occupied the space. "I think half of the crowd went home!" Agothe yelled.

Laman stared at her, unflinching. Schoeff, who felt

powerless over anything physical, didn't look at Agothe anymore. It was his role to not look. The Mind would punish, he thought. Other than someone taking her own life, Schoeff tried to create a crime in his head worth punishable. But he couldn't place any.

"Father, God have mercy," Randolph said. "Why has this happened? Who was that woman?"

Schoeff breathed deeply. "A drugstore clerk from Maryland."

39

Father Lamantiaragski

He was on his knees in the six three hours of Monday. He mumbled original prayers till dawn. When he couldn't think of any, he turned to Hail Mary's and Our Father's and thought these prayers were defense mechanisms for unexpected misery. Yet, he still couldn't find himself after yesterday's incident. Dr. Xya, the psychiatrist-turned-ambulance-driver, said that he had chosen him because he had the charisma to face the worst of people.

Even preach while there was evil in physical form? With that evil mocking?

Now he faced this Monday, and there wouldn't be anything in it to mock about. Trust a psychiatrist and he will give you rest, even on this day, Schoeff thought.

Someone knocked on his door.

"Come in."

The knob creaked. It was Father Laman, with a tray. Schoeff identified a teapot, a cup and an egg on a holder.

"You need these," Laman said. He placed the tray on the end table and poured the pot in the cup. "Think of this as a token of my appreciation. Or think nothing of it."

"What for? You carried the Mass," Schoeff said.

"I did, but didn't decide right away. I feel if you had to take my place, you would have. It disgraced me to be so indecisive."

"Father, if we were all perfect, we wouldn't be here," Schoeff said. "We would all be at Woolworth's buying mink oil to rub on our feathers."

Laman drew closer and sat on the bed. "How do you do it? Escalate yourself to humor at times like this?"

Schoeff sat on bended legs. "I'm sad alright," he said. "This is just safeguard talking in me. A person takes her life and you had it in mind moments before. Your first move is to attend to her needs, counsel her out of the lonely conviction, be at the spot where you think she would land, confuse her aim. But instead you stand still, preoccupied, worrying about your own demise."

"The woman in the veil, who was she? An all-knowing dark spirit?"

"I don't know about all-knowing. But she was...a test forewarned by my uncle."

Laman rested his head on the mattress. His eyes had not made contact with Schoeff's yet. "Tell me of my failure, father," he said. "It seems like I have been living in musty shadows. The unveiling of my years to come, no matter how bottomless, won't make a difference."

"We all have growing minds," Schoeff said, clutching Laman's shoulder. "The idea of stunt growth happens only if our concentration is missing."

"I should know that," Laman said. "There's always that unconditional guarantee, even for homosexuals."

Schoeff didn't budge.

"But sometimes, I get so flustered and enriched inside, especially during ceremony," Laman said, eyes shut. "My deepest sin occurs when I bottle up. Why wouldn't the

Vatican allow retired women from care homes to assist us? Instead of those energetic boys, why not their grandmothers standing at your side for an hour?"

"Father, I don't think homosexuality is your repentance," Schoeff said. "It's the things that make you do or think and feel guilty about being sexual. We are only labeled homo or hetero or bi when sex is in practice, a fact that ninety percent of the nation will tend to forget. Anyway, as ordained fans of celibacy, we're supposed to be incredibly stupid on the subject. Furthermore, Divinity is not big on generalizations. It sees individual heart, soul, mind." Schoeff noticed the teacup and held it in the sun to check for steam. It was still hot. He offered it to Laman. "On the other hand, the future is swollen with generalizations. It's so prevalent that it makes people accept a banner of themselves and go march in parades with those labels over their heads."

Laman, in the midst of his future, took the tea unknowingly. "Am I making you go out of your boundaries in these talks, Father Schoeff?" he said. "I am being open to you because you yourself seem to be all-knowing. I'm delving into an area which you are not particularly inclined."

"What area is that, father?" Schoeff asked.

Laman sat still, suddenly realizing the cup in his hand. When he couldn't bring himself to speak further, Schoeff understood and skipped his offer of contrition.

"Father, we are all lustful," Schoeff said. "If I feel impure urges toward the same sex, I would do the same if I had them toward the opposite sex. Pray, improve the mind."

Laman, who knew that this was not just improvisation, sipped the tea.

40

The Romanced

It turned out to be a bright Monday in another part of the city. The sun glinted on all the gold poles in front of the hotel and on all the chrome on exotic cars parked on Fifth Avenue. The doorman at the DeVoe-Hilton graciously opened the door of the 1951 Jaguar Xk 120, for their honorary Assistant Manager.

"Good morning, Miss DeVoe."

"Enchanting, isn't it?" Juliane said. "I hope it'll last."

"For you, it will," the door man said. "With the delivery we had earlier, definitely it will."

"What delivery?"

"It's in your office."

Juliane stepped inside the sparkling foyer and into the lounge, where everybody from desk ladies to ushers took notice of her presence. In her office, a tall bouquet of roses was placed on her glass top, facing the doorway so she couldn't possibly escape the grandeur. Juliane gasped and resolved to find the card tucked somewhere in the foliage. She had a heart-rending clue. "If it be too soon," she read, "then I am further in wait. The Guilliam Suite at 9 for starters."

Juliane never took poetry in college and was not all that familiar with free verse. Carl Sandburg and Hilda Doolittle had each stayed at the hotel and had shared a conversation or two with her and her father, but these two lines in the card lacked...fluidity? Coming from a published man. In any case, she threw up her arms as if the bouquet were a honeymoon token from her new husband.

She rang Chereb.

"You don't say," Chereb said. "Listen, Julie, I don't mean to be wretched, but I feel this guy is reeling in the line too fast."

"It's been reeled," Juliane said.

"That's what I mean. And he's going to reel you in again in about a week. How about dinner or a Broadway play? If that's not affordable, he could surely take you to a movie."

That said, Juliane felt her friend since prep school had allowed these rendezvouses--or at least, acknowledged that they could be possible for the likes of herself.

41

Howard, 1934

Schoeff as a young man clung to this bilateral rule: to "always be taken care of; therefore, not worry." He saw life as he had seen it in Jessica, a periscope moving toward him, cutting through the colorful oil-slicked water. "Maybe she's the submarine of fate sneaking up on you, ready to attack," his Uncle Dam tried to analyze. "And you're on the Wabash, swimming away like a blue gill." Uncle Dam wasn't always all-knowing.

"I'm not swimming away."

"What are you doing, drowning?"

"It's just that why does she have to be in it?"

"This is not paradise, neph. It's still that garden with the apple."

Schoeff looked deeply disturbed. "What are you saying? She's *not* the forbidden fruit. She could just be a person in my life, that's all. And how do I know I'm in a position to have a forbidden fruit? Maybe I'm just mentally unstable with all these dreams. You know, Mother never took me to that children's hospital down at Indy."

"Do you love the girl?" Uncle Dam asked.

"In a sense."

"Like you could only hear her but not smell or see or

touch her? You're holding back, kid. You're not Father Spencer Tracy yet."

"All right, she's that all-around sixth sense."

"Then love her. I'm sure this *Someone* who picked you arranged this."

"He knows my needs, right? As a man?"

His Uncle Dam ignored this. "Anyway, what troubles you are the laws of becoming a Father Tracy and not the laws of this Someone."

"They should be the same."

"No, one's more flexible than the other. Get wise, kid."

"Am I just being tempted?" Schoeff asked.

"By who?"

As if his uncle didn't know, Schoeff thought. For a once mechanical engineer (before he was a sharecropper), Uncle Dam lacked practicality. Howard for a long time couldn't place his uncle as someone God would use to prep him up for the future. Howard had to rely on those mysterious ways God was so famous about.

42

More Space

"Ooh, I hate walking into a flick," Juliane had said. "Besides, you ought to see the size of the bouquet. It must have cost him a pretty penny."

"Suit yourself," Chereb concluded then. She couldn't well alert Juliane about the calls and Zeyad's new duty to screen those calls. On the other hand, there was that annoying hunch that Juliane might be in danger, and Chereb would have to speak out sooner or later. In fact, jealousy by mistaken identity, which was worse than faux pearls, was the only thing holding Chereb back.

Rapha was at the breakfast table when Zeyad reported no calls for Sunday night. "The police would be happy to take care of this, don't you think?" Rapha said. "But then again they'd have to find room in your bed." Upon his daughter's loathing eyes across the table, he threw his hands out, as if surrendering.

Her father was not taking this seriously, Chereb thought, or else the commissioner of N.Y.P.D. would be having eggs benedict with them by now.

43

The Protested

Oscaro looked out to the dark Atlantic. The fringe of lights to the far left was Manhattan. He thought about what the priest had said to him at Sears. In his weariness, Oscaro calculated the rent could be paid for four months after this visit, and his brother and sisters would have three solid meals each day in those four months. Pilu needed a pair of new shoes. The ones he had had dilapidated heels that they made him lean to the right when he walked. Then there were those chrome cylinder at Milt's Cycle & Parts. The old ones could crack and probably throw him off the bike.

A motor died down in the distance. A boat was coming in. Oscaro stood up, carrying Asha in a thick checkered blanket. He scanned the lit section of the pier. The priest was nowhere to be found. Oscaro stayed out of the light as he was instructed. Asha shivered a little. Oscaro rubbed her arms.

"Good evening, sport," a voice came from the dark. "I hope it wasn't a long wait."

A line was thrown on the pier. Oscaro laid Asha down and tied the rope on a pole. He then gave a hand to the first man getting off the boat. This man, in a dark lab coat this time, approached Asha while Oscaro helped the other person up.

"How is our little patient? Awake, I hope," said this second person, who had a stethoscope wrapped around one hand.

"She is," Oscaro said, "a little cold but awake. Why so late?"

"Any vomiting or rash?" asked the first. "Unusual behavior of any kind?"

"How about youth deprivation?" a fourth voice asked in the dark. It was the main concern Schoeff had in Asha. Addiction, he knew, was still under supervision by these men. Schoeff stepped out of the shadows. "A foggy night for physical examination, isn't it?"

"Who is this?" the first man asked, taking a 60-cc syringe from the black bag.

"Father Schoeff, at your service," Schoeff said.

"He's a priest from the church Asha goes to," Oscaro said.

"Very good," said the first man, getting a corked cylinder from a wooden box that unfolded like a chessboard. "'At our service?' I doubt that, father. We are a very busy medical group, and we don't respond to intrusion well."

"Pardon me," Schoeff said. "It just that your little patient happens to be a friend of mine and is too precious for experimental purposes. So, if you please, put your instruments away. She won't have any at this time."

The three men looked at each other while Schoeff picked up Asha.

"Father?" Asha said. "Don't you have to baptize a kid or something in the morning?"

"I'll always have time for you, kiddo."

"Father, you don't understand. She is under

observation," said the bearded fellow who got off the boat last. "She is on a time-framed schedule. If she stops taking the medication, it may ruin her digestive tract."

"Medication usually means to cure illness," Schoeff said. "And that illness usually happens before medication is applied."

"Listen, we are trying a valuable wonder drug on her," said the man with the syringe. "One that may inhibit excruciating pain from any ailment known to man."

"Ah, a *pre*-benzodiazepine," Schoeff said. "Hoffman-LaRoche will come up with it, and it is not a product from people who spins little girls in a centrifuge."

"One girl," claimed the syringe man.

"Far too many," Schoeff snapped. "What you're doing, sir, is a criminal offense."

"Not when it benefits humanity."

"You call putting a girl in a state of unbearable pain and addiction benefiting humanity?" Schoeff said as Asha clung to his chest. "In thirty years, there will be organizations protesting the use of animals in experiments. They'll have meetings in super domes and rallies in front of the Capitol, and I can sense their original anger rooting from this pier. Forgive me, gentlemen, but it looks bleak. They'll have your photos on their dart boards."

"Hold on, father," said the bearded fellow. "How do you know LaRoche will come out with this *benzodiazepine*?"

"He's the prophet priest," Oscaro said. "The one on the radio. He's not from the area, I know that."

The syringe man laughed. "So, father, you're the fortune teller," he said. "Tell me, who will provide this structure for Hoffman-LaRoche?"

"I'm a little confidential on that one," Schoeff said. "But I'm certain it's not Edwin McVay, William Pahl or

179

Sanford Price. Good evening, gentlemen, your version is too harsh for humanity."

The three men stood still, their tongues tied. "How did...?" the bearded fellow started to say.

Even Oscaro didn't know their names. He gathered his helmet and blanket, looked at the three men, and went after Schoeff. When Oscaro caught up, he slap-patted the priest on the back. "Padre`, you really had them shaking," he said. "They think you're a spirit come back from the dead."

Schoeff stayed quiet. Asha fell asleep with her head tucked at his nape.

"Asha will be okay," Oscaro assured Schoeff. "She's just sleepy. Right, Sasha?"

Schoeff walked on, toward the warehouse where he had seen Oscaro parked his motorcycle earlier.

"Look, you wanted me here tonight," Oscaro said. "It ain't like I came here for my own self." He got in front of the priest, blocking him. "I took no money, all right. If you hadn't showed up, I would have stopped them this time. Father, you got to believe me!"

"Oscaro, will you pray tonight?" Schoeff said. "Pray that you will not be trespassed by this again."

Oscaro looked up and hid his frown from Schoeff. "Right thing, father," he committed, teeth clenched.

"Get a cab for your sister and me, Oscaro," Schoeff said. "It's late."

44

The Carefree

Ira was caught off guard when Juliane suggested that they go out instead of just lounging around in the Guilliam Suite. "An honorable idea," he said. He was in a black cashmere sports jacket with crusted gold buttons, a lamb gray mock-crew pullover shirt and tailor-made trousers of fine black material. He crossed his legs and wooed Juliane with his lavender socks with yellow streaks running down the sides. The shoes were none other than alligator, also gray. "Shall we?" he said.

At Tavern-on-the-Green, which was walking distance from the hotel, Ira offered a late dinner. But Juliane, already sold on his generosity, settled simply for brandy, bread and salad.

"You seem spirited," Ira said.

"Spirited? Usually people don't describe me that until they've taken me out for an hour," Juliane said.

"You mean you could be peppier?"

Juliane sipped her brandy, smiled devilishly, abandoning her first thought.

"There has to be a source for this gladness," Ira said.

"Whatever do you mean?"

"I'm certain that our meetings are no secret. Other people know, perhaps your closest friends?"

"Perhaps."

"Perhaps, your blonde comrade at the jewelry store. She seemed like a treasure to gossip with."

"Who? Chereb?"

"Yes."

"Chereb is more of an announcer. She's the newsy type. Everything has to have solid ground with her."

"Unlike you."

"I'm carefree."

"Would she have been as sensuous as you?"

"Ira?"

"No, take for instance," he insisted. "If she were you on the first day we met, at the penthouse, would she have done more, or less?"

Juliane gasped.

"Hypothetical question. To tell you the truth, I see poetry in everything. Variation in women interests me a lot." When Juliane didn't quite have an answer, Ira added, "By the way, did you pass her my invitation?"

"Oh, yes," Juliane squeaked. She didn't know where to place the emptiness. "Are you sure you didn't overlook me at that jewelry store?" she asked, hoping the tone in her voice possessed anger.

Ira searched the meaning, muzzled his bourbon, and eyed Juliane's yearning look. "You're the one I followed," he said.

"But you're interested in her."

Ira put forth an honest gaze and said, "More than sexually."

"How dare you?" Juliane snapped. "What am I?"

"Go on," Ira said. "Release that green goblin!"

Juliane took her brandy, hoping it was lit, and splashed it on Ira's face and neck.

He still laughed boisterously. "Shall we go back to the hotel?" he said. "I think you've finished your drink."

Juliane managed to calm her nerves. "Chereb," she said, "thinks you're an unstable man. And don't take that for jealousy, but I feel you don't have the slightest chance with Chereb. I know her taste." She breathed deeply. "And as for myself, I know I am a little naive. But I know you are way below my standard." She gathered her purse, stood up, and walked away.

Ira grasped his bourbon and rattled the ice.

45

Angels at the Ceiling

Schoeff asked for revelation that night. "Where are you now?" he said in his prayer at the choir balcony, facing the nave. He had no intention to be there that late. It was just a spot with wide open space. Expanding mind was sure to hover there with the greatest of ease, he thought. "I know I can communicate without you being in physical form, but I confess it's more comfortable to speak with flesh," he whispered. He looked toward the altar, saw no movement. "Dear Lord, the *Times* says the deceased was a career woman, a mother of two, a public accountant, an attorney for a husband...the papers left out where the eldest son went. Durham. I was more informed." He bowed down resting his forehead on the rail where choir members placed their arms. "Forgive me, if I sound pugnacious. I am still learning things, and things still surprise me. Frightening that I have to step back, suddenly faithless from what I've gathered. If you were there, in physical form, let's say as...a reporter, a dignified role, you would have flashed your camera, snapped me out of my stare, maybe say, 'Listen, you're doing a job for Me. Where is your concentration?'" Schoeff looked up to the ceiling. The cherubs there without bodies were fluttering around gargoyles with sad dogfaces.

"Agothe Mir," he said. "Even her name needs concentration. I bet her friends call her Gotie. I bet at the sight of hair follicles on her chin, angry people offer their shavers to her."

He could not even laugh at his own joke.

"You say why am I in remorse? Okay, honesty. I'm laying it on the line. This is from a man who cannot tell when he is to die, because he is mortal." Schoeff opened one eye to see any movement at all. "Here it is," he said. "It… happened…on my watch. There you are, Lord, pride wrapped in black cloth."

It wasn't his usual bedtime consultation, but in the depth of the hangover from grief, he believed the Mind was not a great fan of redundancy.

"God," he said lastly. "I'm not in any way funny."

46

Designer of the Mall

He expected Asha to attend his Ascension Thursday mass and was anxious to know how she was. In his benediction prayer, she came to him like a fresh, bright dawn because he knew that she was safe. During the sermon, he found a way to blend in future hostility. "Christ thought he had stayed long enough," he said to the congregation. "Forty days, and he felt it was time for a breather. That's my thinking. Christ, of course, knew exactly when to go up. But for us, we feel He left too soon. He didn't take us with him. And thus began our testimony. Some sixteen hundred years later, a little town was borne off the coast of a fertile land. It had muggy summers and harsh winters, but, hey, for twenty-four bucks, it wasn't a bad deal.

"Two centuries more, this little spot had become a metropolis, the biggest in the nation. Yet this department store, if you will, slowly became unorganized in a sense that the management had lost its grip. Hardware was telling Sporting Goods to keep their balls from bouncing into their aisle. The beauty salon was complaining about sauerkraut stench from the cafeteria wilting their Zga Zga Gabor wigs. In the early nineteen seventies, we will come up with something called the Mall, where there will be walls between these departments. But people will still lose their patience, and in our patience for Christ to come back, we suddenly need our space, to walk from store to store, to wander without feeling uneasy because of the things we can't help politically or personally. And for us who think Christ ascended too soon and may never come back, we break glass panes and tear down walls. Others who think otherwise will drive trucks into federal buildings and fly airliners into skyscrapers and cause unprecedented damage, primarily, because of envy. Envy of what? Freedom. We will go outside of the mall and track down somebody unprotected and threaten his life for his athletic shoes. We'll always take away the freedom others may have by letting out the steam we have inside. Along the way we will trample on innocent lives. And someone in the turmoil will say, 'Hey, wait a minute! This is not the purpose we've started the fight for.' But it's too late. Freedom has been halted. We have said good-bye to Christ, blipped him out of our thoughts, even though we haven't heard yet his reply."

After this intense sermon, Monsignor Randolph was at the rear waiting for him. "You're a natural mouthful," he said when Schoeff came out.

"Too much?" Schoeff said.

"Nope. Yep."

Schoeff frowned for a second.

"I didn't get the significance of the athletic shoes," the monsignor said.

Schoeff indulged him. "A jam king by the name of Michael Jordan will make athletic shoes cost more than what we charge for weddings."

"Ah." The monsignor looked puzzled for a moment. "By the way, a young lady is waiting for you."

"Asha," Schoeff said happily.

"No. But she said the baptismal room would be perfect. I asked her why, and she said it just is."

47

A Friend in Danger

In the baptismal room, waiting place for parents and godparents, Schoeff didn't find Asha. Chereb stepped forward instead, unveiling her face of pink veil. "Father, I needed to see you," she said.

"Miss Antonisz, what a surprise. How are things?"

"Kind of unimaginable. I think I've placed one of my friends in danger. Juliane Devoe. Remember Julie, the talkative one?"

"Fascinated by Disney."

"Yes! Well, she's missing and has been missing since Monday night. I called her at her apartment, at her sister's in Hartford, and when I called her at work, they tell me she hasn't been seen for three days." Chereb placed her hands on her cheeks to calm herself. Schoeff earnestly waited for her to continue. "There's this man whom she met at my dad's jewelry store, and this man is not the right type for her or anybody for that matter. He's sort of kinky, kind of not you."

Schoeff grinned.

"Juliane informed me that they had met at the hotel once for, let's say, blissful purposes, and were due to meet again Monday evening. But the weird part is he's been calling me late at night and thinks my name is Gwendolyn."

"That's why you think you've placed Juliane in danger," Schoeff said, "because this man is drawn to you and calls you instead of Juliane."

"Exactly."

"Has he called since Monday?"

Chereb smiled. "I guess that's one information you wouldn't know," she said. In the next moment, she shrieked, "No! What got me spooked was when her father, Mr. DeVoe himself, called and asked for the whereabouts of Julie. Then I knew I had to see you."

Schoeff stood silent.

"I mean, you have the expertise." Chereb felt she had coddled in his presence. It was just a matter of trying to feel at ease and be herself.

"Dear Chereb," Schoeff said. "My expertise in reading the uncertain is only for the sake of the future. It has to benefit the future of this city. I could try to find Juliane, but I don't think it'll be approved."

"By God?"

"Yes."

"Tell me, father, what does it take to know God, to really know him inside and out? To have cappuccino with him at the Village, at the drop of a dime."

"I think he's more into Swiss mocha."

Chereb held her seriousness. "I know you can't just be yourself. Take it as it comes and enjoy it while it's here. You have to be a camel through a needle, as they say."

"Hard to imagine, isn't it?" Schoeff said, surprised. "But 'being yourself' is not quite far off. It depends on what motivates your heart while you're being yourself. Everything depends on what you select from the outside."

190

"Zed is a camel."

"Mr. Mughrabi? How is he?"

"He's so surreal. He does things out of this planet. Like he kneels in the subway, and all the other bums kneel with him, thinking he's seeing a vision of Mahatma Gandhi."

Schoeff had to laugh. "Mr. Moghrabi's faith is his heart," he said. "In the Middle East, it beats with rhythm."

"Father, I came into this room thinking that it's a sign since that other priest showed me into this room. I mean of all the rooms here, he had to pick this one. I thought I could be Catholic and be baptized. But I realize I could never be a camel, not even a Jewish camel."

Schoeff bowed down to hide an uncontrollable grin. Chereb sensed this. "Forgive me, father. Enough with the camel talk."

"That's all right."

"If I can't have cappuccino with God, I can have one with you," Chereb said.

"Ah, yes."

"You're free for the rest of day, aren't you?"

"Actually, Chereb, I have dinner to attend to at six with a parishioner family and a wedding consultation before that."

"Well," Chereb said. "Maybe in the future."

"Thank you," Schoeff said. "As for Juliane, it's better to have a solid clue before drawing conclusions. I'm sure something will arise before you know it. Check back at her work."

Her hold on him didn't disappear when she left the room. In fact, Chereb and her plea for the whereabouts of her friend stayed with Schoeff when he was putting out the candles. When he got to the candelabra at the back of the altar, a funny thing happened. He blew on a flame and another candle, completely out of range, went out. He backed away, astounded. He tried again. This time, he blew and a candle went off on another candelabrum, totally opposite, across the aisle. He turned around. All the doors were closed. Impossible for a swirl of wind to linger this long. He closed his eyes and tried to envision the purpose. After a moment, he whispered, "She's in the picture!"

He kneeled before the altar and said, "Roger." He ran down the aisle.

48

A Friend of Use

Out front, in the rosy sunlight, Schoeff tried to track down Chereb. She wouldn't be walking east on Kingsbridge on her way home or north on Valentine or even down Grand — where the suicide had taken place. Chereb wouldn't be walking. But to his right, Schoeff spotted a clean aqua-blue Chevrolet, its white walls clearly unseen at this end of Grand Concourse. Before he could reach the car, Chereb tapped him on the shoulder. He jumped. "I'm sorry," she said, covering her mouth. "I dropped some coins for Mother Mary. It seemed like a Catholic thing to do."

"As you can see, I'm not up for coffee," Schoeff said. "But I just had premonition about your friend."

"Fantastic."

"Do you mind driving to where she is employed?" Schoeff asked. "I think I have an idea where she may be. For credibility's sake, does she own a burgundy top-down?"

"A Jaguar!" Chereb said, astounded.

"Flames from candles told me the color," Schoeff said.

"Oh no, something is wrong."

"I'm not sure."

It was true that he had a dinner to attend at six and a

meeting with a couple heading for matrimony before that, but he felt he had to take part in uncertainty. "When you lit one candle, did another one go on by itself?" he asked Chereb in the Bel Air.

She shook her head no. "Why?" she said. "Don't tell me this visit is also in the plan."

"Not clear on that," Schoeff admitted. "But what I foresaw was luxurious with dark-wax candles blowing out. The windows are closed and there are no vents. There is a huge bouquet, purple roses set in a gray vase. The room has burgundy curtains and matching carpet and throws around a fireplace, and a white porcelain statue of a girl pouring wine from an urn."

"Sounds like one of the suites," Chereb said. "She mentioned that this guy liked plush."

"Juliane must like burgundy," Schoeff noted.

"I don't see Juliane as having an attachment to a color."

"He must like burgundy."

"Maybe."

"Do you like burgundy?" he asked.

"Who, me?"

"Trying to see if there's connection."

"I don't mind it," Chereb said. "It's a color I'd choose for a late-evening dinner at the Astoria."

"Me, maybe at Ash Wednesday," Schoeff said. Chereb looked at him strangely.

When they arrived at the DeVoe-Hilton, a long, black Mercedes-Benz limo was parked in front. Chereb pulled right behind it, and the doorman, who recognized her, gave her the okay. Schoeff, who got out as soon as the car stopped, went around and opened the door of the Bel Air for Chereb. "Mr. DeVoe's car?" he asked. Chereb nodded, and another strong premonition came over him. Now, I should worry, he thought. He wasn't very good at clairvoyance.

They entered the hotel and hadn't reached the receptionist desk when Mr. DeVoe and two other men came up to them. Mr. DeVoe was scowling. He had a suit but his collar was unbuttoned. "Miss Antonisz, isn't it?" he said.

"Yes." Chereb had never been this up close. He was always the moneybag recluse Juliane seldom talked about but had alluded to him from time to time.

"Where the hell is Juliane?"

"I'm not sure," Chereb said. "But this is Father Schoeff. You've heard of him in the news. He has an idea where your daughter is. He's sort of an onlooker."

"To put it safely," Schoeff said.

Wordless to Schoeff, Mr. DeVoe shook his hand and turned back to Chereb. "What is this? I have called every known nightclub, every hotel establishment around the area, asking for her. I've contacted NYPD to look out for her car, and I'm thinking of hiring detectives. But you, Miss Antonisz, offer me a priest?"

"Mr. DeVoe, her car is parked in the adjoining garage where one of the valets had left it three days ago," Schoeff said. "Awkward as it may seem, your daughter came back here Monday night when a different valet was on duty. This attendant parked her car in the back instead of her personal spot up front, which was occupied at the time. It should be on the third floor of the adjoining garage."

"Father," DeVoe said, "from experience, I've never trusted a person who gives information based on telepathy."

"You have my assurance that I'm not big on that," Schoeff said. "I am certain that you have a room with the theme color of burgundy or violet."

"The Guilliam Suite."

"Is it occupied?"

"We'll check the desk."

According to the registrar, it was. But Mr. DeVoe ordered that he be connected to the room. Upon speaking to the guest, who had just arrived and who happened to be a movie director, Mr. DeVoe gave an apology and offered a complimentary dinner if Schoeff and Chereb could be let in to investigate the room.

"For how long?" DeVoe asked, covering the phone.

"Oh, two minutes," Schoeff said.

DeVoe gaped at the priest. He thought Schoeff would need the place longer for an extensive divination or something. They went up to the second floor and found the director waiting in the hallway. He wore a thick green robe and an athletic headband that hugged his thinning scalp. "Search as you please," he said.

Schoeff went in first. Deep purple astonished him more than he had envisioned. He stood in front of the bed with the sheer canopy and sensed a heavy feeling. He closed his eyes. Upon seeing him, DeVoe refurbished the idea that he should have checked the garage for his daughter's Jaguar first before letting the priest go ahead with this intrusion.

"Chereb," Schoeff said, peering down at the mattress. "Don't take this to heart." Tears began to bead in his eyes; a tinge of anger halted them from falling. His conscience already had a spike through it from Sunday's incident. "Please. Step out in the hall," he said. "You and Mr. DeVoe. I'm terribly sorry." He waited, but the two didn't budge. Schoeff had no other options but to stoop down and reach under the bed.

Chereb gasped.

At first, he pulled out a gray-felt high heel, which Chereb recognized as Juliane's. Chereb still didn't budge.

This was merely impossible. The place would reek, wouldn't it? she thought.

Schoeff found the two ankles, pressed them together, and hoisted Juliane's body out with the hem of her skirt tucked in his grip.

Chereb stifled a scream, whispered Juliane's name.

"Oh, no," Mr. DeVoe said, collapsing to his knees. Schoeff found a pill canister in one hand. Juliane's face, composed as if she was only sleeping, was drawn to that hand as it appeared. Schoeff checked for pulse at the neck, then he placed his palm on the forehead and said his contrition. He then took the pill canister from Juliane's curled fingers. "Chloral hydrate," he read the label. "Sleeping pills. She must have slept for two days."

"She didn't touch…narcotics," Mr. DeVoe said. "Beside your usual mixed drinks, she's very much into…air!"

"Don't doubt yourself," Schoeff said. "You know your daughter well."

"Father," Chereb, who had stepped out finally, called from the hallway. Schoeff got up and came to her side. "So, what's the deal?" she said, holding back her sorrow. "Outside of church you said something about Juliane being involved."

Schoeff nodded.

"Being a part of this, your assignment with God, doesn't she have a *ticket* to be brought back? You know like with that Laertes guy?"

"Lazarus," said the movie director beside them.

"Right, him," Chereb said.

"Oh, my Chereb, for one thing," Schoeff said. "I don't have the privilege. For another…"

"Yeah, but you said God could make himself be in us," Chereb said. "Wasn't that what you said? Won't this be a good time for him to visit?"

"Miss Antonisz, I can't just call Him in."

"Call me Chereb."

"Chereb, I cannot will Him at a moment's notice."

The movie director clasped his chin and elbow and paced around them.

"Chereb, you're taking this to yourself," Schoeff said. "You're feeling blame."

"Yes, but not particularly. I just thought, what convenience, father. You're here, and I have a dead friend." She was at the point of her second round of tears. "The odds of that happening again have to be a million to one."

Schoeff felt that this was more than blame. He saw a plea, a deep longing to which humans usually surrender. Above other struggles Chereb might have given up on in the past, this one still had hope, and she had this unflinching belief in him. But how was this possible? It wasn't in the contract. He would only subject himself to genuine fakery. "Um," he said.

"You'll do it?" the movie director asked.

49

How to Convey a Message

Schoeff went back in the burgundy suite. Chereb and the director followed him, and so did the desk manager and the bellboy.

Schoeff placed a hand on Mr. DeVoe's drooping shoulders, gestured for him to get up. Mr. DeVoe, although blinded by tears and absolutely at a loss on what was to be performed, rose and let the priest kneel over his daughter again. Chereb and the rest gathered around. Schoeff in the meantime could not help but pray for himself. He had a hard time concentrating on just the idea of recalling a soul. He knew calling the Almighty in was out of the question. He grasped Juliane's two hands and placed them on her stomach. Then he shut his eyes and began to deal. He bargained that the last time, last Sunday, in front of St. Jude's, he was totally helpless and did not have a prayer in saving the woman who had fell from the top of the building. In return for the awesome favor, this time, he offered from deep within his overlooking Sunday that morning. He offered that his speech on cardiovascular aerobics was not the grandest of choice for that day, and lastly he asked forgiveness for despising Agothe Mir up to now and promised to love her as an enemy should be loved. "This is what I have," he said over Juliane's body. "Though it may not be all that important, not enough to resuscitate life for sure, but consider the sacrifice of these people. They need life in a friend, a daughter and an employee. Juliane, we need for you to get up."

Stillness happened. No one moved except for the director, who suddenly had the urge to sniff on the pipe from his robe pocket. "Oh, don't mind me," he said. "Habit." But upon lighting, his mouth lost grip of the pipe and it fell on the carpet when the young assistant manager came through.

"Hello, there," Juliane said, as if she just walked into work. Everybody's jaw dropped. "Oh, this is just temporary," she announced. "She's with me."

The bellboy, who was leaning on a brass coat-and-hat rack, fell with it over the French tufted chair. Schoeff snapped out of his amazement and helped him up.

Juliane rose from her position and sat up on the bed. "My heavens," she said.

"Julie, baby, is that really you?" said Mr. DeVoe, who had felt the absence of a pulse on her daughter's wrist ten minutes ago.

"Of course, Daddy. It's wonderful."

"What is?"

"Life. It's practically headache-free. I went out with this massive headache, and the relief is astonishing. Mumsy is okay."

"Who?" DeVoe said.

"Your first wife. But enough of the afterwards already, I have to chat this thing out with Chereb."

With renewed spirit, Chereb kneeled and tightly embraced her close friend, speechless.

"Thanks so much for the begging," Juliane said. "A

200

true confidant you are. Here's a word of wisdom — don't ever fall for this Ira guy. He's just an empty jewelry box. He writes bad poetry!"

"Did he try to kill you?" Chereb asked, looking up to Schoeff to check if she was doing the right thing.

Schoeff, who couldn't stop asking his mind of how could this be, nodded his approval.

"He certainly did," Juliane said. "And we must part because of this, his sordid lame work...of a passion."

"What do you mean?" asked Chereb.

"Simple, all things must end. Fish, plants, koala bears, you name it. Why should I disturb balance?" Juliane said. "I had enough trouble balancing the ledger." Suddenly Juliane felt faint. She put her chin up and closed her eyes. A gust of air seemed to have entered her nostrils and tilted her head. "Oh, yeah, there's a great sale on wearable art at Oldham's," she said lastly and fell back slowly on the bedspread.

"Juliane, are you there?" Chereb asked. But the air that came into Juliane replaced the revisiting soul.

"What is this?" asked DeVoe. "Where is she?" He pushed his way among his employees to get to Schoeff at the other end of the bed. He took hold of Schoeff's arms and asked, "Why is it just temporary?"

Schoeff, in return, held the man to ease his anxiety. "She could no longer be with us," Schoeff said. "Her interiors had been poisoned and could no longer sustain life. What you heard was your daughter aided by a being. She, alone, could not continue."

"Who are you?" DeVoe demanded.

"If it's any consolation, my friend," the movie director said, "aren't you a bit relieved that there's a better place than this, and that your daughter and wife are in it?"

201

After a moment, Mr. DeVoe got hold of himself and straightened his striped tie. "Perhaps, Mr. De Mille," he said. "It's just that my daughter's being, as I've known it, felt it a moment ago, is…preferred."

Mr. DeVoe in his misery tried but could not leave the Guilliam Suite.

50

The Unneedy

What was more preferred was that Chereb had the chance to communicate. Everything seemed calm after. At an outdoor cafe on Sixth and Park Avenue, she sat across Schoeff, who was working on a cinnamon root beer float. Four fingers, two from each hand, were on a long straw. He gazed at waddling pigeons that pecked for tidbits on the sidewalk against striding legs that came their way. Chereb had picked the flavor for him.

"Miss Chereb?" Schoeff said. "I am not anywhere like Christ in the garden, or reflect a view that I am somewhat like him, no. Far down the pole. Mr. DeVoe had that conviction in his face that I could control his daughter's fate, that I could make her stay. With that said...who do you think I am?"

"A good speaker," Chereb said.

"Exactly."

"And a priest."

"Yes! Now I know why I am in your company this very moment," Schoeff said.

"And a man? Who can feel love?"

He smiled. Chereb looked away toward the Merchant Building on Time Square. The ad there consisted of a lippy face shocked beyond her fabulous looks because of flying saucers to the left of her head. It promoted a hairspray brand that would hold *even in the most terrifying moment.* "I just don't know in what order," Chereb said to herself, "but I know you did this all for me."

Schoeff looked up from his float. "Pardon?"

"That store Juliane mentioned, Oldham's. I've never heard of it. And wearable art. What is wearable art?"

"Are you sure?" Schoeff said.

"Yes. I know this town from end to end. Clothes stores are landmarks to us."

"I have a feeling it hasn't opened for business yet. It would sell items not of this day and age, my guess."

"You mean Juliane talked about fashion beyond her time?"

"Maybe."

"I think we have company," Chereb said.

From Schoeff's back, a horde of reporters and cameramen were crossing Park Avenue. A patrolman had to whistle off traffic from both directions to make way for them. Schoeff turned in his bistro chair and stood up. Should he stay and get trampled? "It's show time," he said.

"What took them?" Chereb asked seriously.

The pigeons scattered.

"Father Schoeff!" one reporter yelled. He introduced himself, "Will Sagorny, WABC."

"How are you?" Schoeff said. They gathered quickly, sticking their prods into Schoeff's face.

"Fine, sir," the reporter puffed. "It's been said that you have brought back to life a deceased woman at the DeVoe-Hilton. Can you confirm that?"

The sun had not appeared the entire day, and it was near dusk. Floodlights blazed before Schoeff could answer the first question. He shaded his eyes and said, "The best way I could describe it is that it's a graceful riddle."

"What do you mean by that?" an energetic, petite woman asked. She had managed her microphone right up front. Bothered by the brightness of the spotlight, she turned to the man holding it and said, "Would you shut that thing off? He's human! He's got eyes." She turned to Schoeff. "Father, why a woman in a plush hotel? Did she need the miracle more than, let say, a less fortunate being?"

"To answer the first question," Schoeff said. "I don't think it was a phenomenon as we know it..."

"The bellboy saw it, said the dead woman rose up and argued with her father," a voice came from the back.

"It was miraculous in a way that it was utilized," Schoeff said, sticking to the same question. "And that was to relay a message."

"What message was that, father?"

"Dreary as it may sound, I think God was trying to say that we must depend on Him alone, for death alone is permanent. A mind stopper."

"I see," said the short woman, who had become the spokesperson for the group. "Father, were you related to the woman?"

"No, I just knew her through acquaintance."

"A female acquaintance?"

Schoeff delved in the aim of the question. "Yes, very much so."

"Is she the one with you now?"

Chereb, in the background, entertained another reporter.

"We were having floats at this fine spot, perhaps to relieve her of queries of what happened," Schoeff said. "And I myself needed the breather."

"From what we gathered at the hotel, it's been said that there's a probable crime in the event. The woman took barbiturates, but a note was found tucked under the mattress, not in her handwriting. It consisted of a poem? Can you comment on that, father?"

"Your guess is as good as mine," Schoeff said.

"I doubt that."

Schoeff looked over his shoulder for Chereb. He called her and turned back to the crowd. "If you please," he said. "I could chat with you all evening, but I have a dinner to attend to. Thank you." He started walking toward the street, hoping a taxi would sweep by. Chereb followed, cutting ties with the one reporter. Schoeff heard singing from the back. He started to cross the street hastily. Chereb clung to his side.

Suddenly someone screamed from his left, so loud and desperate that Schoeff had to stop in the middle of the street. Traffic had to be held back by two patrolmen now. Their spent energy added burden on Schoeff. But he felt he had to identify who was screaming. "Holy Father Schoeff, holy Father Schoeff!" came through the crowd. "You got to see me!"

Something told Schoeff that he shouldn't have stopped. It was a young man, seventeen or eighteen, with a bulldog collar around his neck. He shoved his way through the crowd, still with the achy yells. He pushed Chereb accidentally and said he was sorry. When everything came to his attention, he leaned on another person to catch his breath. His skin was bland, yokes in his eyes deep and gray. "Father Schoeff, glad to meet you," he puffed. "I'm the man in that hospital window you've been talking about, yes. Except...except I'm here now and not fifty years," he swallowed, "and today, this evening, this day and age, when

I heard you raising up a dead rich broad, well, that just blew my mind. I said to myself, you gotta be my man. As you can see, I'm a cripple."

"What made you that way?" Schoeff said.

The young man grinned and flinched. "You got me there, Father Schoeff," he said. "But my guess is this, this wicked town made me this way, good old New York, the core of your prophecy. But I am *it*. It got to me before your warning. Now you can heal me." On both of the young man's arms Schoeff identified red dots. Some spots were swollen.

Dusk became night, and the people, stimulated by the arrival of this young man, waited Schoeff's reaction. "I don't even know what made you this way," Schoeff said honestly. "How can I heal you? I'll pray for you in the hope that you'll pray for yourself and your health."

"What do you mean, man?" the young man said to Schoeff, who proceeded to walk toward the curb where a cab was parked. "Just touch me and I'll be okay. Hey, where're you going?" the young man let go of the person supporting him and took off toward Schoeff but fell on his weak leg. There were murmurs from the crowd.

Schoeff quickly turned around, anger apparent on his face. "I did not raise any dead!" he said. "Forgive me if I tried. It was taken wrongly. The Mind said, 'Hey, I'm here. Why do you need another person? I'm sociable. I can tend to your mishaps. See! I can even speak through the dead!'"

Chereb looked on, speechless.

"I'm just here to tell you of what is to come," Schoeff said. "And you, my man, how can I begin to help you if you don't help yourself? Salvation is not at the touch of a finger. It's work. It's resisting the bad things around you. It's a day-to-day."

The people were shocked at the tone of voice Schoeff had acquired.

"Guy, I just want you to heal me of my limp," the boy said from the blacktop.

But Schoeff opened the door of the taxi for Chereb, let her by and got in himself. He didn't waste another word till he directed the cab back to the hotel.

51

Mrs. Antonisz

Zeyad, who had been reading the *Post* at the Antonisz' residence after work, sought to take a little nap at Rapha's den when he heard ringing from upstairs. It came from Chereb's room, he was certain. It was muffled due to the pink tufted walls. He hustled up the stairs, almost tripping over a throw rug. He was inside Chereb's room within three rings. "Hello, may help you?" he sang.

"Goddammit!" Ira said. "Where is *she*?"

"May I know who is calling?"

"Listen, you burnt fruitcake. Tell her it can happen again around her precious social circle if she doesn't heed to me."

"What can happen?"

"Just tell her!"

"I don't understand," Zeyad said. "Miss Chereb has no obligation."

"Gwendolyn!"

"Who?"

"This better be her next time, holy man!"

The voice seemed less confident. It was strained. Zeyad pictured a man locked up in one of those steamy bath places, in his undershirt and maybe a sweater and on top of that, a coat, and his only way of communication were through the handpiece of a telephone, the wire sticking out of the porcelain tiles.

Someone knocked on Chereb' s door. Zeyad jerked, putting the phone down. It was Mrs. Antonisz, who had come from watering the azaleas in the terrace. "My apology, Zeyad, for scaring you," she said routinely. "Who was it? Was it him?"

"I am afraid it was," Zeyad said.

"What did he want?"

"To speak to your daughter."

"Did you tell him that he's upsetting her with all this nonsense?"

"I did not have the chance, missus. He sounded a little wild."

"Well, if he adores her, then he might ease off the mystery bit. It's unhealthy. I heard he's a college man."

Zeyad got up from the bed. "Do not see him as healthy at all," he said.

"I know, I know. You have no worry in this. This is just the city. I think it's a good idea not to tell Chereb he called this time. She has more important things to occupy her mind. Instead you can entice her to follow some of your activities. Set her on the right foot to apply at Columbia, God willing."

"Miss Chereb will apply if only she wants to," Zeyad said frankly.

"She said she'll get around to it. But that could be 1966, who knows."

"Missus, this man doesn't frighten you?" Zeyad asked.

"Only when he confuses my daughter. But it's only

the city's doing. He's just a whiner, a wimpy fellow. There is more muscle in the mystery than there is in the man. Believe me, Zeyad. You and my little Reeby are braver." Grace Antonisz was certain of herself.

52

Gwendolyn Brooks

Moments before they arrived back at the DeVoe-Hilton, Schoeff took out a piece of paper from his breast pocket and showed it to Chereb. "It is not his," he said. "It's Gwendolyn Brooks'."

Chereb unfolded it and tried to read under the passing streetlights. She read:

> I label clearly, and each latch and lid
> I bid, Be firm till I return from hell...
>
> My taste will not have turned insensitive
> To honey and bread old purity could love.

"Gwendolyn?" Chereb said. "That's the name he used."

"Yes," Schoeff said. "But, don't worry. He was in there twice and might have registered. If so, they should have him in custody by tomorrow."

"She's that poet from the *Voice*," Chereb said.

"Yes, this year's Pulitzer winner. But now it seems *you* are her in this person's mind. You may be competition to him."

"Father, you're confusing me."

"Or, he may have placed you as Gwendolyn so he can have a fixation on you and envy you at the same time." The cab pulled in under the veranda. Schoeff looked at Chereb in the dark. "Would you inform me if he happens to contact you again?" he said, careful not to say her name at this time, careful not to confuse her further.

"Why? Who is this person?" Chereb asked. "He's just a loser to me."

"He may be premonition, I'm not sure," Schoeff said. "Not to muddle things in your head more, but Mr. Othem is the same person who tempted me in the crowd outside of St. Jude's two weeks ago."

Chereb gasped.

"What will it be?" the cabbie asked.

"Pardon us," said Schoeff. "The lady will be getting off."

"Father, he's a woman?" Chereb said.

"I don't know."

"You mean I'm stuck between Juliane passing and this lunatic having the hots for me, as Gwendolyn Brooks?"

"Hm, we see evil as being complex. But...evil can be put through therapy?" Schoeff wondered deeply. He looked at Chereb and said, "but for now, sorry, get in your nice car and drive home safely, which you will."

"Is that a guarantee?"

"It's a guarantee," Schoeff said. "You're a caring and compassionate being. I'm glad I have made your acquaintance."

"Mm, I bet you say that to all the Jewish girls you ride in taxis with."

Schoeff let out a tireless laugh. Chereb swiveled around and kissed him twice on the forehead. Yet when she lowered her lips and felt the warmth of his breath, then catching his eyes, Schoeff had no choice but to laugh it off again.

"Good night," Chereb said.

"Yes, likewise."

Chereb turned to him one more time before getting out. "Oh, don't forget to pray for that guy on Park Avenue," she said.

"Yes."

The cabbie gave Schoeff a peculiar twist of his connected eyebrows from the rearview.

Chereb in the Bel Air wished her life hadn't become so complicated. She wished it were three weeks ago, to the moment when she found herself doodling a name that sounded so uncomplicated. Yet when she rechecked it on the bulletin outside of St. Jude's, the spelling amazed her still. It only made her think more of this person, to whom she thought had been the sweetest to say goodnight to.

53

Street Tempests

Grand Concourse never looked so empty. The chill got to Oscaro finally. He jogged in place under the streetlamp with the wind on his face. It blew from the ocean. He took the night off from work. When the doctors called him at the station, with all their formal greetings and hospital words, his Italian boss thought they were from D.C. and had an important message for the boy.

Oscaro peered down the huge street. People in cars rolled by, shouting out comments. One man even flicked a lit cigarette at him. A prostitute had crossed the street to check him out and said she would lower her standards to do him if he had the cash. Instantly bugged, he swore her off and checked the road instead from both directions. He could find better-looking Latina girls with nicer mouths at the piers. What pavement, he noticed. The sky, void of even a cloud, would not wet the asphalt for another day or two. Rubber would just scream dry for a block.

Finally, a black Mercury sedan rolled by. He stepped back. A window opened. "Good evening, Oscar. Have you thought more about the project? The one we've started and never finished?" said the man.

"Yes, but no can-do. The priest is like a pigeon up above. He sees everything."

The man laughed with the driver. "Do you really believe him? His very existence in this area, in this city, is ludicrous. You see saints like him only in Portugal or in your Lourdes of France or some mountainous province in Albania where a village needs water for their dying crops. Not in the Bronx. The Bronx takes care of itself. You don't really believe that this city will come to an end at the turn of the century, if two million people right now don't follow his advice?"

"I believe in something."

"Then, why are you here?"

Oscaro stopped swaying back and forth and looked up. "I don't know," he said. "Something might change my mind."

From this, the doctors let him in.

54

The Misinformed

In the morning, in her own room, Asha placed all the pencils and sharpener and protractor in the carrying case even though school was no longer in session. She placed the open box on the bed, its edges aligned with the stitched design of the quilt. Upon slipping into her daily duster, she still admired the sight of utensils and neatness. The year had gone by, yet they were still free of doodle marks and finger smear. She put on her pink robe when she heard the door opening in the living room. Her mother scampered that way from the kitchen, and not a moment too soon Mrs. Gutierrez let out a scream. Asha ran out of her room. It was Oscaro, lying on the floor. He reeked of whiskey. He had not been at work.

"Come here, Sash," he said from the floor.

Asha, who had pressed her cheek on the wall for security, hesitantly walked toward her brother's side.

"How do you feel, Sash?"

"Fine," Asha said.

Oscaro nodded. "Sasha, I've been reading the papers." He had the *Times* clipped under his arm while still on the floor. He got up and spread the front page for Asha.

217

"Who's that?" he said. "Does that man look like our padre`? And it says here that he's been running around downtown with this blonde lady in the picture."

Asha looked closer at the photo and read the caption. "That doesn't say anything. It just says that he was with her at an ice cream shop."

"After they've been in a hotel," Oscaro said. "Some kind of a party went on in that hotel, I don't know. They wouldn't write it up."

"What party?" Asha said. "Oscaro, you're making things up."

"Is the picture lying?" Oscaro said. "It hit the headlines. A priest don't do that."

Asha, nearly in tears, said, "I am not going."

Her brother peered at her.

"Why, Oscaro? No more," Mrs. Gutierrez said from the doorway. She added a string of dialect to stop Oscaro from answering.

"*Ang experimente` wala pa tapus,*" *Nay,* he said.

Hindi na! Mrs. Gutierrez insisted. "*Wala ka gid deus. Tan awa siya. Mamatay na kong e continue mo pa!*"

Oscaro passed Asha the *Times* to look at. "Just look for the apple on the fence," he said. "If you don't see it, it won't be today."

"Apple?" claimed Asha. "There's no more school, Oscaro!"

"It'll be over soon. One more time, that's all they want." Oscaro looked at his mother and said, "*Ikaw, ma, tanawa. Siling ni la ma* come through *sila.* Extra bonus *kuno,* guaranteed! Okay?"

Asha went back into her room and put away her things.

55

The Air-Conscientious

Monsignor Randolph sat back and prayed over his buttered oatmeal within closed windows. It was his staple environment due to the chronic illness he kept forgetting he didn't have anymore. To the other patrons at the table, the morning could be a time for fresh air, and it was up to one of them to break silence and remind the monsignor that open windows were actually good for his health. But the monsignor couldn't be disturbed during his lengthy break-of-dawn prayer, and Father Lamantiaragski, Father Gado and the rest just had to be patient.

That morning, it was Schoeff who broke the lingering pause. He clattered down the stairs and jumped on the floor from the third step. "Monsignor, there'll be controversy today, this morning," he announced. "So be ready for anything."

"Controversy?" the monsignor said, looking up from his oatmeal. "On what, this time?"

"First of all, the only bluebirds in New York are chirping outside. Do you hear them?" Schoeff said and went over to crank all the long windows open. "Ah, hear them."

"Schoeff, all I hear is the garbage truck collecting Mrs. McAllister's cans," the monsignor said. "Why all this enthusiasm? And in that jogging suit again?"

"To bog down the controversy."

"What controversy?" asked Father Laman.

"Yesterday afternoon, I was seen at Park Avenue with Miss Antonisz, and the press, an invincible factor second only to the Big Mind, has printed a story with a few details missing."

"When?"

"Yesterday. I felt it in my dreams. I'm warning you that there may be disturbances."

"The Pope is the factor second to this 'Big Mind'," Laman chided him.

Schoeff ignored this.

"So, what is jogging around the block going to do?" asked the monsignor.

"You read my mind, your grace," Schoeff said. "By jogging around the block, maybe up and down Valentine, I will put out that nothing is wrong, which is true. I was just consoling Miss Chereb after the death of her friend."

Two of the priests made the sign of the cross. The monsignor, still bothered in the face, followed suit. "Start from the beginning, will you?" he said, slamming down his oatmeal spoon.

"Well, sir, I have to get going before any more of the neighbors pick up the *New York Times*," Schoeff said. "I'll fill you later."

Before anyone else could utter a word, Schoeff was out the door.

"What was that word he mentioned last week?" Randolph wondered. "Aerodibs, aerodics...something that had to do with air. If people would be air-conscientious in fifty years, things will be less serious, more playful, I would imagine. Just think, a basketball player would be president."

56

Milo

In his jog toward Valentine Avenue, Schoeff finally saw his path of thorns. It was projected on the first face he met down the cathedral steps. The face, owned by a tuna vendor who happened to be a hefty lady in her sixties, took him back to his pre-teen years, when grandmothers and aunts with cellulite were fiercest in guilt trips. He remembered one August night when he had taken his father's 35MM camera with the wide-angle lens to snap a picture of a girl undressing.

It was a time when school was anticipated after an empty dragging summer, and Milo, a middle-schooler he knew, had a two-year-old crush on one of his neighbors: a damsel who always took ballet lessons. Now Milo was used to hanging out with the younger kids, and Schoeff was reared to respect anyone older than him. As long as Milo didn't rack him for money or chocolate, he was a standout guy to Schoeff. But it so happened that Milo was at the verge of breakdown over this girl and couldn't possibly go on without a snapshot of her before she would leave town again for a dance school in Cincinnati. Schoeff's house, his bedroom for that matter, was only a pine fence away from this damsel's den and bathroom windows. "Why that late?" Schoeff had asked before the mission. "She dances in her living room around eight-thirty."

Sure enough Milo got the hour he wanted. Schoeff put up a ladder against the fence under the sprawling oak. The shadows completely hid them. Schoeff searched the den windows with the zoom lens, adjusting it every inch he moved to get the clearest snap. But the girl wasn't twirling anywhere. Milo moved the lens to the right when Schoeff was still focusing. Upon seeing a blurry slender figure, Schoeff suddenly looked up from the camera and found it aimed at the bathroom window. "Howie, ain't that a beauty?" Milo said.

To this day, Schoeff couldn't figure out Milo's obsession that summer, an infatuation for this girl for two years only to make a freezeframe of her for the sole purpose of masturbation. And how could he, himself, be a tool to the act so unthinkable at the age of twelve, especially when his Grandma Cecil witnessed the whole episode from their living room. He had forgotten that she was an occasional night owl, one that could screech. At dinner, it was her face that made the depths of guilt unbearable.

Inevitably, Schoeff's father punished him by making Milo and he walk over to the girl's house and apologize. Milo, of course, ditched him. Thus, Schoeff had been the only pervert that showed up at the steps of the damsel's house two afternoons later. He said he was sorry and was only a word short to fully describing the event he was sorry about. Masturbation wasn't in his vocabulary yet. Schoeff's father thought if this wasn't done, the boys would do it again. Milo's absent was purely a freak miscalculation.

57

How to Woo a Crowd

And this morning, it was the unnerving face of a vendor lady that made him regress to that misconception of blame. But this time around, it made more sense.

"Good morning," he said to the lady. The eyes glanced away coldly, as if they had destined to make him fall in the next manhole and break his collarbone.

Overall, guilt was good, he considered. It had a function to restore human goodness. The only trouble was that guilt couldn't be guided and was dumb as a pew not facing the altar.

On Valentine, after greeting a few passers-by without much response, he approached a sidewalk market and thought if he could jog through it, he was ready to return to Times Square. A woman shopper, in a hat and scarf, gave him a curve of her lip but did not offer a greeting. When he reached Babar's Grocers, at the cabbage and lettuce section, the owner who knew him well ignored his browsing entirely. A businessman in a gray double-breasted suit recognized him and asked, "How was it, father?"

"How was what?" Schoeff said.

"The blonde dame," the man said. "How was she?"

Schoeff looked around, saw other people had taken

refuge in this man's boldness. This was a Catholic community in southwest Bronx, and most of these faces had pleaded, bowed, and eaten bread at St. Jude's Cathedral, and were probably at the gathering where Agothe Mir had wreaked havoc. For a moment Schoeff thought this face-the-music (before-it-becomes-a-jam-session) venture wasn't a good idea. He kept jogging in place. "She was quite well," he answered the businessman. "In fact, she seemed to have regained her spirit after the death of her friend."

The owner of Babar's grocers came forth with a copy of the *Times*. "It says here you was seen with her *in* the hotel," he said. "In this Guilliam Suite, in fact."

"Mr. Babar, that's where her friend was found," Schoeff said. "If you would only compare stories and headlines, you'd find that they're all different."

"How about that lame man who asked you for help?" another bystander said. "You turned him down because you had to get into the cab before the cameras got to you."

"I assure you that young man will find cure if he truly seeks it."

"Oh, knock it off, father," Babar said. "The damage's been done and printed. You showed your way of life round town and made us look bad up here. You had us believing in yourself and that hocus pocus thing about raising the dead. You think you're Jesus but you're not even a priest."

"Did I ever say I was Jesus?" Schoeff said.

"You gave the signs," Babar answered. "The damage was us, father."

A construction worker at his side responded with, "You made us think and believe that the Yankees will win ten more World Series. Now what kind of a crackpot holy shit is that? The Giants will cream them this year."

"No, they won't," a teenager on a bike protested.

"Just between Rizzuto and DiMaggio, Giants ain't got crap."

"What do you know?" the construction worker grunted.

Those around Schoeff were not amused. "Those are hopeful predictions, especially from mid-season," he murmured.

"Oh, c'mon, father," said the construction worker. "You know the Giants got this year. You're just weighing with the wind here."

"Oh, get off the baseball nonsense!" a stiff woman yelled from the back. "We're talking unholier than *thou* here. The man is obviously sacrilegious. Look at him, mamboing in his shorts like he has done nothing. We should hang him by those shorts!"

To Schoeff, this was all still tamed farce. The crowd that was developing laughed at him, giving the woman a breath of pride. Schoeff tried to lift another knee but came to a halt. Trains were clanging. Cars were bustling in the streets. Monday had begun, comfort zone for work. He looked around and found a sturdy crate under one of Mr. Babar's tables. "May I?" he said.

"Be my guest," Babar said.

Schoeff placed the crate evenly on the ground and got up on it. He raised his hand like a schoolboy and said, "I apologize for being here at this early hour, try to replenish you with my existence and purpose. But this, New York, is a free man, with faults and mistakes. He was born to this earth luckily without any complications or any birth defect, but he can't walk on water or raise the dead…"

A huge ripe onion skimmed him on the shoulder before it hit Babar's tin roof.

"Yet he was commissioned to do some prophecy," Schoeff said with a smile. "In the hope that he may save a disaster or two through the coming...."

Radishes came his way, one striking his chin and another, his chest. Other kinds of produce came flying, some caked with mud.

"Go home, father!" a cafe owner from down the street shouted. "Go back to the radio station and entertain us more!"

"Through the coming decades," Schoeff went on resolutely. "The Almighty obviously thinks our ancestors are worth saving, and he doesn't need me to haggle with him on how many good people this city has in order for it to be saved."

With all the flying debris, the shouting and the threats, Schoeff stood on the crate without much thought of balance. A small tomato splatted on his temple, its seeds trickling down his cheek and neck. He just jolted back, went on. In the process of moving his head and dodging what he could, he spotted a patiently calm boy standing right below his chin. He had on khaki shorts and a torn, loose sweater. There were no socks at his ankles, just red high-tops. Schoeff found appeal in the boy's look.

"You're doing fine," the boy said. "Don't ever think twice like you did a moment ago."

"Yes," Schoeff said. At that second, a piece of concrete the size of a tennis ball whopped him below his left eye. But because of his headstrong gladness, he did not fall back from the crate. He managed to swing his right foot back to the ground to support himself. His head throbbed painfully, but he managed to squat down.

"Sorry about that," said the boy. "You're my dove in all of this. Will you accept my deepest?" The boy began to shed tears without changing his expression. He quickly reached and touched the cut on Schoeff's face.

"That's quite okay," Schoeff said of the sensation. "Just --"

"Cringe," the boy ordered.

"Yes," Schoeff said, cringing.

The crowd had settled down to take notice of the conversation. They huddled around the boy. Most of the people in the back thought Schoeff was out cold, and they closed in as if to see an auto wreck. The boy looked up and said, "Can't you see this man needs air? Give him room!"

"Who are you speaking to, nigger?" said the scrawny construction worker.

"The less stupid," the boy answered.

This somehow silenced every tongue in the huddle, replacing the noise with just stares.

To Schoeff, the boy whispered, "One more tomorrow talk, then go back to daily chores. This is good, but this ain't healthy." The boy let go of his shoulders and motioned to leave.

"A moment, please," Schoeff said.

The boy turned around. "You don't need to apologize," the boy said. "It's Milo that has to." Then in quick steps, the boy crawled into the thickness of people and disappeared before Schoeff could mellow in the euphoria he was left with.

"What did that colored kid do to you?" asked Babar, who was now holding back the crowd.

To this Schoeff smiled, blood trickling around his eye. He stood up again and said, "I feel you need something before the playoffs, before McHermott takes the mound in October."

"Oh, spare us, father," said a round-bellied man, obviously still bothered.

"It's in the making," Schoeff said. "I don't have any

outstanding news before the playoffs, but this Friday, Mary Kate Singly will have triplets at the Bronx-Ashbury at 1:53 PM. They will be a boy and two girls. The boy will weigh five ounces more than the first girl and seven ounces less than the second."

"What kind of a prediction is that?" asked the cockier construction worker.

"A safe one," Schoeff said. "But don't crowd the maternity room when the time comes. The head nurse there is liable to throw basket fruits at you if she feels suffocated."

58

Mourners

Chereb reached out to her society circle. Rachel Browning was off to Hollywood to cameo in a Bergen film when the tragedy occurred. Chereb had phoned her but didn't have the nerve to break the news long distance. She had rung Rose Mary in the Virgin Islands, and knowing that Rose was a steel-plated petal when it came to horrible news, Chereb did fill her in.

At La Guardia, when Rose Mary Getty got off the DC-8 and saw Chereb and Zeyad behind the gate, she came running and sprawled her arms around them. "Oh, God, how maniacally sick!" was the first thing that Rose Mary said.

"I know," cried Chereb.

Zeyad took hold of Rose Mary's handbag and led the two hugging women out of the crowd.

"Only in New York does a man write verse and poison," Rose Mary said. "And *he's* established in his own right. Senseless little dick."

"You know him?" Chereb said.

"Oh, yep. He was like the sweetheart in one writers' luncheon in town a few years back, when his precious little volume came out. I think I even shook his ejaculating hand."

"Rosie," Chereb said.

"No, he's that seedy. Juliane knew it. She was hyped for a little fling, and that son of a bitch took advantage. I can't imagine putting Julie in past tense."

"It's better not to dwell," Zeyad offered.

Rose Mary, who wasn't a hundred percent in favor of a little theistic proverb from anybody at the moment, just kept silent.

Zeyad read her thoughts and said, "Or is it better to talk about it?"

"It's okay, Zed," Rose Mary said. "Either way, we all end up smoking pot in our penthouses to escape life's realities, right? But that's a sorry vacay if I've ever heard of one. Down deep right now, you know what I feel like?"

Zeyad shook his head no.

"I feel like frying up poet balls. I hear most of them don't need a pair."

In the limousine, Rose Mary tipped her chauffeur with a bottle of coconut whiskey for picking up Chereb and Zeyad to be her welcome party. "Just don't drink it while you're at the wheel," she said. "It might scorch your mustachio when you jam on the brakes."

"Yes, Miss Getty," said her chauffeur, who had been with her since her teens.

"And don't run any red lights either, make excuses for yourself."

"Certainly not, Miss Getty."

"Are you always this sarcastic when you're in mourning?" asked Chereb.

"Damn, I'm in mourning," Rose Mary said. "So, what's our agenda for tonight? We're still a threesome, with Zeyad here."

"That's another thing," Chereb said. "The police had advised us to keep indoors. This guy knows all our faces."

"That's one hell of an advice," Rose Mary said. "I've been roasting under the sun for I don't know how long and got whistled at and honeyed by nothing but mambo climbers all that time, and all this city can say when I get back is to keep my mug indoors? They have no link whatsoever in arresting this guy?"

"He was taken in for a while."

"For a while?"

"No solid evidence. The paper said that Gwendolyn Brooks poem was nothing to them. They handed it back to Father Schoeff."

"How about dusting for prints and all that jazz?" Rose Mary said. She rolled her window down and lit a joint. "How is the father anyway?" she said, holding a plume in.

"He has become their source closest to dusting prints," Chereb answered. "The only thing is he's also unavailable."

For the rest of the ride down to Manhattan, the three were silent. Rose's chauffeur dimmed the overhead light to give them calm.

59

Milo, 1931

It was like a huge oily funnel, the dream Schoeff had as a teenager. He was in it scaling the inside hopelessly. Milo, the older kid, was with him. Schoeff's hand had slipped off Milo's hand when they were helping each other up to the top. Milo had that *ces't la vie* expression on his face when Schoeff disappeared out of sight into the hole.

"Girls," Milo had said. "You can't touch them. They're afraid of us just like we're scared stiff of their...*prissiness.*"

They must have been older for Milo to know that word prissiness. Usually, Schoeff dreamed of people jumping off ledges—or people fleeing from each other like they were in between two stores with big seasonal sales. But this time it was Milo with his girl obsession and his religion. In retrospect, Schoeff thought that the teenager couldn't have the two living in harmony.

It was like himself and his Uncle Dam's ideology of not clinging to the "service clubs of routine": two items that were totally opposites. By "clubs" Uncle Dam referred to (to put it in full circle with Milo's own dilemma) were religions. "It's okay to be a naughty in your own backyard," Uncle Dam had said to Schoeff. "But once you're in the front yard, neighborhood kids might think you're nuts, and you won't be popular."

"Do girls make the hair on the back of your neck stand?" Milo asked.

Bored, Schoeff nodded.

"I bet when you see their tops off, other things stand up."

Embarrassed, Schoeff turned away from Milo. "Can't you think of something else?" Schoeff asked.

"If I go home, I can't think about them," Milo confessed.

"Why?"

"I'm not allowed to think that way, sport," Milo said, as if it was common knowledge. He admitted to Schoeff that his mother would smell his shirt for perfume before he'd come into the house. She wasn't strict. It was just that her faith wasn't that of any churches in Logansport. Who was to judge her and the way she was bringing up her son? In fact, their house, which was big on white lilies, was like a shrine of worship. Schoeff had been invited once.

"Yeah, but you think it anyway—in the gym, in the library, *anywhere,*" Schoeff said.

"Not in the house, sport."

Schoeff slipped farther down the funnel, his nails collecting grub. "Don't you talk to God?" he yelled, determined to get an answer. "Listen to him?"

"You won't go through!" Milo only yelled back. "The hole is not big enough."

Schoeff woke up screaming. He swung his legs to the side of the bed and slipped into his pair of flipflops. He realized what day it was and what had happened the week before. The Logansport Gazette called it "an unfortunate accident" as requested by Milo's mother. Schoeff knew it had been "requested" through his Aunt Phyllis. But when a person drives a Ford sedan through an acre of corn just to reach the Wabash River and plunged into it, it was hardly an accident. As Schoeff remembered, Milo couldn't see the end of his fight. The going away of the ballerina neighbor, the person Milo was in love with for the longest, personified the steep hill Milo was climbing.

Milo and his "damp" suicide interrupted Uncle Dam's vision of the future and Schoeff's as well.

60

The Well-Off

Ira concentrated in the high-rise apartment he shared with his mother. There was an enemy again to his focus, perhaps, his entire dedicated being. It came in the form of a meat tenderizer. "Ira boy, would you like your steak well or medium rare?" came from the kitchen. "I can make the omelet correspond with the meat." Her voice was like a jackhammer.

"For Pete's sake, Mother, I'm trying to write!"

"Onion soup is at simmer. Ira, you do care for onion soup, do you?"

Ira sprung up from his mahogany school desk, banged a few cabinets in his room and ran out to rapidly kick the kitchen door, which swung open and shut. His mother, in the heat of the turmoil, spilled the onion soup on the floor and on her arm.

"You meant to do that," Ira said upon seeing her.

"I did not!" shrieked his mother. "You're a *wicked* character!"

"Yes, Mother, only when I'm concentrating. Poetry doesn't stand for soup!" He grabbed a towel, soaked it in cold water over the sink and applied it on his mother's loose-skinned arm.

"No," she said. "You wouldn't have done what they've accused you of."

"How do you know this, Mother?"

"You're too finesse for that, too affluent, a man of letters." She touched his head while he mended her, her fingers getting oily in the scented pomade of his hair.

"Faith' is a fine invention, when Gentlemen can *see--*," his mother recited.

"Don't!" he snapped. "It's not time to be quoting her. The woman deceased was a nice, respectable person. Demure, naive to the hilt, but…"

"Yes, unstable like all those other wealthy people who rely on alcohol and barbiturates to get them through their day. Why so bothered? Everything has to be in the right tempo with you."

Ira whisked his head away from her hand. "There is no right tempo," he said. "Being rich doesn't make you unstable, nor does being beautiful. It's in the crevices of the mind. Once they're filled with nothing but wisdom, it becomes boring, Mother. Wealth and beauty beg in the dark corners of this city. Wisdom robs them and slits their throats."

"What are you saying?" She became appalled.

Ira pressed the towel on her arm again and said, "Let's eat, Mumsy. I think the steaks are parched."

61

Voices, Seen and Unseen

Schoeff was certain that evil was two of the same person. He didn't go further in finding evidence than in their names:

IRA G. OTHEM - AGOTHE MIR

He snapped out of the mixed emotions he went through the morning before. His left cheek had swollen, along with a few other places on his body. The cut above his right eye was long but shallow. He was spared from stitches. It would be nice, Schoeff thought, if it would leave a scar. It would always remind him of divinity's answer to anesthetic. Acting the pain sequence but with no pain. A child would lead us and give us procaine too, he thought. In any event, he was ready for a serene, consulting afternoon.

In the dark confessional booth, a tar-raked voice went, "I gave up my wife two years ago, and I'm not sure if I have been forgiven for that. For one thing, I slept good the first week she wasn't in the house. I was more relaxed, had more time for myself, my job was easier at the binding company, and my blood pressure was down."

Schoeff listened intently. "Go on," he said.

"In those first months I attended Mass regularly and asked forgiveness regularly, but I didn't have that uplifted-lung feeling every time I walked out of this church."

"So, you think you have to feel neglected, uncomfortable and stuffy to be forgiven for your divorce?" Schoeff said.

"In a sense."

"When you first mentioned this separation, did the priest happen to suggest you reconcile with your wife?"

"Yes."

"Obviously, that hasn't taken place. Do you feel any sense of guilt that it has not?"

"I thought about it. But you know how these things are. Once you say something and contact a lawyer and pay him, it's hard to take things back."

"Why is it hard to take things back?" Schoeff asked, his genuine self, taking over, away from his Uncle Dam's middle-ground safety net. When the voice didn't respond, Schoeff added, "Obviously, you feel incomplete or else you wouldn't be here. But here's a doozy. What if your lawyer, through the kindness of his heart, would return your fee, would you go back to her, as the priest had suggested? Even assuming that you are the one wanting to part ways."

"Honestly?"

"You're in the right booth for it."

"No, I don't think so, father."

"That, my man, is your confession. Deal with that first, then come back for the others. For your penance, look at pictures of your ex-wife, preferably ones with her smiling or tossing a ball at the beach. Go in peace."

Next came a younger, dapper voice. "Forgive me, father. I have done an alfalfable thing."

241

"First of all, are you tall enough to see my nose?" Schoeff said.

"Grandpa told me I can talk to you."

"Oh, in that case, what is this *alfalfable* thing you've done?"

"I tried to sit up my sister."

"That's a horrible," Schoeff mused. "Why did you do that?"

"To make her eat her cereal properly."

Schoeff thought for a second. "Is your sister ill in any way?"

"Yes."

"Mm, does she have tremendous pain when you tried to sit her up?"

"Yes. She screamed, and she doesn't stop. She's with our auntie right now three houses down on 15983 West Melbourne Street. We moved her there so you could see her."

"I see," Schoeff said. "Is your Grandpa with you?"

"No, he's three houses down with her. He's angry to come here."

"Tell me, are there any more people out there waiting for me?"

"Yes, a lady."

"May I know your name?"

"Samuel Ralph Woodward."

"Well, Samuel Ralph Woodward, through the love of Jesus, you are forgiven. Now, will you wait for me while I attend to this lady?"

Samuel nodded, which Schoeff could barely make out.

62

Away Clean

Serenity was suddenly gone. He could only think of the seriousness involved in order for Samuel's grandfather, likely a person of different faith, to sway a kid into a Catholic church to confess a trite act. It didn't seem to be an emergency. Samuel's voice didn't sound too hasty. Therefore, Schoeff listened on.

"Hello, father," came a woman's voice.

"Hello."

"It's been awhile since my last confession, maybe eight years, give or take. You see I'm not very much into breaking sins like breaking news. Confessions are more like a private conference to me."

"You don't have to tell me of your sins. But don't report me to the Vatican for saying that. They have the largest collection of sins, figuratively speaking."

The woman laughed lightly. "When I heard that you were the kingpin of priests in New York, my stars, I said, I just had to come."

"How long are you here?" Schoeff asked earnestly. The voice could still be anyone of the tens of women parishioners, but no....

"It's that I've never really known someone close...who was capable of raising up the lifeless."

"That's a rumor," Schoeff said.

"Rumor? Half of Manhattan is crazed over it. They either think you're a phenomenon from Venus or the Second Coming. I see you're still a man of still waters. You're in here *listening* while the whole city clamors over your identity. How do you manage that?"

"Mix of psychology and spiritual brawn. I took a beating yesterday. I guess once you feed in, they eventually get full." He paused, then asked, "May I see you? To talk of things."

"I'm only here for a day, and that day is coming to a close."

"Yes," Schoeff said, returned to peaceful thoughts. "Well, don't be too harsh on yourself in the private conference." He paused, expecting her voice. But the woman had already slipped out. The dimness in the cathedral favored her escape. Schoeff sprang out from the booth, took off his sash, and looked toward the front nave. She had slipped away clean. Even the candles, under each bas-relief Station of the Cross, did not flicker. Only a boy stood there peering up to Schoeff.

63

Raoul of Fire

Out on Selwyn Avenue there was a bonfire that could be seen from Asha's window. It started burning before dusk. It wasn't an ordinary huddle fire, to which people in the alley took comfort. It had been there for meaning and protest. Asha could hear a man shouting. She barely made out what he was saying. Her mother was at the window, too, flanked by Pilu and the two younger girls. Asha came out of her room and joined them. Oscaro was not with them. Evenings were always on edge in that part of town, with or without the strange fire.

Two blocks from Selwyn, Oscaro, on his feet, carried a torch and paraded with the others around the huge blaze. In their hands were books, religious ornaments, and even a small pew. Anything that seemed to have come from a church they tossed into the fire. They yelled over and over again that they were not ready for an end.

"This ain't the time, this ain't the place," shrieked a bearded fellow in front of the fire. "We choose to live on, we choose not faith. The earth is ours, the moon is yours!"

They repeated the bearded man's chant as if somewhere in the low threatening clouds a big ear was listening. A man in an army coat spotted Oscaro and approached him. "Hey, Raoul, what do you know? Didn't I see you with the priest the other night, not too long ago?"

"My name ain't Raoul," Oscaro said. "And I don't know no priest."

"Raoul, it's in my stars to have sharp eyes," said the man. "I always remember a doped-up face once I see one, especially when he hangs around a prophet. But it's okay, I see you're in our team now. People change their views. Have you changed your view?"

Oscaro shuffled on his feet, bothered in the face.

"We are weak," said the goateed man. "We are flesh, but we have minds that go deeper than anything else on this planet. They go so deep that the heavens above can't lay a hand on us. We have a thing called free will and nobody can mess with that. If we don't want it, we ain't having it. You love being here?"

Oscaro nodded.

"Then relax. Yell your guts out. 'This ain't the place, this ain't the time!'"

Oscaro took out a flask from inside his coat, removed the cap and gulped down vodka. Others lugged around bottles of rum, but he was the fortunate one who carried his liquor in sterling silver. He knew that this was crazy. He knew that the minds of these rousers were tripping. In the morning, they would wake up to their jobs and realize that their scare was based on one man and all the lopsided stories about him. Oscaro would return to the garage himself after two nights and conjure up some excuse. Mr. Pinelli was soft, with the daughters and all.

What Oscaro didn't know was that a very rich man by the name of Antonisz had visited the garage during the missed days looking for a private mechanic. Rapha, who was a flexible person, would have taken Mr. Pinelli's

247

suggestion as to whom was best fit to service Rapha's four cars. Because of this unannounced absence, Georgie Pinelli was not likely to pick Oscaro no matter how good a mechanic Oscaro had been.

All things would not settle in the morning. The fire would just die out in the rubble.

64

The Relatives

Schoeff stooped low while walking with Samuel. Schoeff was uncertain but felt obligated to be guided by the boy down the two blocks from St. Jude's. There was no fire to draw his attention, but black-and-white vehicles patrolled the area, watching out for possible outbreaks. A gathering in front of the church lot had peace on their minds and candle wax in their hands. They sang hymns of joy, certain that there was a sacred being inside. An occasional person would hurl trash or shout offenses at them, but the group held firm. Schoeff kept ducking.

With Samuel leading the way, they entered the back gate of a house. The unpainted fence reminded Schoeff of Logansport. He was surprised such a spacious backyard existed in the Bronx.

"Do you think your grandfather will ask me to cure your sister?" he asked.

"Yes," Samuel said.

"Do you think I'm the right person to do it? I have no medical degree."

Sam banged on the screen door. The overhead light came on. A woman in a striped dress opened up and told them to come inside. This person, whom Samuel addressed as aunt, was fit and had an air of mission to her appearance. "Down the stairs," the woman said to Schoeff.

The cellar was no basement limited to laundry and storage but a warm, cozy room with cedar panels and Berber carpet. In one corner flanked a rollaway bed. An elderly man stood by, over the disfigured body of a girl, younger than Samuel. The mattress sagged in the middle where her body weighed most.

She was awake. Her eyes were moving, but the rest, hands, arms and legs seemed to ache in inconceivable pain. A face expression would take an effort.

"How long has she been this way?" Schoeff asked.

"Since birth. It worsens little through the years," said the grandfather. "But to be honest with you, I'm not a believer of what's been happening out there. You are here on a gamble."

Samuel's auntie turned to the priest. "Don't mind him. It's been a hectic, heavy week."

"I'm sorry," Schoeff said.

"It must be turmoil for you out there," she offered.

"People are reacting too soon." Schoeff said. He turned to the elder and confirmed, "I came to see your granddaughter. Why, may I ask, do you have this anger toward me? I just came in."

"I have gone through a lot of phases, a lot of years of tribulations and sometimes defeat," Samuel's grandfather said. "I have traveled the world over, have seen many things. But I've never experienced the presence of a God-sent person, nor have I witnessed a miracle. I saw my daughter jump off to her death not too long ago a block...." His mouth trembled but kept himself under control. "These are her children, Samuel and Georgia," he continued. "They have been left in my care because their father is too occupied with his profession. I was happy, but one night I was preparing Georgia for bed, sponging her clean, applying medication to her sores, making sure I don't make a move that would hurt, well, Annie visited my mind. She reminded me how awfully sudden, how mysterious her leaving was. Then she reminded me of you down there seven floors, a concourse of believers on the ground and you in the middle. You must've heard her."

"I didn't," Schoeff said.

"You were aware of her presence."

"Yes. In truth, your daughter was bright, kind-hearted...yet she was an instrument, to test me of my duty."

"To hell with your duty!" the grandfather said. "You owe us. You owe Georgia here and the rest of us. You can't turn away from...that young man...you can't. The papers said he begged you on hands and knees."

"I admire the preservation of your faith in me," Schoeff said. "I am certain that you know why I had to turn away."

"If you're implying that Georgia is in the same position as that man in the street...."

"Sir, I don't mean your granddaughter. I feel your remorse, but the one who is undeserving, needs no bed bath or ointment on his sores."

The grandfather's eyes widened. "How dare you," he snapped.

Schoeff peered at him. "It's never my intention to dare," he said.

"So, what does it take, father?" Samuel's aunt cut in.

"I came from confessions," Schoeff said. "My devotions are still fresh."

"What kind of a man are you?" the grandfather said.

"A priest never yanks off sin from anybody. It's a man's property, always!" Samuel's grandfather then put his trembling hands together and gazed at Georgia in bed. The aunt got up and wandered to the other end of the cellar. Samuel went after her and jumped on the recliner with a comic book, leaving Schoeff to stare at the rug. After a moment in solitude, trying to release his mind from the negative vibes in the room, he walked over to Georgia and slouched over her without touching her. He clasped on the edges of the rollaway bed and asked. Pleading was not necessary.

"What the hell are you doing?" snapped the grandfather.

The aunt scurried back and held the old man. "He's doing it," she said.

Georgia looked up to Schoeff. The uneasy closeness of this man in black didn't frighten her. She tried on a smile to which Schoeff responded with a bright, gratifying one. "Hello there, Representative Woodward," Schoeff whispered. "I have to mend your body before you could plant those spruce trees on Lexington Avenue." Schoeff kept looking at the girl. "In the year 1998, I believe," he said. "Don't worry about the other fellow. He'll be busy cleaning up after the riots he'll provoke." Schoeff then closed in and embraced the girl. Georgia let out a shriek that caused the grandfather to get up again. Schoeff clasped the girl under his chest. "It's okay, Georgia," he said.

Samuel's aunt held on to the grandfather.

"Think of running and jumping," Schoeff said, holding tight. "Think of water-skiing in the Chesapeake." He began to sweat. "Sir," he said aloud. "Why so much pain?"

But Georgia lessened her screams. Her legs began to extend slowly at the sides. When the elderly man saw this happening, he grabbed his mouth in shock.

Schoeff laughed hysterically as he got off the bed. "Oh, Georgia, you're going to be a physically straight person."

The girl grinned with ease. Her arms were now limp on the bed, very thin but had the flexibility of any girl's arms. "Ahn know wwwhy," Georgia spoke, "so much pain..." She moved her neck and found it handy. The three adults stood around the bed waiting for her to finish her sentence. Georgia resumed grinning when she said, "Because we could laugh it off."

The grandfather knelt down by her and caught Schoeff's glance in the process. "She will serve in the future?" the grandfather uttered, not looking up.

"Yes," Schoeff said.

"Her mother had aspirations to be a politician," the old man said.

Samuel went over to the side of the bed and showed his sister a page from the comic book. The aunt was left to converse with Schoeff. She offered to shake his hand again.

"I think Georgia needs milkshake at this point," Schoeff said.

"It was severe cerebral palsy," the aunt said, suddenly tearful. "You never knew my sister, did you?" she asked.

Schoeff shook his head no. The woman turned away, overwhelmed. Schoeff was left to show himself out.

65

Writers

Rose Mary and Chereb decided on The Blue Parrot on Amsterdam and Ninety-fifth Street despite the police's advice for them not to be seen in public. Zeyad tagged along as their bodyguard, under the assurance that he be given twenty minutes of devotion at the back patio of the Antonisz' house before heading out. At that point, he decided he would aspire to build a mosque in the Bronx. For once, he saw purpose in his long stay. Rose Mary said it was a great idea and felt her morale uplifted by just hearing Zeyad described his vision. On the way to Manhattan, Zeyad wondered out loud about her faith.

"I'm not quite as pasty as Reeby here," Rose Mary said. "I don't have a religion that hasn't changed since Moses. I'm sort of a free agent at the moment."

"Free agent?" Zeyad said.

"She's not Jewish," Chereb pointed out.

They had borrowed a limo owned by one of Rapha's business cronies, to be incognito. The chauffeur that came with the limo was Armenian and was a pro at door opening in front of nightclubs. Chereb wore a sparkling lame` dress that came just below her knees. Zeyad didn't have the nerve to look her in the eye then, and when they arrived at The Blue Parrot, he got out quickly before Chereb could attempt to go over him inside the car. In America, women always went first except when they were wearing short skirts.

"Zed, is there something bugging you?" Chereb asked inside the bar.

"Not in particular," he said.

"So, why can't you...*look*?"

Zeyad kept a stiff neck and checked out the other people instead.

"Let's find seats," Chereb said, vexed. She walked toward the lounge area. Zeyad followed. Rose Mary recognized a few faces but managed to stay with the two.

While they sat and read the menu, with the waiter standing by, Zeyad still had a straight back and a grimace that irked Chereb. "A Bermuda Blast would loosen him up," Rose Mary offered.

"Three," Chereb said to the waiter. To Rose Mary, she said, "This just happened while we were getting out of the car. Something ungodly took place."

Zeyad flinched. "What something ungodly?" he asked.

"You. Your unpredictable attitude."

Zeyad started to open his mouth but stopped himself. He uttered instead, "It's better for me not to say it. I will keep it in myself and enjoy. I am not accustomed..."

"Not accustomed to what?"

"To speak my mind or else it will defeat our purpose here."

"Yes," Chereb said. "I agree."

Rose Mary leaned over to Chereb, whispered, "I think

you're in love with Zed."

Chereb glared at her, then nonchalantly, asked Zeyad, "Is it my dress that's making you stiff?"

Zeyad snapped back his face from her. "We are paying respects to Miss Juliane tomorrow. Aren't we supposed to be grieving?"

"Oh, shit," Chereb said and covered her mouth at the thought. Her own face broke to tears.

"I think it's time for heavy drinking," Rose Mary suggested. "The culture clash here could only be stabilized by weed. Since we don't...Zeyad, this is part of *our* ritual. We do this because we believe Juliane wouldn't have it any other way. If I had died instead of her, she would be here instead of me. If you would have died, I believe Chereb and I would likely be grieving the way you would prefer us to do."

Zeyad looked puzzled. The open-mindedness of this Rose Mary had reached boundaries further than his judgment of her. He put on a scowl of plea and asked, "What is Bermuda Blast?"

Rose Mary laughed, winked at Zeyad.

"Tangerine nectar with gin, rum, vodka, you name it," Chereb explained.

Their waiter seemed taller when he came back. "Here you are, ladies and gent," he said, placing the drinks on the table. Rose Mary picked hers up first, and upon looking up, dropped it on the floor, splattering everywhere. "That's quite all right," said the waiter. "It'll be replaced, I'm sure."

Chereb got up and wiped her legs with a napkin.

"What are you doing?" Rose Mary growled.

"Rosie?" Chereb asked.

"It's him. It's him!" Rose shrieked. "Don't you recognize the low life?"

256

Chereb gasped.

Zeyad stood up immediately and guarded the table.

"Relax, sheik, I'm here in good fate," Ira said. "What better way to break the ice than to serve you."

"You're not worthy of being a waiter," Rose Mary shot back.

"Ah, Rose Getty. The epitome of literary mediocrity, but a name to look out for."

"You son of a bitch. How did you find us?"

"Simple, I looked out of my window and saw this spot with a turban drifting into The Blue Parrot, followed by this incredible, snow-blonde spot, and I thought, how could a guy be so lucky? I live on the ninth floor of The Canon-Delmar across the street."

"Let's leave," Chereb said. She stood up. Zeyad let her by.

"Whoa," said Ira, getting in her way. "I didn't end your friend's life, if that's what you're insinuating. She was fine when I left. The police found nothing on me. Big misconception here, if not prejudice, against me."

"Yes, that's why you're stalking Chereb now?" Rose Mary said.

"Get out of my way, please," Chereb said.

"I don't stalk," Ira said, catching a glimpse of her green eyes. "If I am..."

Zeyad pulled Ira by the arm to which Ira didn't resist. He stepped aside and let the girls by. "Let her be," Zeyad said to him after the two were well on their way. "You are frightening her. That is not a very good sign of affection."

"No," Ira said. "What do you know about affection, eastern man? What do you know about what's going on inside me? I have a place for her inside me."

"Do not call her anymore," Zeyad said, calm but

stern. He gathered his cloak and walked out, saying pardon every chance he could before reaching the exit.

At the front, Rose Mary couldn't spot their borrowed chauffeur. She paced up and down the walk. Chereb managed to lean on a canopy pole, holding her skirt together.

"What do you want to do, huh?" asked Rose Mary. "Shall we inform the law or what?"

"Let's just get home," Chereb said.

"Get home and what? Isolate ourselves?"

"Let's go to Bitter End, then."

"Are you up for it? Where the hell is that driver?" Rose Mary turned, and there was the chauffeur behind her.

"Is anything the matter, Miss Getty?" the chauffeur asked.

"Yes," said Rose Mary. "Your car is not quite here."

"It's parked around the corner, madam."

"Get it."

"You always tend to make me laugh at odd times," Chereb said.

"Thank you, my peach." Rose said. "But is he coming?"

"I do not think he'll follow," Zeyad said.

"Why? Did we embarrass him?"

The limousine rolled up, and the three got in. Rose Mary ordered the driver to Bitter End. Halfway down the block, she clicked the limo fridge open and found a pair of Spumantes. "Why does it always have to be poppers?" she said.

66

The *Fun* Girl

At Bitter End, at a quarter past one, Zeyad sat by himself while the girls found partners to sway to Nat King Cole. Chereb's Greco-Roman cheek-to-cheek was a regular at the place, while Rose Mary's was an old medical-student friend, now a gynecologist at the Upper East Side. He was more of a long-nighter to Rose Mary, a hopeful for daylight. In fact, she said buenos noches to Chereb and Zeyad and parted with the doctor.

"What's in your head, Zed?" Chereb asked, winding down in her chair. "Is Rose Mary good on your list?"

Zeyad raised his brows. He knew exactly what Chereb meant. "She is very well-read, very mature in spite of what I see, and very, very...what do you call that? Road, road...?"

"Streetwise."

"Yes," said Zeyad.

"Why, Zed, that's too many very's for a friend of mine. Are you sure those are just lemon-limes?"

Zeyad was certain his church companion was just tipsy.

"How about me, Zed? What do you think of me? I

have to be very something to you?"

Zeyad was trapped again. It was hard enough for him to sit there hours after his usual bedtime, let alone being asked a rhetorical hip question. And to think he had to wake up considerably early the next day to meet this beautiful being's father's demand for Old World jewelry. "One thing that is in my head," he said. "I am sure you are very fun."

"Fun?"

"Yes, fun."

In their ride back to the Bronx, the word "fun" seemed to have disappeared from the warm, limbered body seated next to him. He didn't know why of all the adjectives he was familiar now in the English language he had to choose one that wasn't even in his list of important daily use.

"Zed, I can't be *fun* to you," Chereb moaned, leaning her head on his silk-wrapped shoulder. "What am I really?"

He had another chance.

"What was I to you when you stepped in front of that Ira...guy?" she asked.

Zeyad closed his eyes. "You are something to die for," he bravely uttered.

Chereb brought her head up, nose touching Zeyad's semi-goateed chin. "I am?"

"Yes, but I am speaking behind a glass wall. Everything that I see, I cannot touch."

Chereb bobbed her face up again, giving Zeyad a curious squint. To take a stab at figuring out that proverb was asking too much in her state of mind. Chereb groaned, "Thanks."

Up the front steps, as the mist shifted inward from the Atlantic, he carried her into the house from the limousine.

67

Intoxication and Poetry

Ira, whom Schoeff finally had sensed as part of the forecast this city had yet to withstand, had the habit of taking cover under faith. It so happened that they shared the same religion, to which Schoeff didn't give much thought because it was as for everybody "to each his own." Ira's distorted thinking could dip high and low. His chameleonic existence, Schoeff saw, lingered in the now nonchalantly.

Ira met a woman after the run-in with Chereb. He couldn't waste such precious thinking hours, and when a sullen-eyed brunette dared to approach him, he couldn't refuse returning the advance. In the cool mist on 42nd Street, he had his arm around her. The strapless chiffon she wore was not exactly suitable for the weather.

"I thought you said your place was only across the street," the girl said. "Where're we going?"

"To the earth's core, my Gwendy," Ira said.

"My name is not Gwendy!"

"I heard it's nice this time of year."

"Listen, I'm going to call it a night. I've been up since eight this morning, and you yourself could use...."

At that moment, he dropped his Old Overholt bottle, and it shattered on the curb, swiping her ankle with a sharp piece. She looked down and saw the slit begin to bleed. She shrieked in icy pain.

"Ah, a sign of truth," Ira said. "Our ticket to paradise tonight. A sweet rendezvous like 'parting is all we know of heaven, and all we need of hell.'"

"What are you...shit."

"A little trite, isn't it?"

"I have to go," cried the woman, ducking from his arm.

"Don't you dare," he said. He bent down to pick up the neck of the bottle.

The woman took off running in her heels. Before he could sense the pulse of going after her, she disappeared into one of the neon-lit doors. He looked up at the tall buildings. "And I thought she was...lovely, trite. Gwendy in her. No rhythm anywhere." He laughed at the lamppost overhead. "You're leaving me empty here!" he yelled. The lights were unreal at that spot. He staggered toward the dark. "You're leaving me alone! I need to be with *her*. What's her name? Her Jewish name? A Jew in a cathedral. That's my faith. Miss Dickinson!"

With the bottleneck still in his hand, Ira stumbled over a sleeping man on the sidewalk. "Hell with you!" he said, upon being startled by this man. "You have no right occupying that spot."

The derelict, who appeared to have a hearing problem, raised a rough, calloused palm.

Ira squatted, looking at the rough face. The derelict couldn't speak as well. His tongue bobbed out now and then. Ira found this alluring. He took the man's raised hand and picked the middle finger. He ran it on the spiky brim of the bottleneck. The derelict flinched, his eyes closing tightly, and then easing them open again as if the scraped cut had healed. He took up a pleasant grin again, eyes still shut.

"Isn't that sanctimonious?" Ira said. "Are you one of these misguided citizens I'm hearing about? Do you look up a crucifix and renew yourself?"

The tongue was moving again.

"Okay, old man, let's deal with life. What sort of things do you find interesting in life? Are you into paintings, Cézanne or Delacroix, or perhaps pottery? Women are certainly out of the question. For one thing you need a close shave. No *mademoiselle* would come near you with that frisk." Ira, laughing, pushed the derelict's chin up with his thumb and felt the texture of the skin there. "You do need one. Nod for me, yes." He moved the derelict's chin up and down. Ira looked behind him. The remainder of the night could not ask for a more stimulating act.

"I've never experienced a 'brusque burial with *pity* for little encomium,' have you, old man? What words!"

Ira raised the chin again and with the tug of his wrist, the man's throat bled. Ira tilted his own neck back as if cold rain were to come down on it.

At this same moment, back at St. Jude's, Schoeff, in his sleep, felt the destined emptiness of any city left unwarned.

68

The Gardener

On Friday morning, as a guided citizen, Jack from the Curb ultimately got hold of Schoeff at Patornak's Florist & Nursery in Weehawken, New Jersey, a short bus trip from the St. Jude's.

"The other priest with the Polish name told me that you'd be stopping here," Jack said. "Things got a little distorted, eh, father? People just don't know how to take what you have to say. They're scared stiff, I say, for nothing."

"For that point of view, Jack," Schoeff said, looking under shrubs for their tiny trunks. "You deserve a medal." Schoeff wore a brim straw hat, white shirt with the collar unbuttoned and baggy khakis, dirt smudges at the knees. Dangling from his back was an army knapsack, strapped tightly.

"They really don't know what you try to put across," Jack said. "I mean Al, a friend of mine, we go back to Bataan. He thinks, what's to worry? Fifty years ain't tomorrow. It's fifty years."

"But we don't think that way, do we, Jack?" Schoeff said. "We do our arithmetic homework long before Mrs. Smith can think of whipping out her discipline stick. The earlier, the better. And we get to watch the television

265

afterwards."

"I know what you mean, but look at the problem here. Look at what you're going through. They've stripped you of your holy clothes, got you hiding in bushes."

"I always dress like this when I shop for *bonsai* prospects."

"*Bonsai* who?"

"Little Japanese trees," Schoeff said, checking a juniper bush. "Good for gifts, which reminds me...."

"One advice, father," Jack said. "Enough of images of people falling off buildings. By the way you describe them, well, that one makes New Yorkers turn their stomachs to something severe. Where was it? Abbey Street, Lower Man, there ain't no huge scrapers there."

Schoeff grinned.

"I've done lost them, okay," Jack retorted. "I had them locked up in a chest, and I put that chest up over a cabinet, and I flung the key in a closet full of her clothes." Jack swung his arm to pantomime the throwing of the key. "But somehow, I found that key glinting in the morning, and the next thing I knew I was tagging a horse at Belmont with pawned money. Father, I'm hopeless. I don't deserve a daughter."

"Jack, what are you doing in New York City?" Schoeff said. "Why not in Atlantic City where there are tons of chips at your reach?"

Jack, who had found a sturdy planter to sit on, looked up in the sun at the priest with a straw hat, and said, "I guess I'm a big-city creature. There're things here to occupy your life through."

"Those things are your daughter's. With you coming over to the Jersey side and looking for me tells me that you haven't forgotten that one purpose in New York."

"I'm long ways from that now."

Schoeff unbuckled the knapsack from his back and handed it to Jack. "It's on your account," he said. "Show that one to Heny. She might even become handy with them."

Jack got up and shook Schoeff's hand. "Whatever this city thinks of you, father, they don't know. You're my savior." Jack nodded at the other shoppers. "See here, this man can tell the future in precision," Jack praised. "He's New York's only hope. God bless the Big Apple!"

Schoeff ducked while onlookers shied away from Jack.

"All the same, Jack, hang on to those tools," Schoeff said. Jack handed him back the empty knapsack, then moved on toward the exit. The cashier with spectacles, obviously the owner, did not take his eyes off Jack till he was on his way out. In the meantime, Schoeff spotted the perfect shrub, purchased it and slipped it in the knapsack.

69

Fence Jumper

For one thing, he was certain he wasn't the Christ embodied. He had to sneak. Jack was right about him skimming, by the fact that Schoeff was downplaying his identity, not hiding, but downplaying his role as a clergy.

Before catching the bus, Schoeff stopped by a souvenir shop and picked a shallow pot for the juniper.

There were two Ford sedans parked in front of St. Jude's Cathedral when he got off the corner. He ducked behind a mailbox. One car was unmarked. The other was dark blue with NYPD seals on the sides. Schoeff couldn't make out the titles under the seals through the legs of the crowd. They had been there, this crowd, since the evening after he had jogged through the produce market on Valentine Street.

He decided to cut through between houses to get to the alley that led to the backcourt of the church. There was a chain-link fence and two cranky poodles he had to worry about. Facing them topped being approached by misinformed believers.

His identity as a sun-drenched gardener was shot when he fell over the fence. Although his landing was a silent one, Father Laman, who happened to scratch the backside of his head at that moment, spotted him from the long windows. An interrogation was being held at the dining commons.

Father Laman excused himself from the group and walked briskly toward the backdoor in the kitchen.

Duck! he mimed to Schoeff from the window above the sinks. Schoeff saw and stooped down like a paratrooper. Laman went outside and crawled along the fence till he reached Schoeff. "They're talking about a probable imprisonment in there!" Laman muttered.

"On what charge?" Schoeff whispered.

Laman was astonished. "They say you withheld evidence, an alleged murder case. Does that sound right?"

"I'll go speak to them," Schoeff said, about to get up.

"No, stay down!" Laman demanded. "It'll only make them stay longer."

Schoeff noticed a wide, soaked spot running from Laman's collar down to his third button. At that instance, Schoeff bowed and prayed.

Lamantiaraski sensed this. "Father, if you were an ordinary man having to face daily problems and temptations, would you be scared of the things you couldn't possibly know as an ordinary man?"

"Not now, father," Schoeff said.

"Oh, yes," Laman said, head pressed against the wood. "What led them to believe that you withheld information?" he asked.

"A poem by Gwendolyn Brooks was found at the bed next to Juliane DeVoe. They checked it out, saw no real importance and handed it back to me. I guess now they see the real value. It's up in my bureau."

"That's unthinkable," Laman said. "A poem? But, of course, they have to respond to the press, right?"

"Their minds are too preoccupied on me. You yourself don't have a thing to worry about."

"Is that a prediction?"

"F.Y.I. only."

Laman could still hear voices from the dining commons with the monsignor entrapped in them. "You must be starved," Laman said, to which Schoeff nodded.

70

Clergyman in the Dark

He had no time to worry about the police or Laman. He did Laman the favor of staying in the backcourt till the cops left. As long as he stayed in that corner and was in gardening clothes, and with Laman getting him food, Schoeff thought he might as well start on the project. From the shed behind the statue of Christ and St. Jude wading on the Jordan, he found a bucket and some clippers. He filled the bucket with water. For soil, he took some from Father Gado's rows of sprouting corn and eggplant. He set the kettle in front of him and began creating from intuition.

"What are you up to?" Laman asked upon arriving with a plate of reuben sandwiches.

"I'm making bonsai."

"Whatever that is, but at *this time*?"

"Let me tell you a secret, father. This tree will live to see Ronald Reagan become president."

"The actor?"

Schoeff thought it wise for Laman to know a piece of the future, maybe entice him to look forward to it. But Schoeff did not dare to bring up outlooks that would make the frail priest nervous. If Laman brought up the subject of temptation again, only then Schoeff would touch upon a forecast most related to Laman's anxiety. Laman knew that the issues Schoeff had been sharing around town did not completely leave out his concerns. But throughout the excavating, re-potting and pruning of the juniper, Laman's questions were related to botany.

"What are you going to do for grass?" he asked Schoeff, who created a true leaning-trunk specimen.

"Moss, of course."

"Wonderful," praised Laman.

71

The Faithless

It was quarter to ten the following morning when Schoeff arrived at Selwyn Avenue. There was no detour separating it from Jerome anymore, but Schoeff still had to hike a block before reaching the row of apartments where Asha lived. Mrs. Gutierrez answered him with a surprised look on her face. She briskly waved for him to come in. Asha, with her brother and sisters, was at breakfast in the kitchenette. "Father?" Asha got up from the table.

"Yes, it's me," Schoeff said. "And this is for you and your family." He lowered the bonsai in his hands for her to see. Asha gasped at the sight but refocused her eyes on him.

"You're in a zoot suit," she said.

He was surprised she knew the term. "Yes, I have to be undercover." He nodded to Mrs. Gutierrez. "People are a little uneasy when they see a priest these days." He walked into the living room and set the bonsai on top of the Zenith television. He got down on his knees and said to Asha, "This, my friend, will see the day fifty-six Elvis impersonators prance around Central Park for their annual roustabout."

"What's an Elvis?"

"A mortal who will inflame teenagers with his rock-n-roll music later this decade." Schoeff checked her arms. He found no needle marks.

"Rock-n-roll?" Asha said.

"You'll be teenage when this musical king arrives on the scene," Schoeff said. "But remember, this person is just mortal, just like his son-in-law four decades later. The king of rock-n-roll's daughter will link herself to the king of pop. His name will be Michael. No need to throw any garments at either of them if you happen to see them perform. Concentrate on your MIT studies."

"Oscaro would likely be an Elvis?" Asha said.

Schoeff laughed. "Likely," he said.

Mrs. Gutierrez brought in tea and Emerald Gold crackers for their visitor, and Pilu, Asha's little brother, strolled into the living room and stood in front of the miniature tree to admire it.

"How about Pilu?" Asha said, trapping Pilu to her stomach. "Will he be an Elvis?"

"No, I think he'd be more like Michael Jackson," Schoeff said. "Pilu, can you gyrate or moonwalk?"

At that moment, Oscaro was at the front porch stomping his muddy boots on the abaca mat. He looked beat, and upon seeing Schoeff in the room, he threw his jacket on the floor. There was a thickness in his face Schoeff hadn't seen before. The furrows were deeper, the hue of his skin grayish. In the kitchen, his mother uttered a sentence in their dialect to calm Oscaro down. He yelled back at her. Asha held Pilu when Oscaro walked back into the living room. "Eh, padre," he said. "You shouldn't be in this neighborhood. People know you out there, and they come in here and talk to me."

"Oscaro, you mean I'm not welcomed in your house," Schoeff said, "while the rest of your family has already welcomed me in."

"What do you want? Haven't you done enough?"

"He brought us the tiny tree," Asha said. "It's the tree of tomorrow."

"Tomorrow, my ass," Oscaro said. "All I hear from you is what's tomorrow going to be like! Padre, think for real. Tomorrow is nowhere. People are still going to look at other people in the face and throw insults for no reason. Kids will still shoot heroine up their arms and blow up their parents! All these warnings ain't doing this town any good, 'specially when they see you, their own priest, running around with *puta*!"

"Oscaro!" Asha screamed.

"No, Sasha, I am right," declared Oscaro. "Your priest is not your regular priest. He has some answering to do to the people out there. It's not right for a padre to be with a woman!"

Schoeff gathered his patience. "Oscaro," he said. "Have I been away so long that you've lost faith in me, even as a priest?"

"Padre, I have no confessions to make to you. It's you that has something for me."

"That woman was a friend," Schoeff said. "She came to me in a time of grief, and she needed my help. What you read in the papers are untrue."

"What I saw in the papers is you holding hands with this lady," Oscaro said. His mother shivered at the door to the kitchen. "People saw you with their own eyes. People took pictures." He drew nearer to Schoeff, jabbing a finger at his shoulder. Asha began to cry. "And word around here is you are not here for the sake of us poor immigrants. You make fun of us, make joke on everything like nothing is holy anymore. You are here for the rich and the well off. Not here

275

for our sake!" Oscaro's voice deepened in fury.

Asha tried calming him down. "Oscaro!"

Mrs. Gutierrez came and hugged her away from between the two men. She placed Asha behind her and took hold of Oscaro's flinging arm, but he whisked her off and, in the process, hit the bonsai tree off the television. The soil was all over the carpet. The kids were stunned to silence.

Schoeff bowed, unmoved, while Oscaro barked on. Schoeff had no more appealing choices but to bring his palms up to try to quell the rage. Oscaro flipped them away. To this, Schoeff backed off and made himself useful by picking up the pot and the uprooted bonsai. He placed them at the foot of the television. Oscaro looked on. Upon getting up, Schoeff asked, "Who are these people you've been speaking to?"

The white in Oscaro's eyes glowed, but with Asha crying in the back, the realization of the plant falling finally got to him. "The locals, padre," Oscaro mumbled.

"Do they know me more than you?" Schoeff asked.

Oscaro shook his head in distress. "I don't know. They think you are bad news. They parade up and down the street, cursing the sky like they're *maniacs,* and the only way they can get what they want is to get everybody to join them." Oscaro let out a frustrated sigh. "You're no-name to them, but they wouldn't be out there if they didn't believe you, you know what I mean? They're scared stiff."

"How about the men in lab coats?" Schoeff said. "Have they bothered you?"

"No. Why should they?"

"Just asking."

"No."

Schoeff took a deep needed breath. "These are times of confusion, Oscaro. You have to be sound among the confused. This is just for a while longer. People will get back to their normal lives once they know I'm here for safety. Stay out of the street when they protest. They think I can hear them when I'm only a priest. I'm no Big Ear in the sky."

"You talk like nothing is wrong."

"Nothing is. See me as good news." Schoeff took hold of the repotted juniper. He asked Asha to go to Oscaro's side. "And this, my friends, is growing still," he said, referring to the bonsai. "Would you happen to have a little shovel, maybe some moss?"

Oscaro thought, *amazing.*

72

Vacant Throat

Schoeff never had solid proof that there was *presence* in Uncle Dam. But God knew Schoeff liked his Uncle Dam, through all the imagination in making Schoeff laugh as a kid. Schoeff, even with his back on the floor and chortling his sinuses out, took meaning in, "Howie, are you gonna be my mind someday?" Uncle Dam's baby talk was far from being devout. But somehow Schoeff felt down deep that his uncle was the megaphone of his calling at that early stage. When Uncle Dam passed away, Schoeff saw the humor of life slip away on ice. It was up to him to maintain balance and not fall.

It had occurred on a February day. Nothing meaningfully pious, but his uncle no longer in existence made Schoeff ponder in the booth long after the last person had gone.

Also, Schoeff wasn't too sure if that was Jessica's voice he had heard last Wednesday. It sounded like her, spunky and obsessed on being clear. The wit was hers, but there was no trace that they were ever intimate. Why didn't she mention his name? If someone came all the way from Florida to see him in the Bronx, the least she could do was utter "Howard."

Schoeff walked out of the Gutierrez apartment with this feeling. Helping to cure a future bright engineer would lift him up from such a void.

He was sure that his assignment was done. At the moment, Asha was safe and unharmed. She had twiddled with the lapel of his zoot suit and seemed well nourished, by the rosy color of her cheeks. Oscaro was lost, but the handle in finding his common sense could be grabbed. A wing of a guardian angel was in him, and that was all the assurance Schoeff needed.

Back at St. Jude's, he waited for the monsignor who had been officiating a funeral. Schoeff slipped on a yellow and purple gown to match the ones the monsignor and Father Gado wore. He came in during the breaking of the bread. The monsignor was surprised to see him and thought for certain that solemnity of the grieving family would be disturbed. But the ceremony went smoothly enough. A few grievers eyed the seams of the coffin when Schoeff shook the canister of ash over it, but the coffin stayed shut.

"Nice Eucharist, I must say," Schoeff said when the monsignor put away his garments.

The monsignor scowled heavily. "Father, I take it that you have nothing to do," he said.

"I do...not," Schoeff said.

"By the way, where were you when the police were here?"

"In the backcourt."

"You were hiding?"

"Those officials were flexing their muscles. It's just for show, or else they would have searched every inch of the church."

"They went up to your room."

"Oh."

"And found what they were looking for, with a note attached to it, informing them that their visit was expected. How can you be so bold as not to warn *me*?"

"I apologize, monsignor. With all the activities going on, I missed that one."

"So, what's the occasion this time?" Randolph asked. "What brings you to my aid? I must admit you make a pretty good altar boy."

"Experience," Schoeff said. It didn't change the expression on the monsignor's face. "I came to bring you good news, father. My duty is done and over."

"Your duty?"

"Yes, this thing with New York. I have this tremendous feeling in my chest that my being here has been worth the while. I feel all will function accordingly. You see, the child whom I have been so frantically worried about is in her mother's home, safe from the ordeal that I thought she couldn't live through."

"You feel all will function accordingly?" the monsignor said. "With all the commotion, the city still in a big question mark about our parish here, with your fan club outside not knowing how to pray and what to pray for?"

"They'll acknowledge my message soon enough."

"So? What now?"

"I'm not sure," Schoeff said. "Maybe become a normal priest, maybe start on that CCD class you've mentioned. Maybe fulfill my dream of climbing the 40 Wall Street Building, up to the ninety-ninth floor and have a picnic there with the elevator man."

"Have you heard from God, telling you of this…rest?"

"No, sir. Last was this." He pointed at the red contusion on his left temple. "Up to now, I feel no pain from it."

"Don't you think you should wait?" the monsignor said.

"That's why I came to you, your Holiness. I thought perhaps He would…use you."

"In what way?"

"Convey a message through you."

The monsignor scratched the back of his head again, peering at the downcast in the window. "Nope," he said. "No Spirit up this throat."

"I know He comes and goes at random," Schoeff admitted. "It's just this one time, I thought I would welcome Him."

"Sorry," said his holiness, "but no dice."

Most obvious Schoeff really thought that his card could be punched out.

73

The Unbothered

To look alive on 42nd Street, a body had to face the ongoing traffic of walkers in order to be noticed. It couldn't lean against the cinderblock tobacco factory and appear to be only drunkenly asleep. Dripping life on the wall had dried, and it was logical enough: an alcoholic too soused to find his freight box had resorted to Red Indian snuff in the early morning hours and had passed out. Citizens as such were better left alone.

West of here, in his mother's apartment, not necessarily called The Canon-Delmar, Ira thought it wise to take a break from his writing. Since he got over the hangover only to spike it with bourbon, writing unorthodox free verse was like remembering what he had last done last night.

He picked up the phone and dialed the exclusive number.

"Dear, would you kindly get the Post?" his mother called from her bedroom. "I'd like to read the news before I play bridge."

Ira slammed down the phone. "Mother, goddamn your timing!"

"What was that?"

He eased himself out of bed and went down but stopped himself. "Mother, I don't want to see any paper today. It would only disturb my thought."

His mother came out of her room, funneling her ear. She was dressed to go out. "News can inspire you. I hear poems on current events are sure to get attention these days."

"That's amusing, Mother. But I tend to be original. I don't write to promote Truman's charisma in public or to show the many cuts and edges of an abortion done in some corner home."

"Yes, dear, that makes sense. We all should see literature more profound than those."

He didn't mind being under her wing. She was easily persuaded, a pushover with an intellectual forgiving mind. She was once a teacher. Surpassing her in education was a great feat in his life, and he did it without the assistance of his proud father, who died in a shelling accident in Annapolis. He never knew him in a fatherly sense, but he once identified his soul in a dark poem he wrote three days before the corporal's death.

Finally, alone, he huddled in the desk, thinking daylight could be on his side. But a moment later, he got up again, snatched the phone with newfound hope, dialed.

The busy tone pierced his brain like a siren from an ambulance.

74

Religion over Ham

Did I pass out on you last night? Chereb mimed across the table to Zeyad.

"Yes," her father said at the head of the table. "He had to carry you up."

"It was a tiresome evening, wouldn't you know it," Zeyad said.

"What time is the funeral?" Mrs. Antonisz asked.

"What?" Chereb said, snapping back to life.

Her mother checked Rapha's reaction. "Vigil for Juliane," Mrs. Antonisz said. "Isn't there going to be a vigil? She's a Christian, right?"

"Ma, don't mention..." cried Chereb, stretching her temples back as if to get rid of a massive worry.

"Forgive me," Gracie said.

"It's from one to three," Zeyad announced. "Last night, we mourned for her."

"You did?" Rapha said. "By the looks of her face, it must have been a real sad affair."

"What Zeyad means is we tried to forget the whole mess. Juliane was with us, alive and dancing a storm. We felt her presence, and that made us happy."

"Did she do the shimmy?" Rapha said, picking up his coffee.

"Don't make fun."

Rapha turned to his wife. "You may not realize it but you're breaking the law of nature in this room. In any religion, being drunk is never a substitute for lament. Ask Zed here."

"To tell you the truth," Zeyad said, "I broke about four rites of Sufi grief last night, and I did not even do the shimmy."

"See," Rapha laughed.

"But after I had a little misunderstanding talk with your daughter, I realized that there was another side to grieving, and one can take it for his own comfort without feeling religious guilt."

"What are you, American?" asked Rapha.

"Papa, the truth is Juliane is still with us. It was confirmed by Father Schoeff."

"Yes, the modern-day Saint Assisi of the malt shop," Rapha muttered.

"Don't be lame like the public," Chereb said.

"I know, I know. He's compassionate in what he says. He's a priest. He has to be sincere."

"Don't be Catholic, Rapha," his wife said. "They'll miss you at the Jewish Yacht Club."

All laughed. Chereb stayed rigid. "Everything has to be religion with you three," she said. "You lose yourself when you talk of rites and guilt. For your info, Father Schoeff never once tried to sell me his faith. That one time, he was just there for me. I don't care what kind of trash you read in the papers. I don't care what anybody says, that was Juliane I heard speaking. Father said it was God reminding everybody that He's still around. But why would God suggest apparel that didn't exist?"

"You're confusing me again," Rapha said.

"As for me," Zeyad said, "I think Miss Juliane has become a part of the future Father Schoeff is so insisting upon us, and God was using her personality in order to be not so much in the room. It's for us to believe his availability or not."

"Very profound, Zed," Chereb said. "Pass the pork, please."

"We don't have *pork*," Mrs. Antonisz answered her sarcasm.

"Just for the argument, I mean, to portray," Zeyad clarified.

"So, we forget about religion in this talk," Mrs. Antonisz said. "The best thing for us is to live this day with Father Schoeff in our conscience."

"Mom," Chereb said. "For that, we should celebrate and have roast pig tonight."

Her mother glared at her.

75

Admirers at the Quay

Zeyad wasn't in a hurry to gather all the dishes and bring them to the kitchen sink, a duty he insisted on doing since moving in the Antonisz house. There was the tight legroom under the table and the scooting back of his chair he had to worry about. He waited for everyone to finish. Rapha finished first. He threw his linen on the plate and rose. He went into the den with the Wall Street Journal. And Mrs. Antonisz was forking her last bites of scalloped potato and peas. At that instance, Zeyad decided to make his exit, almost tipping over his chair. He picked up his dishes, placed them on his left hand, one on top of the other as he usually did. Chereb took notice of his trembling. He caught her looking and a saucer fell to the carpet, unbroken. Chereb frowned, coping with the last phase of her hangover. Zeyad hurried into the kitchen.

Minutes later, Chereb strolled out into the patio. The sun was high and hot. The northeastern breeze brought coolness from the sea. She couldn't find a better time to walk the narrow, stone-clad quay her father had constructed when she was only twelve. She slipped off her skirt, leaving it at the patio, and descended to the path only in her leotards. Midway down the slope, there was a small, grassy plateau to which she jumped on in her bare feet and almost collided with Zeyad, who was in a squat. He let out a shriek and scurried back to the wall of the cliff. Apparently, he had been in solitude.

"What's the matter with you?" Chereb said. "You're jumpy again."

"Why did you follow me?"

"I didn't follow you. I'm going to the beach," she said. "Hey, thanks for not mentioning the incident last night. I think that one would have scared them to the hilt."

"I should have told," he said.

"Thanks for nothing." She turned to continue on her way.

"What do you see in that man?" Zeyad asked. "I notice that you are protecting his identity."

"What are you talking about?"

"The man who claimed he lived across from The Blue Parrot."

"Zed, for a foreigner in America for less than half a year, you draw some bizarre conclusions."

"Is it bizarre for you to believe that he had no responsibility whatsoever in your friend's death?"

"What are you getting at? Are you insane?"

"Maybe I am," Zeyad admitted. "Last night in the limousine, I spoke to you about a glass wall. But because you were intoxicated, you might have slept through its meaning."

Chereb walked to the sandy edge of the plateau where the breeze teased her hair. "To answer your first notion," she said, turning back, her eyes thin against the brightness, "Why do you think the phone in my room is left unhooked? Why did I go to Father Schoeff and tell about this horrible thing I'm going through? Why did I bawl miserably the moment I got home two or three nights ago, huh?" She turned back to the sea. "And as for the second notion," she said, barely audible, "I wasn't that drunk."

Zeyad lifted his head.

"Why couldn't you be near?" Chereb asked loudly as if still bothered. "This glass wall, what the pork is it?"

Zeyad advanced toward her.

"No," she said. "That's not what I mean."

He halted. "What do you...?"

"I mean nothing could..."

He was unstoppable once they were a foot apart. She welcomed his embrace. Zeyad clutched before she could utter another word. The first thing that came to her mind was that she was standing on quicksand. When the kiss ended, she panted, "Zed, this is just for the moment, right? I mean this is nothing to think deeply about, right?"

"Do you mean I cannot think of you as my prospective bride just as yet, the one I will bring to al Basra to meet my mother and family and help me raise llamas out in the tundra?"

She pushed him off. "Zed!" she yelled. "Don't be that!"

Zeyad frowned, then smiled, then laughed. "There are no llamas in Iraq," he said. "I don't know. They might have imported some during the months I've been gone."

"You're sick," Chereb said.

"Yes, but you took me seriously for a moment," Zeyad replied.

After all were said, there was nothing else to do but to continue to what they were doing, before the kiss.

Zeyad, in the later course of his life in America, would meet another famed Muslim by the name of Yusef al Mussar. They would have extensive arguments about interpretations of certain parts in the Qur'an, mostly from the Surah of *Al Kahf*. These meetings would take place in an apartment where Zeyad would make plans to build a mosque — mainly for the convenience of Bronx worshippers. Al Mussar would accuse Zeyad of being in this country too long that it had warped his beliefs. Zeyad would comely say his Sufi ways were deep-rooted and had always been the same. What al Mussar would feed into Zeyad's orderly conscience would be in fact new trend. Zeyad Nadeem Mughrabi, forty-three years into his life, would later believe that this brief encounter with Chereb at the quay was his ultimate soul cleanser.

76

The Proponent

Father Laman had to go to another one of his urgent community calls, this time in lower Staten Island where an orphanage for city-stranded children was at. Schoeff, who thought he was on a probable vacation, took over a baptismal duty for his colleague. "You know how Father Laman is," the monsignor said. "If he wasn't so excitable, he would be the church's answer to emergency last rites."

"What a Catholic thing to say," Schoeff thought to say.

"Is that a criticism?"

"On the contrary, father. I'm just pointing out the convenience of our religion. As you well know, I couldn't have had convenience like this. Well, in any case, it'll be my pleasure to bless the little tyke."

"Whoa," said the monsignor. "What convenience are you talking about? And why are you not part of it? You mean you haven't been practicing the faith in all of this?"

"I have, sir, but God, I'm sure, is not following the faith step by step."

"He doesn't have to," Randolph retorted. "He's the one being followed."

"Yes, but in order for me to follow His orders, I have no choice but to bend some of our well-defined, critically sound rules."

"Don't soften the argument with meaningless compliments."

"My apologies. But to put it in the line, God, I think, is non-judgmental on religions because like the very souls of men, not one religion measures up. As we know it, everything on earth falls flat before God."

"Don't lecture me on basics!" The monsignor turned to his desk and picked up a pen without realizing it. He looked out the window and started to scribble on a piece of paper, paused and said, "I thought you were a priest."

Schoeff felt heavy. To a priest, this was a wound through and through, to be doubted of your vow. He realized Monsignor Randolph was the negative photo of Uncle Dam, and for a minute there, Schoeff sounded like his long-departed, egg-whacking relative.

Schoeff shouldn't feel misplaced. It was just that he hadn't heard from his source a long time. The only voice he thought that could be utilized doubted him at the moment.

"If there be anything else," Schoeff said. "I'll start up on my duty." He walked slowly out of the room.

77

Jessica Ankenby

Talking about doubt and lack of faith, he didn't quite catch that his own Uncle Dam was an atheist, until Schoeff was at the age of sixteen. The mechanical engineer/sharecropper believed in how-to's and was deep in these how-to's most of the time while in church, when his wife thought he was praying. Howard, at sixteen and up, just let the constant figuring out of life his relative by. His Uncle Dam's all-to-itself mind didn't bother anybody and could do no harm.

Schoeff recited the defenses of the four-month-old girl at the font. With all the saints and patrons guarding this new life, the tyke would surely go through life without ever being doubted, Schoeff thought.

He noticed a figure sitting patiently in the background. Light blue dress and a matching veil. He kept looking over to her. She sat far back enough to not be associated with the baptism. Schoeff thought this person could be the reluctant voice in his confessional last Thursday, or it could well be Chereb wanting to talk more of her crisis. If it was Agothe Mir coming back to take another swing at him, Schoeff felt ready.

After the picture-taking with the family and friends

from all different angles, Schoeff walked down the aisle and approached the figure. Ten pews away, he eliminated Agothe Mir. A feisty drugstore clerk couldn't keep a serious expression this long. The hair became evident through the veil from five rows away, and it wasn't in the likes of Chereb. It was brown, the shade of burnt paprika. She had it down over her shoulders, which she didn't like, he remembered.

"I have a distant aunt in Manhattan," Jessica said. "She more than welcomed me for the rest of the week. I couldn't just leave, not see what would happen next."

"I'm glad you decided to stay," Schoeff said. "It's usually therapeutic for acquaintances. Well, for me, anyway."

"Therapeutic, yes, I'll take that."

"Would you like to go to the nursery? It's more private."

"No one would mind? I hear you're in deep waters these days."

"Tabloids," Schoeff said.

Jessica got up, and Schoeff led her toward the west vestibule. "No one is here to mind. They're either out or taking naps. Only one is watching over us, and He knows me pretty well."

It was never a problem communicating with her. Schoeff admitted that he didn't know women. He could read their minds if they didn't occupy themselves in things only women were favorable to do. Many years ago, this person whom he still cared for, had an untouchable independence even other women would find hard to explain in their female-bonding moments.

"So, how is the world of broadcasting?" he asked once they were in the nursery.

"Oh, good," Jessica said. "I'm heading for a producer's spot next season, and our company is due to rank first in Dade."

"Impressive."

"But you're in the city most of us from out-yonder would trade their right lung to work in."

"Lucky me."

"I'm surprised there's not much television coverage on you. I've only seen you once on the tube, and that story wasn't even near Milton Berle."

"Is it important to be near Milton Berle?"

"Yes, his variety hour is tops."

"Mm," Schoeff speculated. "But I think He was happy with the radio. There's a lot of mustard seed in voice, and they grow plenty in people's ears."

Jessica clasped her fingers together, brought one elbow to the back of the bench, a bracelet of gold dangling from her left wrist. She sat cross-legged in front of Schoeff, who found the slim, cherry-wood pulpit there a good place to lean on. "You really believe in your private quest, don't you?" she asked.

"What do you mean by private?" Schoeff said.

"No meaning. For a minute there, I thought I made your charisma pause, away from the city, away from the rest of the world."

Schoeff bowed. "Much like what you have," he said. "I guess we both have our own missions."

"You could say that. But mine is more self-calling, I think."

"Me agree," Schoeff said, laughed. "And that has made the distance far."

"Yes, Howard Schoeff," Jessica replied in a slower drawl. "But I advise you not to go beyond that. Don't look back and regret unchangeable matters."

"How true, they're unchangeable. But don't you think there are blanks to be filled in?" Schoeff paused, edging off the pulpit. "For instance," he said, "why, in that brisk autumn day, a long time ago, I remember Thanksgiving was just around the corner, why did you call my grandmother and tell her that you had to break it off? I mean, my grandmother. She wore Dad's corduroy kilt and had a blouse on backwards at my graduation."

"Great memory," Jessica said.

"Grandma. Bless her soul."

"No, I mean your Jessica at twenty years of age," Jessica said. "Now I truly see your compassion, Brother Schoeff, perhaps your insecurity. It's me, your source."

Schoeff jolted from the pulpit and leaned back against the corkboard on the wall. "God?" he said.

"I began in 'unchangeable matters,' a few sentences back."

"A few?" Schoeff felt a surge of embarrassment.

"Am I not the one you're longing to hear?" Jessica said.

Schoeff resumed breathing and pushed on his shoulder blades off the corkboard. Pieces of notes that were tacked there fell off his back. "Your Holiness?"

"I still prefer 'sir.'"

"It's just that you took me by surprise, Your Grace."

"Nah. Your Grace is papal or dinner."

"Pardon me."

"You have a strong question in mind."

"Yes, but..."

"Spill it."

"Yes, where is...Jessica?"

"Here with me and not in some bottomless pit. You

have another one urging to leave your mouth."

"Can you bring her back? Not that I hadn't waited for you all week."

"I like it. You're always honest. It will never fail you in the long run. And that long run does not only consist of this life. I will bring back Miss Ankenby soon enough, with the present thought she had, with the self-esteem she is holding. But for now, let's talk about your vacation plans."

"Forgive me. I don't mean to place you second," Schoeff said.

"Forgiveness is to be begged," Jessica replied, "I accept yours due to the fact that Miss Ankenby and I are in a different state of minds. The love you have for me and the love you have for her differ like cantaloupes and walnuts. One is larger than the other but softer."

"There's no question," Schoeff said. "You'll always be the one I'll worship."

"I'm talking about uncontrollable drives, libido. Sigmund Freud coined it as the Subconscious, and he's absolutely right about the 'sub' part."

"Do you mean after all this time I still...crave her?"

"She left an empty spot, and you're constantly visiting that spot. You dreamed that she was your nurse at South Bend General when you had the appendectomy. You see her in Miss Antonisz, and you cater to it, prolonging her stay. You are now aroused upon looking at my dress."

"Holy Father, sir?"

"If it were not for my thought in this voice, you would transpire to physical. Your genitals would likely move that pulpit forward."

"Oh, sir, how can you be so explicit?"

"Relax, Brother Schoeff. Sex is harmless, as long as mannerism has it under control. I would tell you how this body acknowledges your presence. It's dancing here in Miss Ankenby's psyche. Now, how about giving me your gut feeling about little Asha. Obviously, you feel she's free of abuse."

Schoeff couldn't focus on an answer. Jessica was still physically there, having not lost her Rita Hayworth figure since the Thanksgiving in 1944. The dress she wore was prominent, but the sheer material could easily draw the eyes.

"Try focusing on the ears," Jessica said. "You always found those too wide on her." She hooked the hair over both ears.

"Well...Asha," Schoeff started off. "I feel her only obstacle is...her brother, of course, and in my last visit, I found him manageable. He still has anger issues, perhaps from the outcome of him being the provider. As a young man, full of energy, I feel he should be exploring possibilities in his life under a guiding father. Yet, Oscaro was able to see right once it dawned on him."

"Didn't you think his anxiety was strong?" Jessica asked.

"Yes, but it was because I was intruding in his fatherly role. The morning I came, being there cuddling Asha and the brother, Pilu, was intrusive."

"Mm, constructive gut feeling," Jessica said. "But remember the child's earnest thought can still be offset. That voice in her brother wasn't just teenage in conflict."

"You're being level with me," said Schoeff. "You have the answer, but you still want to hear my version."

Jessica recrossed her legs. "Your free will is like an egg with the thinnest shell. It could break upon my touch, serves you no use."

"How profound. I've heard that before."

Out in the nave, a door opened and shut. Schoeff took notice.

"Go on," Jessica said. "It's just a parishioner looking for his wallet. You'll help him later."

"With Oscaro," Schoeff continued. "I feel there is an occupant in him, not exactly Satan himself, just one of his drones. And this drone is loud but weak against Oscaro's guardian angel. I saw an example of the mismatch when I visited."

"Very good," Jessica reasserted. "All has been determined for the time being. With this observation, I shall leave you physically. The message has been said, via radio and all, and that message has been felt. Effectively, I may add. The streets are rumbling in confusion over your voice. I'll prepare your pass."

Jessica tilted her head gently and closed her eyes.

"Whoa," Schoeff said.

God snapped back in. "Still me."

"'Confusion over my voice, I'll prepare your pass?'"

"I'll give you a choice. You can either say, 'Nice seeing you again,' to this body, or you can stay and chat for those blanks to be filled in, which is likely to serve no purpose. Trust me. I'll leave it up to you."

This time Jessica snapped back to her own self without hesitation. "Well," she said, "aren't we a little excited on memory lane? The prophet of the Big Apple seems problematic of the past."

Schoeff grinned and conversed with her more. He entertained her for the rest of the day. He brought her to Daphne's Diner around the corner and had lunch. The people there were not so alarmed by his presence with a girl anymore. They just lowered their chins when Schoeff introduced Jessica as an old friend from college.

78

How to Leave for the Evening

Rapha was amazed by his daughter's carrying on at the restaurant. In the last two days she had been on time, from eleven to four, hosting without putting up much fight with the maitre` d's or him. This was the time of year that he and the missus threw hints of higher education, but Chereb's work ethics that week dissuaded Rapha otherwise.

"What's the matter?" he said upon seeing her reach over for an empty pepper grinder. "Busboys do that."

"A busy night. That's all."

"My little girl being of importance."

"I wouldn't go that far," Chereb said.

A smiling maitre d' stepped in between them. Upon seeing Rapha's face, he wiped the grin off, handing Chereb a note on stationary paper then leaving.

"What's this?" Rapha said. "André is passing you notes?"

Chereb shrieked, "It's Rachel! She's landed a role opposite Mickey Rooney. We're in for some celebration."

"After you clean up on table twelve, you can go," Rapha quipped.

"Where is The Brassery?"

"My daughter, the bar-hopper. Nothing has changed," Rapha sighed. "On Chelsea, near the Huston Building. A friend of a friend owns it. Better take Zed with you. Your mother sleeps better knowing he's with you."

"Not tonight, Pop. This is sort of a private go among us girls. Anyway, Zed dreads staying up."

"He can sleep in the car."

"Nope."

"He brings you home okay. That's enough for your mother."

"You mean you, Daddy," Chereb said.

At the end of her shift, she went in the kitchen and thanked André for the stunt. She used the phone in there to ring up Zeyad at Antonisz' Jewelry.

"Again?" Zeyad said.

"It'd be a different. Different scenery, a different conversation."

"I will come."

"Not if you don't want. You have to have the urge to join us."

"For you, I'll come," he said.

"It has to be what makes you comfortable. You have to *want* to go even if *I'm* not going."

The day before, he had made a pin of gold in shape of a woman's air-blown hair with the strands detailed with tiny pearls and diamonds. He daringly asked Rapha what he thought of the piece. Rapha complimented but never asked on what inspired him to create it. Zeyad would have told him the truth. Now the inspiration of this pin was granting him freedom, and all he could offer in return was his honesty.

Chereb knocked on his door that evening. "Are you

up for it?" she asked.

Zeyad said, "I am grateful that you ask. But tonight, I am due at the mosque. Other people are expecting me."

"Oh, okay," Chereb said. "I appreciate you speaking for yourself. It's the only way we can communicate, really."

"But Chereb, as much as I am dependent to my Allah, I very much like your company. This is like breathing to me. Without, I am dead."

It was the first time he had said her name outright.

"Say no more."

To look *safe*, Chereb walked through the living room at the same time Zeyad did. But Rapha was not around to see this. "Goodnight, Pop," she said at random, and Rapha moaned from somewhere in the den. It was good enough.

79

The Date

With the top down, Chereb grasped the steering wheel and headed downtown. Two blocks, she was already over the speed limit. The scarf on her head reminded her that she was well prepared, even in the slightest detail of controlling her bangs. She coasted down Times Square and turned left on 34th Street to go east toward Chelsea. Once she spotted the Huston Building, she knew there was no turning back. The Brassery sign was in neon against brick. It was attached to a posh hotel.

Chereb parked between two massive cars. She was level in her thinking, or else she could have never parallel-parked. The pantsuit she wore was a little keen for the establishment; the pinstripes flashed when she walked. Underneath the scarf, she had her hair sculpted, appearing like a gangster's coiffure. Her mascara was alluring. One couldn't tell she was only twenty. She crept into the dim bar, clouded in tobacco smoke and peppermint incense. The management obviously failed on this part. Instead of making the place acquire the aroma of liveliness, it stunk like an overstayed carnival. She spotted an empty table at the far left and made for it. But at that moment, a man in a dark suit, held her arm gently. "Please, this way," Ira said, guiding her toward an even dimmer corner in the bar.

"No, I prefer that one," Chereb said, snatching her arm back. She walked over, not losing her poise, and seated herself at the table she wanted.

Ira, who couldn't appear distinguished even in his smart ensemble, followed her without much choice.

"You're very trenchant, aren't you?" he said once he settled opposite her.

Chereb stared at him, long enough to embarrass him in his already nervous state.

"Aren't you going to speak?" he asked.

She let him curdle more. The moment he moved his mouth, she chided, "Why are you doing this?"

"Well...I thought we should meet after all," Ira said.

"You know how stupid I think you are? How moronic, how insecure and disgusting this whole thing you think I see as romantic?"

"Listen," he said, taking the punch. "You accepted my invitation."

"I'm here for Juliane," Chereb said. "She was a loving person, and I want to know what killed her, what delinquent cut short her splendid life."

"Don't say that!" Ira retorted. He took a deep breath to get a hold of himself. "I mean you're not even considering that she was unstable, and suicide was likely in her personality."

"No way. She was splendid until she met the likes of you. Anyway, I didn't come here to defend Juliane's personality. I came to see what degree of a lowlife you are."

Ira became tight-lipped. "You're double talking," he said with a forced smirk.

"And you got away with it.   How sick!" Chereb bombarded on. "You thought I came here because I was charmed by your silly, non-poetic note.   No, I am here to show you that I am not the least bit scared of any sleaze muck that comes my way." She began to gather her purse.

"Double double-talking," Ira sneaked in.

"It's been a pleasure chatting.   But I must be heading home. My sheik is expecting me." She stood up.

Ira, shattered, managed to put his hand in front of her and said, "You mean your priest."

"You're dumb as the rest," Chereb said. "And to think you admire Gwendolyn Brooks and actually read her."

She left him mesmerized.

80

The Provider

Asha developed an affection for her bonsai tree. She would brush any debris off its moss and water it regularly during the scorching start of summer. She placed the tree on top of her nightstand. Oscaro had allowed it since he told her that it was her gift, not the family's, from the padre'.

In the living room, with a fan blowing on his face, Oscaro had placed the two cylinder heads on the rug, their flawless stainless-steel casings glowing. The old pair had a hairline crack from too many rev-ups on Grand. What possessed Oscaro all evening was whether he should replace the mufflers as well to match the gleam. Chrome pipes came in variety at Ron's Cycle and Parts.

"Sasha," he called out. "Eat your dinner yet?"

"Yes, *manong*," Asha said.

"Come here for a second."

With the rest of the family asleep, Asha trudged into the living room. The bags under her eyes were heavy again, and she could hardly see the floor.

"How do you like them?" Oscaro asked. "They gonna move my Indian like lightning."

"They're like statues I see in the museum," Asha commented. "How much were they?"

"Hmm," Oscaro groaned. "More than regular. Since when do you worry about money?"

"I don't know," Asha moaned. "They're nice. I go back to bed now, okay? I have...oh yeah, no more...assignments."

In her room, Asha crept back under the blankets. Before sinking to sleep, she managed to flick off a dead needle from the mantel of the bonsai.

81

Shadows in Central Park

Ira found a follow-through route.

She was within arm's reach a moment ago, there at his disposal, communicating, sharing her day's thoughts with him? Now that spot was cold and empty. He got up and was drawn to the swinging door in the back.

"Let me through," he told the bartender.

"And what's wrong with the front?" said the whimsical, brawny man whom Ira saw as an illiterate blue-collar person.

"It's too public. I hate to be seen in my condition."

The bartender leaned forward on the bar and studied Ira. "You look okay. Believe me, you'll get over that shut-down faster than a bad haircut."

On impulse, Ira took hold of the corkscrew from the porcelain-tiled top of the bar and sprung over to the nearest female, a brunette having a conversation with a foreign-accented man. Ira raised the corkscrew over her and threatened to strike. "I swear I can open her up quicker than you can think up of another advice," he said to the bartender.

The woman shrieked.

"Let me through!" Ira shouted.

Without hesitation, the bartender got his key and stepped in the back to unlock the door. "Okay," he said when he reappeared. "Just small talk. No need to go nuts."

Ira threw the corkscrew at a shelf, breaking a couple of long-stems there. He caused other women to scream.

The air was choked by smoldering heat, enough for any young, day-seizing socialite to leave the car top down. Chereb had skipped her scarf. The wind would just play with her hair on the way home.

But to Ira, her hair was the guiding light from the alley. He thought she had parked in the back. He hustled to the front, cutting through the shadows like a well-attired thief. In the dark, he rammed the passenger door of the Bel Air, before the car could roll back and forth out between two cars. "I do not despise you," he said to a shaken Chereb. "But when you insult me, I have to convey myself. Do you understand?" He opened the door and got in.

"Please, get out of my car," Chereb said, her hands stuck to the wheel.

"No!" Ira shouted. "Not until I convey myself to you." She was open for explanation again. This time, out where no one could come to her aid.

"Okay," she said. "Convey."

"Drive."

Central Park was ten blocks away. The trees mysteriously rustled as if a storm was coming. Chereb swung the car out. The moment there was space, she hit the gas and drove fast. Ira's head whipped back and stayed there. At the park, he requested her to stop in an area where there were still strollers. Chereb didn't hesitate.

Her braking again could cause injury.

"Ease off," Ira said, massaging his nape. "Get your foot off it. Now!" From this, the Bel Air rolled, and he grabbed the steering wheel with one hand to guide the car to a bush-hidden gravel path.

"You'll ruin the hub caps," Chereb said.

"We're not here to worry about daddy's car."

"Yeah, but I have a responsibility whenever I borrow a possession of his, get it? Now take your filthy hand off the wheel!" Chereb punched at his hands.

He elbowed her, causing a sharp vibrating pain to her right upper chest. "Strange as it may sound," he said. "I'm sorry for that." He ordered her to stop the car entirely and shut off the engine.

"Yes, you're a true candy boy at this," Chereb said.

"Please, don't mock me," Ira said. To test my intelligence just lowers my evaluation of you. How can women be so narrow-minded on the less fortunate? My mother, for example, takes my whole literary world as second to her wellbeing, under my care. She would rather rattle pots, pans than give me peace while I'm writing!"

"She does?" Chereb said. "I'm truly bothered. But I have to head home now. My own mother is a worry bunny." She leaned forward to restart the engine. Ira slammed her back. Chereb whisked his hand off. "You push like a girl," she said.

Ira saw mock, but the tremor on her mouth led to unattractiveness he never believed existed in her. "How conceivable," he said. "You don't see anything. You're just ordinary. All this time I've shown my affection. You're as flighty as your dead girlfriend."

"You didn't give her a chance."

"That's totally out of context here." Ira's face glimmered in the moonlight. "I know of you. I've stopped at the jewelry store maybe four times. The first stop I met your father, and he thought I was a young professor from NYU.

311

Anyway, we got hung up on that, he showed me a photo, asked if I thought you could be NYU material."

Chereb kept silent.

"Come to think of it," Ira said, getting up from his slouch and looking around. "This is the place where a woman exerciser gets mauled allegedly by a gang of fifteen-year-olds, according to your priest lover. Your priest is not a hoax." He ran a finger on her shoulder. "Relax, I *am* gentle." He smiled his pearly whites in the dark. "I know exactly what he sees in you. He's too human for his position. Not enough hold back." Ira laughed. "But you aren't mine to use as temptation. You're his...or the sheik's? Never mind. It's sooner than we think, this mauling."

From a black leather pouch attached to his hip, Ira took out a Fina knife, the only brand his mother would keep in her kitchen drawer.

82

How to Rid of Faith

The phone in her room was in the middle of a ring when Zeyad snatched it. He had been in there since ten in the evening, sneaking in there in his soft woolen sandals. Rapha and Gracie had retired early, believing in their precautious minds that he was with their daughter. He listened, then, with anguish, he buried his face in the pillows. The handpiece dropped from his ear. He stood up. The carpet under him shook, but he realized it was only weak thought sent to the bone structure of his legs. He ran out of Chereb's room.

From the staircase, he noticed the *Damdado de Armada* statue in Rapha's den. It was dark, but the glint of the sword made him think.

He remembered a note that he had written a month ago. He had skimmed on this thought before but never gone to the point of pursue. Quietly he went into his room. He poked around for a box where he kept order receipts, a stack of other items fell. The two maids in the next room could hear. He switched on the lamp and rummaged for the note.

Looking for a cab in the middle of the night was like looking for a penny on a sewer grid, the chances of it staying on the gridiron depended on how steady your hand was at this late hour. Zeyad walked on Grand for four blocks before he spotted a parked car with a bar of light on top. He hurried to the driver's side and knocked on the glass. The cabbie looked irritated but rolled down his window.

"Do you know where this is?" Zeyad asked, presenting the note.

The cabbie switched on his dome light. "That's clear across Greenwich Village. You have twenty bucks on you, sheik?"

"Yes."

"Get in."

Zeyad breathed unevenly during the ride, although the cabbie did not notice. "So, what's the occasion?"

"No occasion," Zeyad answered.

"Just out for a ride, eh?"

He pictured her the way he had seen her last. By the way she dressed and made herself up, there was not a hint of trouble. How dare she go by herself? He had been correct in thinking that she had a corner in her heart for this man.

Zeyad got out of the cab. He recognized the name Bleeker Street, but the surrounding was totally different, not the area that Chereb and Rose Mary had taken him a week ago. Neon light from the Blue Parrot was nowhere, and the building that towered in front of him was clean yet vulgar, compared to the ones he had seen on 42nd Street.

The doorman approached him in choppy eloquence, and Zeyad said, "I have come to rescue my friend."

"Pardon?"

"I am looking for Mr. Ira Othem."

"Oh, yes. He just stepped in about fifteen minutes ago. Let me ring him..."

"Tell me, was he with a lady?"

314

"Getting quite personal, aren't we?" said the doorman.

"That lady is my responsible. I am to bring her back to her family," Zeyad said. "I am wondering if she has used the telephone from here."

"Let me ring up Mr. Othem." The doorman went behind his counter and got on the line. Zeyad knew he had only a slight chance of getting in and even a thinner prayer of being invited up. The doorman waited with the phone trembling at his ear. Then the doorman's face lit up on seeing something under the tester. "You're in luck," he said to Zeyad and pointed toward a vivacious person.

Zeyad caught the gawk of Ira. Ira recognized him and resolved to grin. "Ah, the wise man from the East," Ira said upon opening the door.

"Mr. Othem, I thought you came this way already," said the doorman.

"That's me, always on the rebound."

"Anyway, this gentleman wants to see you."

"It's all right, Leonard," Ira said. "He's quite peaceful."

"Where is Miss Chereb?" Zeyad said.

Ira laughed, holding his hands up. "I don't know. She made a rendezvous with me at a bar, and the next thing I knew she was off. It must have been the contrast in our brief conversation, probably her choice of feminine versification."

Zeyad noticed blood on one of Ira's cuffs when Ira raised his hand in wonder. Zeyad grabbed that one hand and pushed up on the sleeve of the suit, revealing the peanut-shaped red spot.

Ira yanked his arm back. "Do you mind? It's not what you think, holy man. I snagged myself in the car door."

Zeyad, blinded by inconspicuous rage, didn't waste any time. From the wide folds of his cloak, he pulled out the

315

sword. The silver sparkled momentarily; then it was embedded, staining dark Ira's bright ensemble.

Ira went into a convulsion, his fingers trying to come together at the sword's handle. The blade had sheared his back, disabling him from control of his hands.

"Oh, Christ on the crucifix, what have you done?" Leonard drawled, long enough for Zeyad to speculate that he was still on the other side of the decorative fence, on foreign soil. Zeyad bolted out the doors toward the street, tripping down the steps and over the curb. He got up. Regaining balance, he took off running toward the direction where he thought the piers would be.

83

How to Become Obsolete

Yet the fog settled on Pier 60. It had shifted in from a lowtide Eastchester Bay. Oscaro had sensed that it would cause shivering late in the night, so he brought along an afghan blanket to wrap around her. He sensed their trust in him had dwindled. He also knew that they weren't finished, and the time they had put in the project was invaluable. He cuddled her, telling that this should be routine to her by now, like doing the table.

"Forget what the padre says," he said. "And you're still okay with him. He ain't just your whole world."

What Oscaro meant, deep inside, was that this life supposed to have a father coming back home, not a priest father.

The lazy fog moved out, back to the sea.

During this first week of summer, the *padre* had time to read the paper. Schoeff found how easy-paced priesthood could be without a sideline. But he felt uneasy. It was too out in the open, this leisure. He would comb through the *Times* and the *Post* and found less and less of him. Gatherings, both peaceful and riot-urging, had slowly worked their way back to miscellaneous, and even to the arts and culture.

The New York Police Department, determined as they were a week before, had not called to continue their surveillance of him. Also, he hadn't spoken to Monsignor Randolph all that time. Randolph was always in another section of the cathedral. At breakfast, Schoeff always chose to do exercise while the monsignor ate. Aside from this, Schoeff felt that the head priest had been avoiding him.

"It is Father Laman that's worrying him," Father Gado pointed out. "Believe me, your outside affairs had been accepted by him a long time ago. He sleeps easier now because you've told him that this was it. You've finished your job."

"Thanks, father, for your faith in me," Schoeff said. "But tell me, what exactly is worrying the monsignor about Laman?"

"Nothing serious. It's just that Mrs. Cimoch, the superintendent at the orphanage, has told the monsignor that a couple boys have been complaining of headaches whenever Father Laman visited. I don't know, maybe some kind of incense he brings over there. No Yankee talk. Father Laman is not much of a baseball fan. They don't like that."

Schoeff thought for a second. "Has Laman talk to the monsignor?"

From the doorway came a groggy, analytic voice. "When did it become Laman?" Monsignor Randolph asked.

"Oh, Your Grace," Schoeff said. "I didn't know you were there."

"Father Schoeff, doesn't every ordained man under this roof deserve to be called father?"

"Certainly, Father Monsignor," Schoeff replied. "I've had the opportunity to be rather compassionate and open with Father Laman in the last few weeks, and I believe he would understand that his name has more syllables than any of ours."

"Father Gado, would you excuse us, please?" Randolph said.

Gado bowed and left the vestibule. He shut the double doors behind him.

"Father Schoeff," Randolph began, "Has it occurred to you that in every answer you give me, no matter how respectful it may sound, it always has an annoying defense?"

Schoeff did not speak.

"As if they're just boomerangs. They come back and hit me."

"I apologize, Your Grace."

"I'm not your grace. I'm your stepping stone to this *mission* of yours." The monsignor walked toward the oak-veneered wall. "And no matter how you slice it, you have this hidden arrogance in you that makes you walk upright. In all my experience, I've never come across a man of God who wasn't humble and selfless. It's only natural for a man in *your* position to be modest, giving!"

"If I'm not selfless, I think God would have picked someone else."

"There you go again."

Schoeff stopped himself from uttering another "defense." "Sorry," he said.

"The police commissioner called me," Randolph said. "He asked me for a way to get you out of the public's mind without defaming the Bronx, our church here. As you know, there are people who accept you and there are people who don't. But the problem lies between two groups, and it becomes violent three out of five."

Schoeff had no will to tell the monsignor about his name disappearing from the papers.

"So, what has to be done is inevitable." Randolph had his back against Schoeff when he said this. "I have a strong belief that you are beyond your priesthood, that the position you hold now is just your nest which you fly from and go back to whenever you please."

Schoeff, aching inside, still held his tongue.

"Therefore, I'd like you to consider leaving your obsolete post."

"Monsignor Randolph," Schoeff said. "My post is St. Jude's Cathedral. Here."

"You'll always be welcomed here."

"What about the C.C.D. class for the kids?" Schoeff asked. "What about my Saturday Mass?" Randolph did not turn around. "Father, am I being excommunicated?" Schoeff asked.

"Not in a sense that you have done something wrong," the monsignor said. "It's just the fact that your position is obsolete to you and us, and the city needs to return to its normal state. Officials feel the city will take comfort in forgetting that there was ever a commotion over...you. Your voice has been heard, and that's the important thing, true?"

Schoeff nodded. "But the commotion, as long as the city is breathing," he said, "will never be over. I've stopped my speeches, but it would take a while...."

Randolph ignored this.

"When do you want me to leave?" Schoeff exhaled, tremors down his throat.

Randolph did not answer as much as a moan. He just left the vestibule like Gado had.

84

Reaper of Soil

Out in the backyard that afternoon, Schoeff found Father Laman hoeing in between rows of giant green peppers. He was breaking down soil that had already been purified by the diligent hands of Father Gado. "I am not fit to be a priest," Laman said. "I lack that one-to-one approach, the thing you're very well-gifted with. I am not what you call a compassionate offeror, just some *cultic* being."

"Does this have anything to do with Mrs. Cimoch?"

"So, you've heard." Laman dug on. "Father, I'm just brittle. Those boys – and girls—think I am what I have boldly confessed to you weeks ago—a ninny, one who cries in the bathroom."

"Father, did the children inform Mrs. Cimoch of their discomfort?"

"I beg your pardon?"

"I don't have the ability to read into these circumstances."

Laman stopped hoeing. "My dear priest, there is no circumstance, no contradiction. I, I told that lard-bearing ostrich Mrs. Cimoch of what only may happen if I continue my duties at her orphanage. I drew her a catastrophic picture of me. Which I shouldn't have."

Schoeff grasped his mouth.

"Father, your advice has concealed my sins," Laman said. "I am in control of them totally!"

"I'm sorry," Schoeff said. He resolved to hug Father Lamantiaragski, who began to sob.

Though Schoeff couldn't read into parallel human emotions, he appreciated Laman's braveness in preventing what might happen. Milo had that same braveness. Milo just didn't see or had not grown to see that disgrace was good humility as well.

85

Chereb in White

Gradually was the word that the monsignor used on just how Schoeff was to leave. It didn't have to be urgent. As for Schoeff, who still had church duties for the week, the freedom to leave anytime was still conditioned. In the west vestibule, he thought of Christ's love and how unique it was. The instructions were all there, yet through all technicalities and rules, it was still love that could be described as unconditional.

He watered the rubber plants along the hallway. When Chereb came to him all dressed in lace and white shoes, his gladness was soaked like the soil in the pots.

"Father, I need to be baptized," she said. "That may sound bizarre and urgent coming from me, but to tell you the truth in all my life, I think I was destined to be Catholic."

Schoeff frowned amusingly. "Is that so?"

"Yes!" Chereb shrieked. "And I cannot waste any more time. It has to be done now, today." She kneeled down before him.

He let her, with the cold floor and the balancing on her kneecaps. "Well, as long as I have this can," he said.

Chereb closed her eyes. "The day we met, the day I heard you speak, I knew I was somehow connected, and it took me all this time to figure it out. With Julie and all...I had to go through a lot."

Schoeff noticed a bruise over her left eyebrow covered by mascara, and on her chin, there were three cuts, an inch long each.

"The thing had to be seen in the dark," she went on, "just like our God's own sacrifice for our souls."

Schoeff put down the watering can and grasped her shoulders to bring her up. "What did you have to see in the dark?"

She opened her eyes. "It doesn't matter. What matters is that I'm here now, ready to accept your Catholic Lord and Christ."

"Yes," Schoeff said.

"Your way of seeing things dug up something in me. I never knew I had a faith side."

"What brought this urge to Catholicism today?" Schoeff carefully rephrased his words. "I know for certain Christ accepts you the moment you let him...but, why today?"

"He does?"

"You seemed overturned."

Tears welled up in Chereb's eyes. "Three nights ago, I saw him. The guy who left that poem. We got to Central Park, and there, father...he pushed himself on me. But that's alright..." Chereb paused. "All I could think of is *meaning* to replace it, and it's you! How you would always have your arms open for me."

"Mercy," Schoeff said to himself. "Oh, Chereb, forgive me."

"Quite alright. You weren't there. The prick was, which brings me to another problem. Zed, my companion, is in jail right now for stabbing the guy."

325

Schoeff stood startled by this second round of news.

"I know he meant well, and I think he's done it because he loves me. But what I think he doesn't know is how serious it was. And he did it for me, father! You need to see him."

Schoeff nodded. "Would Zeyad's love be any way romantic?" he asked.

"I think so. Yes, but I don't love him." Chereb fought back menacing tears, wiping them quickly as they went down. "I'm into *you*," she gurgled. "I've always been reserved about it. I know you're a man of the cloth and I'm just an immature social girl who just happened to see you that day. You might say it was coincidence. But I say it was destiny…our meeting and our way at looking at life. Zeyad sees it totally different. But we, you and I, are alike."

Schoeff was speechless, his gut twisting inside him. "First," he said. "I don't think you're immature. You're a strong-willed palm tree out in the harsh wind."

"I say I love you, and you call me a palm tree?"

Schoeff laughed. "Insensitive of me. But you know, Chereb, in order to be accepted by Christ, you have to love *Him* and not a short, wobbly priest on his way to retirement. Baptism is like a fresh waterfall you walk into."

"Retirement?" Chereb said.

"Did I say that?"

"You did. That could only mean from work."

"You look nice in white," he complimented.

"I love you," she said again.

"I love you," Schoeff uttered back. "When should we...when could we visit Mr. Mughrabi?"

"He's downtown. Daddy's ringing up all his lawyers."

At the door, Father Gado coughed twice. Chereb stepped back from Schoeff, regained her poise, and

326

introduced herself to Father Gado, who had an appreciative smile. "Father," Gado said. "This note came for you."

Chereb resourcefully took the note from Father Gado and handed it to Schoeff.

Schoeff, nerves on end, unfolded the note.

"It was delivered by a man who claimed he was an orderly from Bronx-Lebanon. He said you should be notified," Gado said.

At that second, it was Schoeff's knees' turn to give out, and Chereb had to bring out a hand to his chest for support. "What is it?" she asked.

"I think I'd like to see...downtown," Schoeff said.

Gado, who had not flinched from Chereb's remark, immediately grabbed the bench from under the Virgin Mary statue and placed it under Schoeff.

86

Remnants

The jail cell was in light green, freshly painted. Since there was no opening to outside air, the stifling fumes stayed. Only when the guard would go in and out of the hallway door did the air circulate. Zeyad didn't mind.

Schoeff hadn't known how devastating the message Father Gado had brought. Schoeff thought requesting to see another undeveloped site would ease him of the pain. It was in the future that he would find relief. He had the idea of a bonsai tree changing the mood in the Gutierrez apartment, giving them hope and continuity. But he was human who erred. He couldn't know everything. The news of Asha overdosing, as the note indicated, had sent him to his quarters in the middle of the day. He never revealed what was said in the note to Chereb, who, judging by her sorrows, had the urge to wait for him. Within the hour, Schoeff came down and found her still by the rubber plants.

At the Lower Eastside precinct jail, what Zeyad minded was that he couldn't see the sun. He had refused his meals in the first two days, so time to him also became guesswork. He figured that he was three prayers behind in the *salat* — and that itself added to the guilt.

When Schoeff came to see him at about four in the

afternoon, Zeyad was on all fours on his small rug, with beads in his hands. Schoeff approached cautiously, motioning to the guard to keep the silence and that he'd be okay from there on. Irritated by the gesture, the guard rattled the lock hard to Zeyad's cell. Zeyad looked up.

"Pardon us," Schoeff said.

"Yes, excuse the intrusion," said the guard. He told Schoeff he had five minutes.

"Am I facing Iraq, my country?" Zeyad asked Schoeff. The guard coughed out a laugh and left.

"Mr. Mughrabi, you are the light of your country," Schoeff said. "It is safe to say you're praying toward God."

"Thank you."

"How are you feeling?" Schoeff said.

"How is Miss Chereb?"

"She is quite okay. She's in the lobby if you want to see her."

"No!"

"You're only allowed to have one visitor."

"Father, I will *not* see her again."

"Zeyad, I respect your sacrifice. Though vengeance has no place in my faith as it has none in yours, I respect one's own protection and one's own love."

Zeyad, wide-eyed, stared at the priest, digging deep into his meaning. "Call me Zed," he said. "Father, do you know what you are trying to make right? It is never right to kill like it is never right to neglect one's religion." The words became gritty. "It is like carrying a house on your back once you take a life."

Schoeff nodded. "And as part of this weight, you committed yourself not to see Chereb?"

"Not only for that reason."

"In the loneliest hour you've spent in this room, have

329

you touched on asking for forgiveness? I know that may sound convenient. But I'm sure Allah will take it in consideration."

"What do you know of Allah? Allah does not think that trite."

"In our deepest crises, we tend to think for our God, with our exhausted minds," Schoeff said, withstanding the smell of paint. "I've lost an innocent, bright child today because I thought I knew what my Mentor had in mind. He has this gift for us, so precious and fragile that he himself is afraid to touch it."

"I am not allowed to want anything outside!"

"You have a friend by the name of Chereb."

"You have her," Zeyad said.

"I have a story that may benefit the *both of us*." Schoeff sat down on the cot. Zeyad remained squatting on the floor. "I knew a childhood friend who thought faith and the opposite sex were two sparring enemies," Schoeff said. "It destroyed him, took away his life without ever knowing that it wasn't faith holding the weapon but his interpretation. In memory of him, I'm saying this to you now. Our faith harbors love. It must. That rope is taut. It's up to us to pull and make room for better halves. How big that room depends on how good we are with our better halves."

"What are you saying?" Zeyad snapped. "I have dipped down from my purpose."

Schoeff, near nausea, grinned still, said, "The rope doesn't get pulled in. Everybody stands still where they are."

On seeing Zeyad's face unchanged, Schoeff abandoned the task. He saw the New York state justice system advanced enough to give this man a fair trial. As he was about to leave, the guard unlocking him, Zeyad called out, "Why did the Almighty choose you? Do not tell me that it is inborn when devotion and work matters. Why did God choose you as a personal servant?"

Schoeff saw torment on Zeyad's face, realizing that he couldn't partake in humoring him anymore.

"I have been attached to Allah since I could only hear my father's teachings of the Holy Pillars," Zeyad continued. "I couldn't speak yet. Yet I was Sufi. I am Sufi by heart." His eyes, though motionless, began to develop tears. "I had come here by accident. I thought I could be in Allah's will." Zeyad inhaled, gathered himself. "Why was it you in that position?"

Schoeff brought his chin up and said, "My sense of humor."

87

Human

Chereb waited at the prison lobby, scratching her chin nervously. When she saw Schoeff being let out of a steel door and heard him say something other than it was her turn to see Zeyad, she let out a sigh.

"How long does it take to get to the 91st floor of the 40 Wall Street Building?" Schoeff asked.

"Oh, without delay," Chereb said cheerfully, "about nine minutes, unless you want to climb the antenna, too, which could take another five."

"Do you provide hiking boots?" Schoeff said.

"How is...?"

"Zeyad, your friend, I think for the better, doesn't mind his solitude. It's best to see him in a couple days."

The sun outside the jail coaxed sightseeing. Chereb flipped on her cat-eye sunglasses, then took them off again and offered them to the priest.

Schoeff refused. "I'm over my Grace Kelly stage, thank you," he said.

Chereb stifled her laugh, smiled instead.

"Shall we take the bus?" Schoeff said.

"Or we could walk. That building is just around the

corner. By the way, why the 40 Wall Street Building? The Chrysler Building is more grand and glittery."

Schoeff paused uneasy before stepping off the curb. "Not all is certain," he puffed. "We, priests, go for function. The Chrysler Building had arches added just to be taller than the 40 Wall Street, and that threw my respect for one over the other."

"If you like respect," Chereb said, "the Empire State Building then?"

"Hm, that name. Sounds like world power. It's tall, but the name has no height."

The pedestrian traffic was horrendous to a newcomer, which Schoeff still considered himself to be to the city. Chereb had talent in flouncing through the crowd. "What's the matter?" she asked as they trawled closer to 40 Wall Street. Schoeff felt like he was walking a festive tightrope. "There's a bus stop ahead. We can get on one to go home," Chereb offered.

"I just feel...*drawn* to height today," Schoeff said. Chereb a few steps behind nodded. Suddenly the building wall ran out at Schoeff's side, and he found himself at the foot of the Thirty-Eighth Street alley. He must have known that Jack would be in the vicinity. Schoeff turned around and spotted Jack sitting across a young lady in a tattered biker's jacket and maroon plaid skirt. They were at a hardware storefront with dainty tables and chairs to spare up front. They were talking, a hint of harmony lingered between them. Jack had his hands at his belly. He was half reclined, face amused by the people at the walk.

What was better than seeing a man spend time with his daughter? Schoeff thought, halting.

From the alley, a troop of pigeons sprung upward, as if Schoeff had trespassed their territory. They came out gnashing from the trash bins. He took notice. Chereb focused on something else. At that instant, she wished Schoeff hadn't had such a curious mind toward everything.

Pigeons were used to New Yorkers. They scattered when they were in immediate harm's way. A bus hustling through an alley to meet its schedule was another thing. It elicited oddness. Chereb, screaming her head off, couldn't reach the back of Schoeff's shirt in time. He had a fraction of a second to turn his face toward her, but his hip and leg could not escape the dash of the huge vehicle. Schoeff bounced off it like a beanbag mannequin.

Someone shrieked, a Niemann-Marcus shopper across the street.

Schoeff managed to fall back on the sidewalk, maybe a yard away from where the bus had sideswiped him. The silvery mass that loomed up in front of him had screeched to a stop. He read the destination: Corona Heights-Ashbury.

"*Corona.*

"*High.*

"...*Asha,*" he uttered.

Jack, who had seen a glimpse of Schoeff and was sure it was him, got up throwing his chair back. He rushed across Wall Street. Heny, his daughter, slow-paced and mesmerized, rose and followed. She grasped her father's flannel shirttail as he worked his way into the crowd. Jack managed through and found Schoeff lying with his head awkwardly positioned on Chereb's lap. Jack slouched down, attempted to make him more comfortable by putting his palms gently on each of Schoeff's temples, then straightening the head slowly. But Schoeff only made a face signifying pain that could be avoided. Jack's hands sprang back. "Somebody get the ambulance!" Jack yelled. "Somebody get his doctor!"

It was then that Schoeff identified the face of the bus driver, hovering among other heads. The sad expression of his Uncle Dam, not a day older. Uncle Dam smiled, uttered two meager sentences: "You did dandy. I'll take you up there." Uncle Dam, in his bus-driver getup, referred to the building half a block off but looming already overhead.

But according to Chereb, in tears, the bus driver was getting help. "You know him?" she asked.

Schoeff closed his eyes. "Jack, you found her," Schoeff said.

"Yes, sir," Jack said. "Heny, my pet, came looking for me...and, and I still have the lovely tools. Yes, sir. You must be deep in hurting?"

"Not so much," Schoeff said. "It's one leg, one hip."

"Well, stay still. The old ambulance is on its way, I'm definite."

"How far is the 40 Wall Street Building?"

"The what building?" Jack said. He looked up. "There, up...."

Schoeff brought his eyes as far back as he could, saw the blurred tower behind Chereb. "If I were a lovesick ape," Schoeff said. "I'd climb that one instead." He peered back to Jack. "Jack, how are you at being my leg?"

"What?"

"And Chereb, you can be my hip." Schoeff grabbed Jack's shoulder and pulled himself up before anyone could budge. Schoeff, racked in pain, didn't care for that pain.

"You can't be real," Chereb said.

"It's my only chance," Schoeff gasped.

"That ain't even the building you're referring to all this time," Jack said. Schoeff reached out to shake his hand.

Chereb tried to read him. "What's your only chance?" she asked. "Are you getting some kind of a vibe? Stay down,

335

please!"

Schoeff, still trying to hoist himself up on Jack, grinned at her. He turned to Heny. "And how are you at being...my balance?"

Heny plodded next to her father and said, "I try." She went around Schoeff, looking for leverage, first checking, then taking a grasp.

"Or do you prefer being an elbow?" Schoeff said, still in the humor.

"I *knew* it!" Chereb said.

"May I know what has been known?" Schoeff asked.

"You're not human, are you?" Chereb said. The crowd could hear her loud and clear. "I mean you're human but not in a sense of *being*. Not from New York, not from Indiana, not from nowhere..." She sounded sarcastic.

"He's an archangel on a mission, can't you see that?" Jack said. "And he wants up in there!" He and his daughter started to walk Schoeff.

"Yes, but he can't feel. He's not completely...here," Chereb sobbed. "At least...."

Schoeff bowed.

Jack thought Chereb was a candidate for the hospital of the terminally off the rocker.

"Come closer," Schoeff said to Chereb.

Chereb hesitated but drew near. "In times like these," Schoeff said. "This very moment with you, just you--pardon me, Jack, Heny--I wish I had a place to which I can say affection without feeling I've crossed...listen, the mind above my mind thinks you are that inspiration."

Chereb gazed for a second, trying to catch what Schoeff was trying to relay. "You mean that?" she took a stab.

"I does," Schoeff said. "But now I need to be *elevated*.

336

I need a pleasant tour guide." At that instance, he collapsed. From the paleness of his skin, it was eerie that he was upright at all. Jack and Heny held on. Chereb went around and bear-hugged him from the back. Schoeff screamed in pain. He suppressed it. At a snap, he opened his eyes as if to reawaken. "Ah, lovely day for sightseeing...," he said.

"You do love me," Chereb whispered.

Schoeff, drained, looked up to her, saw the blur of her angel-like features and uttered, "It's no secret."

88

Uncle Dam, 1951

Random is still key to the future. Things had been said, maybe events, but in order for them to take place, they still have to follow the rules of randomness. It's the only way they would become possibility.

Uncle Dam had a way to assure certainty in randomness. If things are aimed to happen, they are just in focus to take place. On the ninety-first floor of the 40 Wall Street Building, there would be a conversation between the elevator man and a retired Catholic priest. It would go something like this:

"It's been years, and you don't look a day older than the day you had that Buddy."

"Still in production."

"Now you turn out to be my St. Peter."

"If you say so," the elevator man would say. *"But first, how do you fit fifty New Yorkers in an elevator?"*

"Ah, comedy, the fruit of my youth," comments the priest.

"Toss a bagel in, with cream cheese."

Both laugh.

"Sorry about the accident. Buses, they go faster than a tractor."

"That's okay. The pain is zilch. Asha would pull through, right?"

"You should know."

The priest looks puzzled, still.

The elevator man would say, "No and yes. Depending on how cracked-open people would be. Between you and I, we did good. Minds, they're made to tiptoe on. There will come a time when they're the only things that'd matter. Bodies would just be candy wrappers, thin on how-to's."

89

Possibility

Zeyad never saw the logic in parole. He was sentenced to twenty-five years for a murder he proudly admitted. Any shortcoming didn't add up to him. He only requested for a window in any cell he occupied. The wish was not taken seriously at first, but after nine years of good behavior and denying parole, the warden made sure that his room sun-drenched. They even provided a cell with a dome-like ceiling in Pekin, Illinois where he was transferred in 1956. After the fourteenth year, something clicked in Zeyad to want freedom. Whether it was the chance to go back to al Basra and see his mother or the chance to start over again, to see a mosque established in the Bronx, the moment was ripe, he realized.

Yosef Mussar, an outspoken leader from Riyadh, wrote Zeyad in prison, applauding him for his "mystic" bravery. Zeyad didn't know what Mussar was referring to at first. Zeyad hadn't actually cared. But before he was released in the mountains of Pennsylvania and brought back to Rikers Island for his final hearing, Zeyad could only think of one thing a person like Mussar would be after, the act that had sent Zeyad to jail in the first place.

When Zeyad stepped out, he didn't realize he had a following to his name. The jeweler who had killed for love was finally free on his own accord. There was a flock of young people to greet him at Grand Station. They had raised a banner with the words "Welcome Home, Zeyad Nadeem Mughrabi" painted on it. He tried ducking away, but he could only escape the thick of them and not the three women who ran after him.

"Mr. Mughrabi," one said, "will you give us a moment?"

"I have nothing to say. This is all press bullshit," Zeyad said.

Two of the ladies, who were shocked by this un-Casanova attitude, shrugged, and stopped following. But one still went after him.

"Please, Mr. Mughrabi," she said. "My reason for wanting to talk," she puffed, "has nothing to do with your gestures years ago. You knew Father Schoeff."

Zeyad halted. A name he hadn't heard for so long came back to him like warm tea. The girl hurried to his side. Zeyad checked her from head to foot, and she was not a girl at all but a woman. The light green embroidered blouse she wore summoned him to gawk, and she controlled her heaving then, mostly because they had separated from the crowd.

"Where is he?" Zeyad asked.

The woman, caught strangely by this question, gave a bewildering "Oh." She peered at Zeyad for a second, then realized she had her purse at her side. She opened it, took out a newspaper clipping and handed it to Zeyad. "It happened the day he visited you," she said.

"Tourist killed by bus," Zeyad read. "He was a chaplain who could see the future, and all came down to this?"

"You're telling me. They gave Rebe Anthony most of the attention. You know, society girl turned Hollywood star."

"I need brand-new glasses," Zeyad said. "I can't. Would you, Miss?"

"Oh, sure," the woman said. She read the clipping aloud under the streetlight, all the while feeling Zeyad's eyes on her. But she knew the blade-sharp concentration was more on what came out of her mouth. She knew quite well that Rebe Anthony was the center of his solitude.

"Where do you go?" Zeyad said when the woman was done.

She thought he was asking about her schooling, so she said, "M. I. T. But it's summer. I stay in the Bronx."

"They provided me money to get a place," Zeyad said. "I'll tell you more of Father Schoeff and in return, you can read for me."

The woman, who seemed cautious of her next, bypassed her first impression of the offer and walked with Zeyad.

On Times Square, they stopped at a newsstand to select magazines. "She used to be in *Metro Eve* a lot," the woman said. "And many times in *Vanity Fair*, of course. But she's not like that."

"Why not...like that?" Zeyad asked.

"I don't know. I find her beautiful. But also, I see her not minding taking the subway!" The woman laughed.

The hotel room they found was sanitary enough. Neon glistened from the window, projecting the escape ladder on the walls. Zeyad switched on the lights and asked his reader to take a seat on a cane chair. "Please," he said, looking out the window. "The streets have changed."

"For better or worse?" the woman thought to say.

"If I had come back to al Basra instead, I would not see much change. People walking are more of different… backgrounds and of different faiths, yes. I see proof of what the chaplain was saying."

"Father Schoeff?"

"Yes."

"He said all would be one in years to come."

"Well, more like all will be better if they become one in years to come."

Zeyad took notice of how the woman was sitting in the chair, her knees touching but her feet wide apart. Zeyad sensed she was uncomfortable. "Forgive me," he said. "Ten years ago, I would not look at someone this way. But please," he begged, "…let me be near you."

On this request, the woman shivered but stood up.

"I think it was partly due to my brother that Father Schoeff was careless the day he died," the woman said. This halted Zeyad for a second. "You see, my brother, had forged a note saying…and someone sent it to the church for father to see."

Zeyad began to embrace her, awkwardly kissing her baby powder-scented neck, rubbing himself on her eventually, all the time asking her pardon. Then he stopped, upset, beaten. "Go. Go now," he demanded.

There was a sheepish quake in the woman's throat when she said, "Miss Anthony comes back to the city from time to time." Zeyad became apologetic. But the woman stayed. She did not resume her place in the cane chair. Zeyad fell to sleep with a scowl on his face. She pulled the

343

covers to his shoulders.

The woman realized that Zeyad was free in this future New York, a place to redefine himself, nourish himself back to etiquette and hope. Only the innocent tone in her voice had made him approach her that way.

Asha gathered her things and took the taxi home.

90

How to Stay in America

In his second month of being free, Zeyad found work as a net-caster for a small fishing company on Staten Island. He would wake at five in the morning and spread the nets on the pier with the cold, smoky sea in front of him. There were dim lights in the fog, mooring tugboats that had ventured out in the night, pulling passenger ships and oil barges. Surely Rapha Antonisz would have known of his release by now.

By daylight, Zeyad would be on a steamer, hauling tuna in. The ridges of his upper arms were sharp, toned by the hammer swinging he did in prison. He had crushed an index finger, and it had lamed the grip in the right hand. He wouldn't be able to manipulate small tools for jewelry in that hand. So, what was the point in Rapha calling him?

Early at dusk one humid day, as he leant over the boat's deck, he saw a figure in white among a group, dressed like her. She was waving a banner and yelling. It seemed as if she was in one of those ship-toasting galas well-off New Yorkers couldn't seem to give a rest. Zeyad hustled to the front and told the driver to slow down. When Zeyad asked if the driver could swing closer to the harbor, the driver sped up and Zeyad had no choice but to run to the rear of the boat. The figure on the pier stood still. She got smaller in size, and she seemed to be looking directly at him. He had fisherman's overalls. She would not recognize him. Silver tides lashing toward the harbor concealed her in the distance.

He would finally snap out of his funk and find himself. For one thing, Zeyad did not forget the reason why he got out of jail and that was to provide convenience to Muslims in the Bronx. But to his cheery disappointment, there were two firmly established mosques in the populated borough already. A lot could happen in thirteen years. Yet Zeyad was determined. In 1969, he picked a spot in Mott Haven, where it was accessible to the devout in Manhattan as well. It would take him two years to receive a moderate grant for the start-up but almost seven years for permission from the state Islamic leaders since Zeyad wasn't an imam by trade. His famous name was always under scrutiny.

All this time, Yusef Mussar had enormous hope for him and would have consultations with him. Zeyad felt his religious ideas didn't really match Mussar's more intervening ones. "I am not the one you should place on a pedestal," Zeyad would humbly say. "My Qur'an sheds only peace for me." In all of this, Zeyad had not had the courage to remind Mussar that the motive of his much-heralded crime (the thing Mussar saw most promising in Zeyad) was for a Jewish girl.

Zeyad thought Mussar would have caught on. But all things considered, Zeyad didn't see Mussar as a cofounder to his new mosque. Zeyad parted ways by gradually not returning Mussar's calls.

Twenty-six years before every citizen across America would feel their sense of security slip away, a hint of that catastrophe would happen in the Bronx district of Mott Haven. One sunny November day, Zeyad drew his palms together, a white cap on his head, in front of a dozen worshipers. They were hearing Zeyad's inaugural thanksgiving under his own blessed dome. A pipe bomb thrown into a window would subvert his brick-house mosque into flames.

The happy and fulfilled first servant would not survive.

At Zeyad's burial, a small American flag jutted out of the thick blanket of marigolds draped over his coffin. Rapha had stuck that flag. He, Gracie, and Chereb—who canceled all her engagements for a week—attended.

EPILOGUE

The Threshold

What she couldn't grasp was how much Father Schoeff had loved her. It had been that rare affection which was now the base of pursuing the endless study of Safety, her giving back. Asha knew the only way she could recapture the light in her otherwise foreboding youth was to become a mechanical engineer. Here she was at thirty-one working at the renowned Bickle Dynamics in Boston, trying to figure out how to hide an aluminum "roller" door that would pop up in seconds to conceal the cockpit.

Three years before, an irate passenger had tackled a standard cockpit door in a Boeing 707, causing the plane to crash land in the Mojave Desert. Fifty-three passengers did not survive the inferno. The news made high-flying vacationers grow cautious. Holiday travels dipped in numbers each year.

Asha had the idea of a second door "materializing from nowhere" two days after the incident in the desert. It was her responsibility, she thought, her calling as a safety advocate. She and her assistant, Henalynn DeSio, worked on the project for some thirty months, and in the spring of 1973, they were ready to demonstrate at Boeing.

In the jetliner in route to the headquarters, Asha's assistant worried if the hydraulics were minimized enough to draw serious interest. "Good, Heny, I admire your nitpicking," Asha said. "But we have a functioning product. It's up to them to see its worth."

Asha reclined in her seat, worry-free, clasping her assistant's hand in notion that Heny should do the same. "Nitpicking," Asha laughed. "I got that word from you."

The two had met eight years before. It was in August of 1965, the nineteenth to be exact, and it would be the first time Asha would actually see the famous Elvis Presley — which Schoeff had mentioned merely to uplift her spirit then. The singer was playing at Madison Square Garden that night. Heny had the same intuition, except she worked at one of the concession stands and could not well see the performance at the same time. "I have to go," Asha had cavorted that morning.

Her mother told her nobody was stopping her. Oscaro would, but he had joined the Army and was stationed at Fort Hood in Texas. It was Oscaro's resolution to rid of the guilt of what he had put Asha through.

When Asha bought Coca-Cola from Heny, Heny was red-faced holding back her anxiety to go into the concert. Mrs. Gutierrez felt this and offered her ticket to Heny. Jack who had vowed through the years never to be absent from his daughter's side took over the duties at the concession stand with Mrs. Gutierrez. In the two hours they spent together, hand in hand almost, the subject of Father Schoeff never came up.

At the Boeing headquarters in Seattle, Washington,

the two ladies received great accommodations. Their model of a sectioned fuselage was displayed with clarity. The "boom door" sprung down just as accurate. Asha thought the loudness would turn off the nine panelists watching the demonstration, but they had to take in account that the trigger hydraulics were exposed, and in actual jetliners, they would not be. The Boeing president approached Asha and told her he thought highly of her project and would let her know of his answer by letter.

"This is it," Asha insisted then. "I have to know if it'd be installed in your fleet. It's totally concealed, a one-time use product, like the black box. Except the safety feature in this is to avoid the black box!" Asha heartily argued.

Astounded by Asha's response, the Boeing president reasoned that the addition might lengthen the fuselage on every model by at least three feet, and that would be expensive.

"But to not install them immediately," Asha persisted, "is dangerous…." At Boeing's high-tech cafeteria, she took the hand of her assistant and asked in a whim what would Father Schoeff do?

Heny inhaled deeply and said, "Father, I think, would have said have hope for the future."